He turned to her. "This is a disaster."

She couldn't argue. Juliet's party had been reduced to a manic free-for-all.

He tightened his grip on her hand and a memory flashed of the day they'd gone to the courthouse to say their vows. He'd held her hand just as tightly then. The promise of a future together had made her giddy, and she'd stuttered when it came time to say "I do."

Standing next to Dane now, so close she could feel his body heat, made her heart race. Just one touch from Dane and she reverted back to a love-struck teenager? She couldn't let Dane get to her. They'd had their moment in time and blew it. She would not let these jumbled feelings for him ruin years of healing the wound he'd inflicted.

No. Not now.

Dear Reader,

Who said do-overs are easy?

When Nealy returns home for her sister's engagement party, she is shocked to run into her ex, Dane. One look at Nealy, the girl who got away, and Dane knows he has to try to win her back. What could possibly go wrong?

Second chances sound romantic, but we all know the journey to true love is usually rocky. And believe me, Nealy and Dane have a bumpy road ahead of them. Joining our struggling characters on their journey to happiness is what we love to read about: the discovery of who the characters are, what makes them tick and most important, whether or not they will overcome the odds and get together. Trust me, Nealy and Dane have their work cut out for them every step of the way.

So, dear reader, welcome back to Cypress Pointe. Pour yourself a glass of sweet iced tea and pull up a comfy chair to spend a few hours with new friends. When you close the book, please visit me at www.tararandel.com and tell me what you think of Nealy and Dane's romance.

Enjoy!

Tara Randel

HARLEQUIN HEARTWARMING

Tara Randel

Magnolia Bride

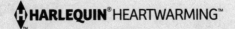

Recycling programs
for this product may
not exist in your area.

ISBN-13: 978-0-373-36685-9

MAGNOLIA BRIDE

HARLEQUIN®
www.Harlequin.com

Printed in U.S.A.

TARA RANDEL

has enjoyed a lifelong love of books, especially romance, so it came as no surprise when she began writing with the dream of becoming published. Family values, a bit of mystery and, of course, love and romance are her favorite themes, because she believes love is the greatest gift of all. Tara lives on the west coast of Florida, where gorgeous sunsets and beautiful weather inspire the creation of heartwarming stories. This is her second book for Harlequin Heartwarming.

Also by Tara Randel

HARLEQUIN HEARTWARMING

10–ORANGE BLOSSOM BRIDES

To my good friends Nikki and Kelley. You are both very special people and you mean so much to me.

PROLOGUE

NEALY HOOKED ONE FOOT over the sill before hauling herself up and out the window. Her heart was pounding with excitement as she landed on the soft grass. She'd made sure the coast was clear, checking on her sleeping parents before slipping away. They'd made it very clear they didn't like her sneaking around and ignoring her curfew, but who cared? Ever since she and Dane had started dating, she wanted to be with him every second. And if it meant getting in trouble, again, he was worth it. No way would she let being grounded keep her from the party Dane was throwing for her birthday.

He'd told her to join him at midnight. Right on time, she jogged onto the beach, her flip-flops kicking up sand as she ran, heading toward the beacon of a roaring bonfire. Once she arrived, Dane pulled her into his embrace.

"Happy birthday."

She threw her arms around his neck. "You are my hero."

He grinned, a lock of his long hair falling into his eyes. "And the best boyfriend ever."

"That, too."

"C'mon." He took her hand and led her toward the action. A group of girls, including her good friend Lilli, hugged her, giggling as they pointed to the boys gathered at the far side of the fire. Knowing the boys as she did, they were most likely up to no good.

"Are you sure this was a smart idea, Nealy?" Leave it to Lilli to voice a concern, always worried about getting into trouble. "When your parents find out you snuck off again, they'll ground you forever."

Nealy laughed. "It won't be forever. Once I leave for college I can do whatever I want."

"Like you don't do whatever you want now?" Marianne, her friend from homeroom, snickered.

"Okay, so yeah, I might have gotten into trouble one too many times this summer."

"Ya think? If you ever decide to go on out to the causeway late at night and get stuck in the mud, be sure to find another driver," Marianne huffed. "My parents are still ticked at me."

Dane swooped in behind Nealy, circling his arm around her waist to draw her close. "No talking about parents and trouble. Tonight is all about you. I have something planned you'll never forget."

"Really? What is it?"

He kissed the side of her neck. "Just wait and see."

Even late at night, the sultry summer heat saturated the air, scented by the damp sand and burning logs. Sparks drifted from the fire, escaping into the star-filled night.

Nealy sighed. She'd never been this happy, or this in love, ever.

This year had been the worst. The more her parents had tried to convince her to go to a college that would ready her for law school, the more she'd refused. It seemed as if they'd always been at odds over this and would never be able to reach a middle ground. But this summer they'd hit the ultimate height in their disagreement. They didn't get that pushing her to be an attorney, only made her push back, or rather, act out. She'd been unhappy until she met Dane.

As soon as Nealy started hanging out with him at work, she developed a crush on him. The night she'd decided to spray paint the pier and Dane showed up to help her, she lost her heart to him. Subsequently getting caught and grounded hadn't kept her from him, which made her parents just that little bit crazier. Served them right for always bullying her to do what they thought was right, never caring about what she wanted. Once she left for college, and freedom, they'd lose the power to make her miserable.

"Ready?" Dane whispered in her ear.

"Are you kidding? I've been going nuts since you told me about this party."

He looped his arm over her shoulders and pointed across the bonfire. "Watch the sky."

She heard shouts. Suddenly a light flared, followed by a whizzing noise as a swirl of red, yellow, green and blue erupted in the darkness. Surprised gasps could be heard all around her. Before she knew it, another colorful burst of sparks shot into the sky, followed by another, then another.

"What do you think?"

Nealy crossed her hands over her heart. "You got me fireworks for my birthday?"

"Yep, since you light up my life."

She snorted. "Lame."

"But true."

Her heart melted as another round of fireworks went off. "I love you," she said. "More than anything."

"I love you back."

They stood side by side, lost in the wonder of being a couple and sharing this special moment. Nealy secretly wished it could last forever, but her hopes were quickly dashed as the familiar-sounding sirens rang in the distance. Before she knew it, she was running, had to before the police arrived. A stitch tweaked at her side and her breathing grew labored as she made her escape, but not badly enough to keep her from laughing.

Best. Birthday. Ever.

CHAPTER ONE

AFTER BEING AWAY from Cypress Pointe, Florida, for more years than she cared to count, Nealy Grainger expected to find more changes in her small hometown. Sure, a few new businesses had taken up residence on Main Street, but the familiar sights of Milly's Gifts and Things, Rascal's Candy Shoppe, Duke's Grill, and Cuppa Joe, her grandmother's coffee shop, remained the same. Maybe she expected more because her life had changed so much since she left. Shouldn't everyone else's life have changed, too?

Late-afternoon sunlight sparkled off store windows while tourists browsed from the sidewalk, some seeking protection under the store canopies to escape the afternoon heat. She drove the candy-apple-red rented convertible toward the north end of town, deeply inhaling the salty air as she cruised past the public beach, the location where countless days had been spent lounging in the sun, splashing in the waves and hanging out at late-night bonfires.

From the radio, Trisha Yearwood's lyrical voice crooned a soulful melody about driving past an old boyfriend's house after many years away.

Nealy snorted.

Yes, it had been years since she'd been home, but the old boyfriend part? The term *boyfriend,* even if she had considered him a quote-unquote boyfriend, would have been used quite loosely. What they'd had was intense, quick and forever burned upon her heart. Boyfriend? No. They'd fast-forwarded through that phase and went straight to the altar. Husband? Yes, with a capital *H.*

Actually, ex-husband was a more accurate description.

Her cell phone rang to the tune of "Surfin' U.S.A.," a peppy Beach Boys song she'd come to love since living in California. She snatched up the phone and noted the caller ID. Her boss's number. If she was calling, it meant some kind of drama had transpired. Nealy had had everything in order before leaving. As executive assistant to the party planner of the celebrities, every detail must be perfect. Expensively perfect.

"Hi, Crystal. Is everything all right?" she asked while silently praying she hadn't forgotten anything.

"Mr. Taylor wants the color scheme changed."

"Now? The party is Friday night." She'd checkmarked each detail with the man weeks ago, from the monogrammed napkins to the rented crystal chandelier he insisted on dangling from a tree on his oceanfront property.

"His astrologist says blue is not a good color for him this month. She insists he should focus on red."

Nealy worked for Milestones by Crystal, a much sought-after event planning company in Los Angeles. They had three huge parties booked for the upcoming weekend and even though she'd put her vacation request in weeks ago, her boss didn't let the pesky little inconvenience of Nealy being out of town stop her from calling.

"Can't Liz handle it?"

"No. Mr. Taylor refuses to talk to anyone but you."

Nealy took a deep breath since she couldn't close her eyes and count to ten. Hollywood clients could be a challenge, but her boss even more so. She'd loved her job when she first started four years ago, but as the company grew, their stress levels had gone off the charts. Her boss knew Nealy had come home to visit her family, yet she phoned as if it were a snap for

Nealy to handle the problems from Florida. So much for her vacation.

"Okay, I'll give him a call as soon as I can. Then I'll get in touch with Marsha at Elegant Linens. She owes me, so I'm sure she'll make the changes. Can you speak to Michele and see what she can pull off with the flower arrangements?"

The rustling of papers sounded over the line. Nealy formed a mental picture of Crystal sitting at her desk, her attention already focused on a different problem while Nealy tried to fix the current one.

"Hmm. Michele? Yes, I'll contact her."

Nealy breathed out a sigh of relief. "Good. I'll call Mr. Taylor. And, Crystal?"

"Yes?"

"Then I'm on vacation, okay?"

"Of course. Unless I need you."

Crystal signed off. Nealy knew it wasn't the last time she'd hear from the woman during her much-needed break.

In the past year, Nealy's workload had doubled. She never complained because she appreciated the steady paycheck. With the prospect of a new client signing with them soon, her workload was about to get even more hectic.

An up-and-coming fashion designer, Ashlee James, popular with young stars, had shown an interest in hiring Milestones by Crystal to plan her clothing launch and then take care of all subsequent events. Everyone at the company had their fingers crossed the contract would come through, especially Nealy, who was tapped to lead the project. Interacting with elite clientele from Hollywood and L.A. had its moments, but Nealy logged long hours arranging an event. Did she have time for a social life? Please. Dating? Forget it. She hadn't seen Sam, her kinda, sorta boyfriend, in three weeks. Though when it came to Sam, her workload wasn't the only cause for the distance between them. He put in just as many hours at his office, which made their relationship status vague.

She pushed her dating woes to the back of her mind. She had more important matters to fret over. Namely, her sister's multiple engagement parties. Yes, multiple. What had started out as an intimate gathering of friends and family to celebrate the joyous occasion soon morphed into adding an additional party to allow the senator—the fiancé's father—to invite his political friends and financial backers so they, too, could offer their best wishes. Between the demands of the two families, her sister had booked both engagement parties for this weekend.

When Nealy's sister Juliet had called to tell

her about the engagement, she begged Nealy to plan the bigger party. Since she was marrying into an illustrious political family, Juliet wanted to impress her future in-laws. She complained because the coordinator she was working with didn't have ideas grand enough to make an impression on the senatorial family. Juliet wanted the glitz and glamour of a Hollywood A-list event. Nealy could make that happen.

Nealy had her reservations; after all, it wasn't as if she lived close by. Juliet put her in contact with the coordinator at the venue where both parties would take place and the two got down to business. Soon, Nealy realized her sister's frustration with the woman. To say her ideas were lackluster was being kind. Sure, a traditional party might be nice for the quaint coastal town of Cypress Pointe, but it would never do for her sister's opulent vision. Nealy took over and before long was working her magic from the other side of the country. Now she had only a few days to finalize the arrangements for the two events.

In addition to the engagement parties, Nealy's second mission involved Cuppa Joe, her grandmother's coffee shop. When her grandmother found out Nealy would be coming home, she asked Nealy to run the shop while she went on a seniors' cruise. Growing up, the coffee shop had been Nealy's second home. She loved the place and would do anything for her grandmother, so she agreed, but secretly wondered if she was pushing herself too hard.

She couldn't remember the last personal day she'd taken, let alone her last real vacation. Was it the first year she worked for Milestones by Crystal? Once she decided to come home to Cypress Pointe for her sister, she'd stood firm on using the vacation days she'd accumulated, knowing once they landed the Ashlee James account, there would be no more free time for visiting family. Okay, so this had turned into a working vacation, but after years of working nonstop, could she picture herself relaxing and doing nothing? Hardly. She'd been born in high gear.

Driving past Swindler's Ice Cream Shop, Nealy noted a young couple walking out the door, hand in hand. Her heart pinched at the sight. How many times had she and her ex met there for what they thought was a secret rendezvous? Another blast from the past. Until now, she'd kept the special memories from that summer tucked away. But really, what did she expect? Had she thought coming back to Cypress Pointe wouldn't stir up a mess of emotions? She thought she'd recovered from her heartache, but driving through town proved challenging.

Her cell phone rang. "Not again," she muttered, and immediately dismissed the leftover romantic notions and adopted her usual business tone. "Nealy Grainger at your service."

"Where are you?" her sister Juliet whisper-hissed into the phone.

"About ten minutes away."

"Step on it."

"Mom getting on your last nerve?"

"I swear, I'm about to break something. Tonight was to be spent visiting with you. It wasn't supposed to turn into let's-interfere-with-every-little-detail night."

Today, Wednesday, the women of the family were getting together to make last-minute tweaks to Nealy's plans for the weekend. The next several days would be a whirlwind of formal social gatherings and casual meet-and-greet time as the families got to know one another.

"When did my engagement turn into a national event?" Juliet asked.

"When you agreed to marry a senator's son."

"I know I asked you to go big, but this has turned into a media frenzy. And who ever heard of a three-day engagement party?"

Their mother. When Nealy's older sister got married it had been a rushed affair because Lanie had been in college at the time, which left their mother disappointed at its small scale.

Now they were going to be related to a senator—her mother's dream come true—so the ante had gone up. And up. And up.

"Where's Grandmother? She's good at distracting Mom."

"She's fed up, too."

Not good if Dorinda Hobart, the voice of reason, couldn't fix things.

"Hold on. Sanity's on the way."

Nealy ignored the usual foreboding that accompanied anything to do with their mother. Instead, she enjoyed the balmy breeze tickling her face. She'd been putting off the prodigal return and the old twinge of inferiority crept up on her, well aware certain family members wouldn't welcome her with open arms. She didn't expect them to behave any differently. She'd burned her bridges years ago and dreaded the cool reception awaiting her.

It doesn't bother me.

Right. If she repeated the mantra enough times, she might believe it.

Instead of dwelling on her insecurities, she turned her attention to her sister. Juliet would be fretting over the details, because, well, that's what Juliet did. As the baby of the family, they went overboard to pamper and protect her.

Then at fourteen, Juliet had been in a horrific automobile accident. Hospital stays and months of rehab had been the norm for her for a long while. The physical scars had healed, but the emotional toll? Nealy wasn't sure her sister had ever recovered. So how could she deny her sister when she begged Nealy to come home, claiming she needed her cool, professional demeanor to deal with a party and a weekend schedule growing bigger and bigger by the moment? How Juliet expected Nealy to keep everyone calm, she had no idea. She was an event planner, after all, not a miracle worker.

As Nealy pulled the car into the parking lot of the Grand Cypress Hotel, the location of all the parties, crushed shells crunched under the tires. Searching for an empty spot in the crowded lot took longer than she'd anticipated but she finally eased into a space. Cutting the ignition, she grabbed her purse and briefcase before exiting the car.

She took a few steps before stopping in her tracks before the main entrance. Wow. The previously modern contemporary style of the hotel now sported a charming Southern plantation facade. When she'd worked here during high school, the place had lost its luster, even though many of the same families returned to the hotel to spend their summer vacations. She'd done shifts at the snack bar, been a lifeguard and parked cars for fancy events.

She'd also met her ex here.

From the moment she laid eyes on him waiting tables in the dining room, she had decided to go after him. She'd strutted below the floor-to-ceiling window overlooking the pool area, twirling her lifeguard whistle to catch his eye. It worked. Boy, had it worked.

Before more memories could overwhelm her, she took a breath and marched on.

Her heels sank into the crushed shells as she took the path from the parking lot. Why on earth had she chosen three-inch heels today? Not that she had a choice. She'd caught a red-eye flight immediately after finishing up an event she couldn't miss. It meant she'd had no time to change from her lemon-yellow linen business suit and leopard-print heels. Huffing along, she reached the wide veranda of the renovated hotel.

Initially she'd been surprised when Juliet booked the engagement party, and subsequent wedding, at this location, until her sister explained the hotel's face-lift. The pristine white exterior with shiny black shutters fronted by a wide veranda dotted with rocking chairs promised a no-stress zone for weary guests.

As she stepped into the spacious foyer, cool air greeted her, along with some major structural improvements. The new owner had removed the old ceiling to create an open two-story master-piece. Nealy's breath caught. Marble floors shone as light filtered through the frosted dome ceiling. A counter nearby, also in marble, had staff waiting behind it to help the guests.

She let out a low whistle. "Not too shabby."

Her cell phone rang. This had to be Juliet worried about her ETA. As she crossed the highly glossed lobby floor, her heels echoed. "Hold on," she said to herself, digging through the contents of her purse, intent on finding her phone, when she bumped into a tall, solid form.

"Whoa," a deep masculine voice said as firm hands grabbed hold of her upper arms to steady her.

"I'm so sorry," she sputtered, pushing her hair from her eyes. "I'm in a hurry and wasn't watching where I—" Her words stopped as she recognized the man holding her in place. *Him.* "Dane?" she whispered.

"Nealy. Been a long time."

Her breathing nearly stopped as she gaped at her ex-husband, Dane Peterson.

No. This couldn't be right, could it?

"What are you doing here?" she managed to croak out.

"I'm the owner."

"Of what?"

"The Grand Cypress Hotel."

Granted, running into Dane made her thinking a little fuzzy, but… "You own this hotel?"

"Yep."

Knocked off-kilter by her first glimpse of Dane after twelve years apart, her legs became shaky. Why hadn't anyone told her Dane owned the hotel? Probably because they figured she wouldn't step foot in the place if she knew.

They'd have been right.

He'd aged well, exceptionally well, as evidenced by the unexpected stirring in her belly. His dark blond hair, highlighted by the sun, was cut short, a far cry from the disheveled locks he'd once sported. Whiskey-hued eyes and tanned skin portrayed the picture of a man in his prime. Even more handsome than the boy from her memories. She still remembered the lanky teen, long hair falling over his brow into his eyes, wearing T-shirts proclaiming the name of a favorite band paired with ripped jeans and sneakers. Today, a mature Dane wore navy pants and a light blue shirt with the sleeves rolled up his forearms. His dark shoes shone.

His masculine scent, so alluring and familiar, had her leaning toward him until she realized her mistake and blinking furiously, she took a hasty step back from the stunning man standing before her and the powerful reaction he evoked.

"How did you come to own this place?"

"It's what I do. Rehab old or failing hotels."

"You renovated this hotel?"

"That's right."

Wow. Talk about total and complete shock.

Nealy shook her head, trying to reconcile this man with the boy she'd fallen head over heels in love with. Her pulse fluttered as the intensity of his gaze made her heart race and her eyes sting.

"Welcome home, Nealy," Dane said in a low, familiar voice.

Her initial surprise at seeing him dissipated instantly as the hurt came rushing back. Apparently twelve years hadn't healed the wound he inflicted when he'd shattered her life that summer. He'd married her, then turned right around and filed for an annulment, dashing her hopes of them spending their lives together. The dream had turned into a nightmare, courtesy of the man standing in front of her.

"Home is L.A. now. If you'll excuse me, my sister's expecting me." She needed to escape from Dane before he noticed her curt tone hiding the traces of old hurt.

"Yeah. About that. There's a problem."

She raised a brow. "What's happened?"

"It's more like who happened."

She shook her head. "You've lost me."

"Remember Angela? The hotel's in-house event coordinator?"

"Sure. We've been working together on both of Juliet's parties."

"Not any longer."

She jammed a hand on her hip. "And why is that?"

"She quit this morning."

Nealy tried to keep from gaping but didn't succeed. "What did you do to her?"

Her sharp question earned her a throaty laugh. "Me? I didn't do anything. You, on the other hand…"

As his sentence trailed off, she protested, "I just got here."

"It seems you were a bit too…zealous in planning Juliet's party. To quote Angela, 'I've only dealt with Nealy over the phone. How much more nerve-racking will it be having her here in person?' Your imminent arrival sent her over the edge."

"Hey, I'm good at my job. I can't help it if she was overwhelmed."

"Overwhelmed or not, I'm minus an event coordinator."

"Thankfully I'm here for Juliet. Her parties will be wonderful despite this upset."

"Easy for you to say. You'll be leaving soon. I'm the one on the hook with scheduled events over the next couple of days and no coordinator."

She tugged the strap of her purse higher on her shoulder. "Figuring out these problems is all in the day of a hotel owner. I'm sure you'll manage. Excuse me." She took two steps when she realized she didn't know where to find her sister. Reluctantly she turned back to Dane.

"Down the hallway," he said and pointed. "Second door on the right."

She headed off, but not without hearing a husky, "Good to see you."

Ignoring the blood roaring in her ears, she hurried to the room. Bad enough the party would be at this hotel, but to run into Dane while she was home? The knots in her stomach tightened. Why couldn't she have gotten a flat tire? Preferably somewhere in L.A. so she would have missed her flight.

Did he have to look so good? Smell so good? And why had she turned into a flustered teenager? Because the man still had a way of getting under her skin, that's why. She pressed her hand against her roiling stomach. She'd worked with top celebrities without so much as a bat of an eye, but two minutes with Dane had her insides screaming as if she were a starstruck groupie. She would *not* let him get to her during her time in Cypress Pointe.

Still, Dane Peterson, owner of the Grand Cypress Hotel. Who would have thought it? And what was she going to do to avoid him?

Before she could come to any conclusions, she crossed the threshold into a large banquet room and assessed the chaos.

Juliet was pacing. Lanie, her older sister, had a box that she was rustling through, pulling out rolls of bunting and crepe paper. Nealy shuddered at the sight. Her mother, Anita, was chastising a tall man with a glazed look in his eyes. Having been at the receiving end of her chastisement, Nealy empathized with him.

"Hey, everyone," she called out. "I'm here."

Juliet shrieked, running over to envelop Nealy in a big hug. "I knew you'd make it."

"Yes, we were wondering when that would be," her mother's voice came from behind her. "We could have used your help this afternoon."

Sure they could have, but then Nealy would have had to stick needles in her eyes.

"Hi, Mom." She gave her a dutiful hug, miffed she let her mother's lack of affection get to her.

Following the pseudo hug, her mother scrutinized Nealy. "You look pale. Don't you ever get out in the California sun?"

Before Nealy could respond, Lanie cut in for her hug. "Welcome home, sis. We could use some major organizing skills since a therapist isn't available."

"Lucky for you I have them."

Juliet put a death grip on Nealy's arm. After their most recent phone conversation, Nealy understood why. Her family had a tendency to be a bit too eagerly involved.

"Please promise me you won't leave my side."

Nealy didn't want to make any promises. Her mother's frown didn't reflect a warm welcome and knowing Dane lurked somewhere in the building made her want to bolt. Then she focused on her sister's worried face, noticing the dark circles under her eyes and that her usually tidy hair was a mess. Nealy lifted her chin. This wasn't about her. Her sister needed her here and for that reason alone she would see this week through. "I promise."

Juliet let out a breath, tears glistening in her eyes. "Thanks."

"Are you okay?" Nealy was genuinely concerned.

"Tired. Work has been demanding. If this party is any indication of what the wedding will be like…"

Nealy should have come home sooner. "Maybe we should—"

"There she is," cried a familiar voice. Nealy

turned to see her maternal grandmother, Dorinda, hurrying toward her. "Come give me a kiss."

Nealy sent one last questioning glance at her sister and received a reassuring nod in return. Once she and her sister were alone, Nealy would get to the bottom of what was bothering Juliet.

"Grandmother!" Nealy wrapped Dorinda in her arms, holding on for dear life. The scent of lilacs Nealy always associated with her grandmother enveloped her. Welcomed her home. This was the person who had cleaned her cuts, wiped her tears and filled her life with joy. "How have you been?"

"Other than missing you, just fine. Talking on the phone and only seeing you for our annual visits is not enough."

Nealy grinned. "I agree."

Dorinda ran a hand over Nealy's wavy hair. "I'm so glad you're here," she whispered and tilted her head toward the women in the room. "Not a moment too soon."

"Are things so bad?"

"Not bad. More like difficult. The usual Grainger women drama."

"As usual, Dad is wise to stay far, far away."

The urge to run away welled up in her, but she squashed it for Juliet's sake. Maybe a few minutes to gather her muddled thoughts would shore up her resolve. "Okay, ladies, before we get busy, I have to make a couple of quick business calls. Be back in a few."

She turned on her heel, hurried out of the room and back down the hallway, hoping she wouldn't run into Dane. Before entering the foyer, she stopped and peeked around the corner. No ex-husband. Expelling a breath, she rushed past the main desk, heading to the veranda for some fresh air and to place the phone calls she promised her boss she'd make. She'd just reached for the door handle when she heard a slow masculine drawl behind her. "Leaving so soon?"

DANE KNEW NEALY would never miss her sister's party. That meant he'd be seeing her again. His regret over how he'd ended things with her had entailed a lot of emotional upheaval, but still he maintained he'd made the right decision to end their marriage before it really started.

What else could he have done but file for an annulment after their impetuous act? Once they'd said their "I do's," the enormity of the situation had sunk in. There was no doubt in his mind he'd been head over heels in love with Nealy, but marriage? At eighteen, he'd had nothing to offer her. No way to support them financially or emotionally. How could he not have considered the consequences? Because he'd let the roller-coaster ride of young love blind him to reality instead of considering what Nealy needed—security and a man with a solid future.

He'd done the right thing by walking away. It had been the hardest decision he'd ever made, more so because he knew he'd hurt her in the process. Yeah, he hadn't missed the surprise and hurt in Nealy's eyes when she'd bumped into him a few minutes ago. She'd never been very good at hiding her emotions. From him, anyway. But she was here now, so how was he going to handle the situation? If her body language and angry tone were any indication, she didn't plan to make any encounters between them easy.

She let go of the door handle and faced him, her lips pressed together, a sure sign she was annoyed. "Do you make a habit of stalking your guests?"

"Only the ones I haven't seen in over a decade."

"There's a reason for that."

"I'm well aware."

Coming back to Cypress Pointe to purchase the hotel had been a calculated risk, like returning to the scene of a crime. But when the hotel had gone up for sale, Dane couldn't resist. After a mere few hours of debating the wisdom of buying a property holding so many memories of love gone wrong, he broke down and placed an offer. It had taken a lot of hard work to get the place looking even better than its former glory, but once he'd started, he never looked back.

Nealy stood with her arms crossed over her chest, one foot tapping. Yeah, she still had all the pent-up energy that got them into one scrape after another when they were kids. "Don't you have some hotel stuff to keep you busy?"

He grinned at her, encouraged by the flicker of interest she tried to hide. "At the moment, you're my top priority."

She narrowed her eyes but the gesture didn't scare him off. She still had the power to make his heart pound with just one glance.

Mahogany-colored hair, cut in wavy layers, swung around her shoulders and down her back. Dane remembered the texture, and his fingers itched to touch the thick tresses. Her slender build admirably filled the suit she wore and he smiled at her choice of footwear. She always did have a flair for the unexpected.

The subtle scent of peaches accosted him, just like that long-ago summer. He also remembered the luscious bubblegum gloss she'd constantly applied to her lips. The bubblegum fad of her youth had faded, but in its place had grown an incredible woman. He could sense she was the whole package. He liked this version of Nealy. A lot.

"How long are you in town?" he asked.

Her chocolate-brown eyes filled with suspicion. "I don't think it's any of your concern."

"Just being courteous."

"And while that's very gentlemanly of you, I'm sure we'll be too busy to see each other during my stay."

"Look, I know this isn't easy for you. I'm sure you feel—"

"I'm trying very hard not to feel anything."

He didn't like hearing those words. She couldn't have lost all feeling for him, could she? The angry glint in her eyes told him otherwise.

"I don't blame you for hating me. I was mad at myself for a long time."

"I don't hate you. I hate what you did to us."

He nodded. "I wanted to talk to you again. Try to make things right."

She raised a dubious eyebrow. "As evidenced by all the phone calls."

"I couldn't. At first, it was too soon. Before long, too much time had passed by."

"Yeah. Twelve years to be exact."

"Are you saying if I'd reached out, you would have talked to me?"

His lips thinned into a mulish line.

"Just what I thought."

From the moment he and Nealy eloped, the situation had gone downhill. He'd been reeling over the loss of a baseball scholarship to the University of South Florida because of a rotator cuff injury. His parents, always at each other's throats, were talking divorce. They spent more time arguing and not enough time focused on their kids. Consequently, he'd missed deadlines to apply to other colleges and scholarships. Spending a wild summer with free-spirited Nealy had been just what he needed to deal with his shattered reality. They'd both been of age, and could legally marry, but running off didn't mean they'd made the brightest move of all time. Look at his parents. They'd married young and couldn't stand each other now. All Dane knew at the time? He was crazy in love with Nealy and the minute she turned eighteen, they'd stolen her dad's car and taken off.

At least her parents hadn't pressed charges once they returned home.

"Well, lucky for both of us," she said, "I'll be very busy while I'm here. Besides, we don't have anything to talk about."

"I need to clear up some things. I think you do, too."

"As a matter of fact, I do." She pointedly glared at him as she swung open the lobby door. "But not today."

He watched her shapely figure disappear behind the door. He turned just as Josh Hamilton, his head landscaper and handyman, strode across the lobby toward him.

"Hey, Dane. Got a minute?"

A minute was about all he had until Nealy returned to her family. "What's up?"

"I fixed the problem in the pool pump house. Anything else?"

Anything else consisted of Nealy Grainger here at the Grand Cypress Hotel. "No. We're good," he said as he kept an eye on the front door.

"Then I'll get back to tending to the ornamental garden by the restaurant."

"Fine, fine," he replied.

"Then I'm going to knock on every guest's door, yell fire and run away screaming."

"Fine."

"Or I could bug the sharp-looking woman who has all those parties planned."

"Get to it, then."

Josh laughed. "Dude. Are you even listening?"

Dane turned to his employee, who also happened to be his friend. "Sorry. What were you saying?"

"Nothing. A little preoccupied?"

"I have a lot going on."

Josh cocked his head. "Anything to do with the pretty brunette walking this way?"

Dane glanced over his shoulder. "You could say that."

"Just did." He slapped Dane on the back. "Good luck."

"I'll need it," Dane said as Nealy headed for the hallway leading to the banquet rooms.

"You again?" remarked Nealy.

"Yeah. I own the place, remember?"

"So go do some hotel things."

He fell into step beside her. "I am. Acting as the temporary event coordinator." Before he could continue the conversation, they reached the Grainger room and Juliet rushed over. "Please, make her stop."

Nealy followed Juliet's gaze to their mother. "What now?"

"She's badgering the caterer for no reason."

"Let me handle it." Dane took off, but not before brushing Nealy's forearm with his hand.

Despite every intention of not letting Dane get to her, his touch sent a tingle of awareness across Nealy's skin. How, after all these years, could his touch affect her?

When the gentle pressure of his hand lifted, Nealy was relieved. Okay, so some things hadn't changed, like a mere touch from Dane raising her temperature. Or the pure command in his every step. Even her mother would have to listen to him. She'd hate that.

Nealy smiled for the first time since arriving at the Grand Cypress Hotel.

"Thank goodness Dane is here," Juliet said.

"Speaking of Dane, you knew he owned the hotel and didn't tell me?"

"I'm sorry." Juliet at least had the grace to look chagrined. "I was afraid you wouldn't come if you knew. You have so many memories tied up in this place and knowing Dane owned the hotel might have changed your mind."

True. Memories bombarded her every step.

"He suggested I tell you but I couldn't take the chance."

So he definitely knew she was coming. Hmm. Still, she wouldn't ruin Juliet's weekend just because the past had caught up with her. Swallowing her pride, Nealy would stick to their plans. By the look on Juliet's face, she was in worse shape than Nealy anyway. "I'd never miss your engagement parties."

"I know he's the last person on earth you want to see, but he's been wonderful. Happy to accommodate two parties. He's so professional."

"Dane? The same Dane who talked me into stealing Daddy's car and eloping?"

"He's not that guy any longer, Nealy. He's made this hotel a success and he's very responsible now."

"But he's still my ex-husband, Juliet. Do you think I should be all smiles and rainbows while he's underfoot?"

"No." Juliet's voice grew quiet. "Maybe it's time to let go of the past."

"Maybe you expect too much." She took a step to escape the room but Juliet grabbed hold of her arm.

"You promised."

"And you purposely kept me in the dark."

"For just this reason. Yes, he owns the hotel, and I am sorry for keeping the truth from you."

The anguish in Juliet's eyes assured Nealy her sister regretted her actions. For that alone, she could forgive her.

"Fine." She softened her tone and privately vowed she wouldn't let Dane's presence rattle her anymore. "What Dane and I had ended long ago. And I have moved on with my life. So has he, by the look of things."

And things looked good from where she stood. As if he knew she was thinking about him, Dane captured her gaze from across the room and his lips curved into that same boyish grin that had once captured her heart.

She broke visual contact, but from the corner of her eye she saw his imposing form coming her way. This time, instead of the urge to run, she stood her ground. She had to in order to get through the next few days. That meant establishing some ground rules.

"Excuse me, I have to, um, do something," Juliet mumbled, leaving Nealy alone with Dane.

She summoned her courage and spoke frankly.

"Look, Dane, I understand this is your hotel and the parties are going to take place here, but I'll stay out of your way if you'll stay out of mine."

He stared at her for a long drawn-out moment then strode from the room.

Nealy watched him go. What, no parting jabs? No last word? He'd given in too easily, which was not like Dane. Or at least the Dane that she remembered.

Maybe he'd changed after all.

CHAPTER TWO

ON THURSDAY NIGHT, Nealy sat in one of the Grand Cypress's private event rooms, the French doors wide open to emit a soft June breeze. Everyone lingered over dessert, delicious strawberry shortcake, that followed a superb dinner of roasted herb chicken and grilled vegetables, catered by the hotel's four-star restaurant. Nealy sipped her coffee, eyeing members of her family and the family of Juliet's fiancé, Brandon Mason. The Masons seemed like nice people, for political elite, but Nealy felt an uncomfortable vibe between the clans. Juliet had been quiet and withdrawn all night. Brandon hadn't seemed to notice.

This couldn't be good.

"Nealy, Juliet tells me you work in L.A.?" Mrs. Mason asked.

"I do."

"Do you know many movie stars?"

Typical question most people asked when you lived in L.A., but in her case, she often met celebrities. "Yes, some."

"How exciting. What do you do that you meet them?"

"Yes, Nealy," said her father, Marshall, who cleared his throat to ask, "what do you do with your business degree?"

Nealy wanted to roll her eyes. The fact that she hadn't attended law school was still a point of contention between her and her parents. Growing up around adults who loved to argue and debate any and every little point of law was both tiring and a bit stuffy. Because of that, she'd never had the slightest interest in pursuing a law degree. Instead, she chose a profession that stirred her creative soul and she'd never once regretted her decision.

Her father knew what her job entailed. He just didn't think she contributed to the good of the world like those nearest and dearest who were socially conscious lawyers. Most of them made no secret of their political and personal causes and platforms and considered her job to be trivial and nothing but fluff. However, they, and especially her dad, had no idea that a high percentage of functions she planned were major fund-raisers for various charities benefitting children and important health issues. Charities she herself had become involved with. She didn't explain or argue because it would only fall on deaf ears. And she wasn't about to turn philanthropy into some sort of petty competition, either. She'd been fortunate to come into contact with a lot of worthwhile people and organizations because of her job.

"Oh, Dad." Nealy did her best to offer a chuckle, but knew it didn't sound convincing. "You know my company handles large events like movie premieres, red-carpet ceremonies and after-parties. Logistics, decorating, refreshments, keeping the celebrities moving in a timely fashion, that sort of thing."

"Now now, you two," Dorinda admonished, then addressed the other guests. "Speaking of celebrities, I have pictures on the wall at Cuppa Joe of Nealy posing with lots of famous people. Of course, I don't know who half of them are, but Nealy likes to send the photos and I frame them."

Nealy's mouth fell open. "You do what?"

"I show you off," her grandmother said.

"Why?"

"Because I'm proud of you, dear."

"You could have been an attorney," Anita sniffed.

"Just like the rest of the family? No, thank you." Yes, almost the entire Grainger gang were lawyers. Her mother and father, sister Lanie and brother-in-law, David. Juliet. Even her boyfriend back in L.A.

"At least you might marry one," her mother said with a wishful tone.

Nealy remained silent, refusing to acknowledge her mother's scheming.

Mrs. Mason, her brows drawn as she listened to the Graingers bickering, turned her attention to Nealy. "It sounds exciting."

"Just think of the billable hours those celebrity clients would bring in," David remarked.

"We aren't moving to California, so don't even think about it," Lanie informed him, using her serious voice.

"But we have a connection."

"Not. Moving."

Nealy rubbed the throbbing over her left eye.

"I told Juliet we should go to California for our honeymoon, but she had something different in mind," Brandon announced as he wrapped his arm around Juliet's drooping shoulders.

Juliet blinked when she heard her name. "What?"

"The honeymoon," Brandon said, raising a brow.

"Oh. Right. The beach condo in Hawaii." She nodded with a distracted air.

"Sweetie, just think of the fun we'd have if we started out in California. Do the whole tourist thing before flying to Hawaii." His face grew more animated as he warmed up to the idea of this trip. "Movie studios. Spotting celebrities. Visiting vineyards." He frowned. "Besides, we practically live on the beach right here."

"Yes, but I think Hawaii's beaches are different."

Brandon shrugged.

Juliet blinked furiously.

Oh, no. Trouble in paradise.

"At any rate, Nealy is good at her job," Dorinda told the group. "We're fortunate she could take time out of her busy schedule to make it back home."

The discussion ebbed and the conversation drifted to local politics.

"If you don't mind," Lanie said to the senator, "I'd like to get your input. I'm thinking about running for mayor and could use a few pointers."

David flinched. "Not that again."

Lanie gave him a stern look. "Yes. That again."

The senator smiled. "I'd be happy to help."

And with his participation, the conversation about the merits of Lanie running for mayor took place.

With the spotlight of scrutiny no longer shining on her, Nealy took the opportunity to slip through the glass doors to the outside patio.

Between follow-up phone calls with her crew
for the event in L.A., flying cross-country and
having to deal with family, jet lag had zapped
her energy. She slipped off the heels she'd worn
all day, and padded to the pool area, empty this
time of night. Smoothing her sleeveless ivory
lace dress, she dropped down on the nearest
chaise to stretch out.

Resting her head against the cushion, she
gazed at the moon high in the star-filled sky.
The sweet scent of a nearby southern magnolia
tree wafted her way. She remembered picking
the creamy, pink flowers when she worked here
at the hotel. The original owner had planted the
beautiful trees around the property. She was
glad to see Dane had kept them in place.

Closing her eyes, she breathed deep to lower
her stress level and curb the tic still throbbing
over her eye. The murmur of voices drifting
from the open café at the far end of the pool
lulled her senses. Her body relaxed from the
stress of the hectic day. She'd started to nod off
when she heard steady footsteps approaching.

"Nealy, I need to talk to you."

She opened only one eye to see Dane take a
seat on the edge of the chaise next to her. He
leaned into her personal space. Her pulse quick-
ened and her muscles shot to attention. Ignoring the tightening in her chest, she said, "What

part of not getting in each other's way while I'm here don't you understand?"

"All of it."

Nealy let out an annoyed breath.

"This isn't about you. It's about your sister's party."

Embarrassment made her cheeks heat. "Oh."

"The caterer is threatening to bow out of Saturday night's big party. He's had enough of your mother's constant interference."

She sat up straight, shifting into professional mode. If his manly presence hadn't already jolted her, this piece of news did the trick.

"How bad is it?"

"Pretty dire, but some quick damage control can fix it, though I don't want Juliet to know. We can handle it without involving her."

"What do you suggest?"

"I'm going to lay down the law with your mother. This is my hotel, my reputation. I just wanted you to know in case there's fallout."

Nealy eyed him, intrigued by his take-control attitude. She'd forgotten how relentless he could be when he wanted something. And right now, he wanted and had her undivided attention.

"Do whatever you have to do to keep things going smoothly."

"Good." His gaze locked on hers. She couldn't seem to break the connection. She caught herself fidgeting and made herself go still. Had he noticed how he affected her?

Amusement, and a dash of rakish interest, flickered in the depths of his eyes. Darn. He noticed.

"Since we're getting along so well," he said, taking advantage of the spark between them, "now's as good a time as any to have a personal conversation."

She crossed her arms over her chest. "You're not going to let this go, are you?"

"Not until you hear me out."

"Why does it matter so much to you? You ended things, not me."

"And I owe you an explanation."

"I'm not asking for one. I never have." She pushed back the frustration. "There's nothing to talk about. We were young and stupid. I was in love when I married you. Apparently you weren't." More like he realized what he'd gotten himself into and couldn't run fast or far enough away.

"I realize you were hurt, but—"

"But what? Do you think I've spent twelve years pining over you?" she asked through a laugh that sounded forced, even to her. "I have a good job. A good life." She paused and her chest grew tight. "A boyfriend."

"Yeah, I heard." A faint hint of disdain filled

his voice. "Made your mother's day rubbing in the fact."

"Look, there's no point bringing up the past." She'd lived through years of dealing with the heartache, wondering why he'd wanted out of their marriage, if twenty-four hours could be considered a marriage. Did she want to relive it? No.

"I'm here for Juliet."

Silence settled between them. The only other sounds were the nighttime serenade of crickets and the surf lapping onto the beach. She glanced his way just in time to see the raw emotion flashing in his eyes before he blinked it away. Maybe she wasn't the only one thrown off balance by her visit.

Voices from the banquet room could be heard, cutting short the awkward moment. The party was breaking up, Nealy thought with relief. Dane's intense gaze remained on her. She shivered, and then rubbed her arms, as if trying to erase the heady sensation.

He leaned forward, his breath, so close to her ear, sending more shivers cascading over her skin.

If she moved ever so slightly, they'd be close enough to kiss. She swallowed hard. The youthful longing she'd quelled now threatened to surface with a vengeance.

As she racked her rebellious brain to come up with something witty and carefree to say, Juliet called out her name.

Dane sent her one final knowing glance before he stood and walked away, his long-limbed stride moving him out of her line of vision. Despite the pain of the past, and her resolve to not let Dane have any kind of hold over her, she'd liked his close proximity.

Disgusted with her own weakness, she groaned and lay back against the chaise lounge, trying to block his image from her mind. She so hadn't signed up for this when she agreed to help her sister.

"Was that Dane?" Juliet asked as she stopped beside the chaise.

"Yes."

"What did he want?"

"To bother me."

"Looks like it worked." She heard the smile in Juliet's voice.

Nealy playfully gave her sister the evil eye. "It won't happen again."

"What won't happen again?" Lanie asked, leading the group as the family moved her way.

"Dane. Bothering her," Juliet answered.

"Think he's trying to win you back?" David asked as he brought up the rear.

"Of course he is," Lanie answered in a sharp

tone. Her husband sent her a puzzled look and Nealy wondered what was up with her usually peaceful sister.

"Who is doing what?" Nealy's mother asked.

"Dane. Talking to Nealy."

"I knew this would happen," her mother said, sounding resigned. "Didn't I tell you this would happen, Marshall?"

Nealy silently counted to ten.

"Yes, you did," her father said. "And I spoke to Dane about it."

Nealy jerked upward and swung her bare feet onto the patio. "You discussed me with Dane?"

"Yes. Told him you were off-limits. It's no secret you're seeing Sam."

She jumped up. "You did what?"

"You're my daughter. I'm looking out for your best interests."

"Again," Anita chimed in. "You always were weak-kneed around him. We had to ensure your protection."

Trying to control her exasperation Nealy said, "I appreciate the concern, but I can handle Dane."

"Please," her mother scoffed, brushing off Nealy's concern. "You never were reasonable when it came to Dane. We couldn't take the chance he might try to lure you into his lair again."

"Lair?" Nealy spat. She would have laughed at her mother's overactive imagination except this wasn't funny. "Trust me, he hasn't tried anything nefarious."

Her mother drew up to her full height, although she was still shorter than Nealy. "You've got a good thing going with Sam. Please don't blow it."

"Don't worry about my life."

"Someone has to," her mother countered.

"Are you kidding me? I can assure—"

Her grandmother interrupted as she broke through the crowd. "Time to say goodnight, everyone. Nealy, will you please drive me home?"

Nealy clamped her mouth shut, retrieved her shoes and went with her grandmother to collect her purse. She couldn't decide if she should scream or cry. Her father had spoken to Dane? How embarrassing. And way over the line.

"They mean well," Dorinda said and laid a calming hand on Nealy's arm.

"There's a reason why I stay clear of this family of buttinskies."

"I know, dear."

Nealy swallowed her bitterness. "I know I disappointed them. Do they have to throw it back in my face?"

"Despite their bluster, they love you, Nealy."

"I just wish they'd back off." She shook her head. "Let's go, Grandmother."

Needing to walk off her temper, Nealy headed to the lobby. The chilly marble floor under her bare feet did little to cool her down. Hopefully Dane had left for the night because she didn't want to see him. Not after learning what her father had said to him. Her family might mean well, but it wasn't their call to make. Her past mistake involved Dane. Her mistake and hers alone. She'd work with him for the sake of Juliet, then she was gone. As she'd told him, she had a life. A great job. A future.

None of which included Dane Peterson.

AS SOON AS she was back at her grandmother's house, Nealy settled into the guest room. Her parents had downsized when all the kids moved out, leaving no room for her to bunk there, which suited her just fine. To be honest, she felt more at home here. Juliet had asked her to stay at her apartment, but Nealy declined. Being at Grandmother's always kept her grounded and centered. She needed some peace with everything going on right now.

After changing into sleeping shorts and a tank top, Nealy sat cross-legged on one of the two twin beds, ready to flip through a scrapbook she'd set on her lap when her grandmother, having changed into her gown and robe, joined her.

"How are you holding up?" she asked.

"Just peachy."

"Are you really?"

Nealy laughed. "Yes. I am."

"Despite talking to Dane?"

Leave it to her grandmother to get to the root of the problem. With Dorinda, no subject was too touchy or off-limits.

"Why is everyone so worried about me and Dane? There's nothing between us."

Dorinda held up her hands. "As long as you're okay with the eight-hundred-pound gorilla in the room, who am I to argue?"

"I have no idea what you're talking about." Nealy twirled a lock of hair between her fingers.

"Of course you don't," Dorinda said in her I-don't-believe-you-but-will-let-you-live-in-denial tone. "The next few days won't be easy so I'll let the topic of you and Dane slide for now."

"Thank you." She patted the bed, beckoning her grandmother to perch on the edge. "Now, tell me about what's going on with you. How are things at Cuppa Joe?"

"Busy, as always. The place keeps me out of trouble."

"Did you read the information I sent on the new coffee system?"

"I appreciate it, but I'm happy with my way of making coffee."

"It's the newest top-of-the-line system available. Upgrading will make your life so much easier."

"Maybe, but I'm old-fashioned. I see no need to learn some newfangled thing. I've said it once, and I'll say it again, my pots work just fine."

"You are stubborn."

"No, just old."

Nealy hugged her, comforted by her grandmother's ever-present lilac scent. "Never."

"Old enough to want some fun before I die," she said with mischief laced in her voice.

Nealy pulled away. "So that explains your interest in a seniors' cruise."

"Some of my friends talked about going and it sounded like fun."

"It will be. To be honest though, I'm worried about one thing."

Dorinda laughed. "Only one?"

"Tell me about these businesspeople bugging you at the shop."

"Ah. The evil Cypress Pointe Merchant's Association."

"What's up with them?"

"They have all these rules and regulations about how the storefronts must look and are always after me to fix one thing or another. I have to admit, I'm thinking about selling."

Nealy's heart twisted "You would do that?"

"Dear, as much as I love the place, I'm ready to retire and you know no one in the family wants to run the shop. I can't go on forever."

She couldn't imagine her grandmother ever slowing down. Or giving up the coffee shop she and her husband had opened before Nealy was born.

Dorinda patted Nealy's hand. "The time is coming."

"I don't want to talk about it."

Her grandmother frowned. "You always were bullheaded. I wonder where you get it from?"

Nealy eyed her grandmother suspiciously when Juliet breezed into the room carrying an overnight bag.

Dorinda rose and kissed Juliet's cheek. "What are you doing here?"

"I asked Brandon to drop me off. I want to spend time with Nealy before she escapes again."

"I thought you two had plans?"

Juliet tossed her purse on the other twin bed and reached behind to undo the zipper of her dress. "We rescheduled. Besides, I'll have a lifetime to spend with him." She threw Nealy a pointed look. "You, not so much."

Dorinda chuckled. "You girls get a good night's sleep. I'm making pancakes in the morning."

Juliet closed the door behind their grandmother then went back to rummaging through her bag. "I'm sorry about tonight. I didn't know Daddy had said anything to Dane." Juliet changed into the pj's she produced from the bag. "Just like old times, right? Parents interfering and Nealy taking off."

The remnants of anger from her parents' actions overshadowed the fatigue seeping into Nealy's bones. "You'd think I would have been prepared. Would have thought ahead. Made a contingency plan." She shot her sister a lopsided grin. "I'm losing my touch."

"You've been gone a long time. Your shields have grown weak."

Then again, they always were when it came to Dane.

Juliet climbed onto the bed beside her. "Anyway, I'm glad we're together. Now we can catch up without interruption."

Toying with the cloth cover of the scrapbook, Nealy cleared her throat. "I do wish you would have told me about Dane owning the place."

"Like I said, I figured you'd make an excuse not to come home."

"I would never do that to you."

"I should have realized. It's just, you've been gone for so long and I didn't want anything to ruin your visit." Juliet twisted the beautiful solitaire diamond engagement ring around her finger.

A nervous habit? Nealy didn't know. What she did know was Dane had never given her an engagement ring. She glanced at her own ringless finger. Neither had Sam. Truth was they barely had time to date, let alone make a formal commitment. Nealy was certain of one thing though, when she finally got a ring, she wanted it to be sparkly, dazzling and over-the-top.

"Besides," Juliet continued, "how do you prepare to see an ex? Maybe it's better this way."

"The lesser of two evils?"

"C'mon. Dane isn't evil."

"Why are you defending him?"

Juliet laid back and stared at the ceiling. "I'm not. I'm simply saying he's not evil."

Nealy grimaced. Tell that to her heart.

The adrenaline from the earlier anger subsided and she leaned back against the headboard. "What were you thinking by booking the Grand Cypress? Did you know Dane owned the hotel?"

"Not at first. I remember visiting when you worked there during summer break and always imagined it would be a beautiful place for a wedding. I know it was run-down back then, but something about it just grabbed me and I fell in love with it. It's everything I dreamed of."

Nealy knew the feeling well. Even at its run-down worst, Nealy always had a connection with the hotel.

"I dropped in to check it out after the renovation. The elegant Southern style is exactly what I wanted for a wedding venue. I met with the event coordinator and booked the place. It wasn't until later I learned Dane owned the hotel."

"Mom must have had a hissy when you told her."

Juliet smiled, with a bit of added mischief thrown in. The first real sign of her old self. "To put it mildly."

"I'm proud of you for sticking with what you want. Not easy in our family."

"The entire process has been a tug-of-war."

Nealy flipped a page in the album, then another, grinning over pictures from their youth. The three sisters playing dress up. Graduations. Birthdays. Weddings. Their parents' anniversary. "So you're handling interference from Mom?"

"I thought she'd be the biggest problem, but…" Juliet's voice wavered.

"But what?"

Juliet stayed silent.

"Whatever it is, sis, you can tell me."

Juliet burst into tears. Waving her hand in the air she sat up, managing a few words between shuddering breaths.

"Don't mind me. It's nothing."

This was a whole lot of nothing.

Nealy placed the open book on the coverlet and turned so she and Juliet faced one another. She reached out to stroke her sister's hair. If she waited long enough, Juliet would open up.

Being the middle and youngest sisters, Juliet the youngest, there had always been a special bond between them. Even through the years Nealy lived on the west coast, they talked at least once a week, if not more. Juliet had seemed fine in the days leading up to the parties, but since Nealy arrived, she'd noticed a change, subtle at first, then increasingly uptight.

"You know you can talk to me about anything."

Juliet swiped at her tear-streaked cheeks. "It's only jitters, right?" She grabbed a tissue from the nightstand. "I mean, c'mon. I'm marrying a senator's son. I should be excited and here I am crying." She sniffled. "I'm only dealing with the engagement right now. What will the wedding plans be like?"

"Has something changed?"

"We've had a few disagreements."

"Like the honeymoon location?"

Juliet pursed her lips. A good sign. "Hawaii is more romantic than rock climbing in Colorado. That was Brandon's first choice. I hate rock climbing. I told him so, but sometimes he doesn't listen." Juliet blew her nose. "It's more than the trip. I didn't tell you up front, but I wanted to have a small engagement party, but Brandon insisted his parents expected a big bash and Mom agreed, so we compromised on two parties. What a headache."

Oh, boy. "Two parties are unusual, but you've got it under control."

"With your help. You've made this fun and I don't know what I would have done without you."

"Anytime, sis."

Nealy fell silent while Juliet rose to pick up her toiletry bag and carry it down the hall to the bathroom.

When she returned, Nealy asked, "You love him, right?"

"Yes, but is it enough?"

Nealy didn't have an answer. Her own track

record left little to be desired. "Tell me more about you two."

"Other than how we met at the law firm?"

Nealy groaned. "Another lawyer in the family."

Juliet hiccuped a giggle. "We worked on a trial case together then went out after hours with coworkers from the office. Eventually, it became us going out alone. He's smart, fun to be with, and Mom and Daddy adore him."

"Of course they do. He's a lawyer," she said through a small sigh. Her parents were happy Sam, her boyfriend, also happened to be an attorney. They'd met at a charity function she was overseeing, had clicked and started dating. As for Juliet, she sounded as if she was trying to convince herself Brandon was Mr. Right.

"Then let's get to the bottom of your concerns. Are you marrying Brandon for them or yourself?"

"I don't know now. I mean, I think he's the one, but could I be wrong? How do I know for sure?"

"I'm not the person to ask. Look, if he makes you happy and you enjoy being with him, I'd say those are strong building blocks. You just never know when you'll fall in love or who you'll fall in love with."

"True." Juliet half sniffed, half laughed. "Look at you."

Nealy straightened her shoulders. "What about me?"

"You did everything you could to stay away from love and lawyers and now you're seeing one."

Nealy laughed. "What can I say?"

"I don't know. You're always cagey on the subject."

"He's a good man."

"Loyal to the end, our Nealy."

"I don't know about that." She'd never told Sam about Dane, deciding early on in the relationship she didn't want to talk about her past. Was withholding information a form of a lie?

"You must like Sam, otherwise you wouldn't still be with him."

"It's not a fireworks kind of relationship, not like with Dane." Her heart gave a heavy jerk because she spoke the truth. She slapped the scrapbook closed, as if closure alone could diminish the time she'd shared with Dane.

"Look, I'm sorry about dumping all this on you. Brandon is great. I guess I've been overwhelmed by having two parties." She tried to brush off her concerns with a shaky laugh. "I'm being pulled in so many directions. Mom's got delusions of grandeur and I don't feel like Brandon's family is overjoyed about us."

"I didn't get that impression."

Juliet took a deep breath. "See. I'm overreacting. Everything will be fine. The parties will run like clockwork and after I'll ask myself why I was a nervous wreck."

Nealy patted her sister's leg. "Try to enjoy the weekend."

Juliet nodded. "Oh, before I forget, I wanted to show you this." She slid off the bed to retrieve something from the top of the dresser. She handed Nealy a shiny brochure from the Grand Cypress Hotel. "You didn't get a chance to see the incredible grounds yet. The landscaper is a genius." She pointed to a picture of the beautifully manicured yard sweeping from the hotel down to the beach. Magnolia trees in bloom. "I know this is a little soon since the wedding isn't for a while yet, but I want to give you a heads-up now so you can start brainstorming ideas for how it will look.

"You know I always wanted this grand, Southern-themed wedding. Maybe not super traditional because the ceremony will be outdoors, but it's what I pictured in my dreams. There are two magnolia trees at one side of the hotel and the lush grass sweeps down to the beach. I couldn't imagine a more perfect spot to say my vows."

Nealy scanned the brochure. Yes, the grounds were amazing. From the pictures alone, it seemed the hotel had everything in place to conduct a full-scale wedding. Atmosphere. Scenery. Romantic ambiance.

How weird. Dane, owning a hotel. *This* hotel. She studied the picture, remembering the span of grass Juliet mentioned. Back when she worked there, it hadn't been as lush and healthy. She recalled playing volleyball in the summer after their shifts. Playing catch with Dane after his dreams to play professional ball were dashed by his injury.

"Seems perfect."

"It is. Brandon wasn't too sold on the place. He wanted the reception held at stuffy St. Luke's banquet hall, but I managed to convince him." She shivered in mock horror. "Heavy brown drapery and musty smell. Yuck."

"Juliet." Nealy stopped as she noted her sister's shadowed eyes. "Take a breath. If you aren't sure, you don't have to go through with this. Think it through."

"I'm sure." Juliet grasped Nealy's hand and squeezed hard. To reassure Nealy or herself?

There was always turning back. Nealy knew from personal experience. One look at Juliet's uncertain expression and Nealy started to tell her so, and then decided to hold her tongue. Who was she to counsel her sister on true love?

"Get some sleep." Juliet hugged Nealy and climbed into the matching twin bed. The topic of conversation was over and Nealy admitted she was kind of thankful there would be no more said on the subject of love and marriage. "I have tomorrow jam-packed with activities. Shopping. Nail salon. The works."

Before long, Juliet's breathing evened out and Nealy knew her sister had fallen asleep. Unfortunately, Nealy couldn't even doze. All charged up from seeing Dane, her family and hearing her grandmother's news, she found herself staring at the ceiling.

"This isn't working." After a while, she rose, snatched up the scrapbook and sat under the window where a street lamp gave enough light for her to view the old photos.

Her gaze settled on a group picture of the entire family taken about five years ago at a picnic in the woods. They'd rented a cabin in the mountains and the whole bossy group had had a good time together. Who would have thought?

Nealy flipped the page and found some loose photos sandwiched between the last page and back cover. She picked them up and sorted through them. When she came to one featuring her and Dane posing in her grandmother's backyard, her smile slipped.

Dane had an arm thrown over her shoulders, his goofy grin mugging for the camera. She had her arms wrapped around his waist, her smile wide and happy. It was taken a few weeks into the summer after they'd started dating. She could tell by her expression she'd already fallen in love.

She ran her finger over the smooth surface, her vision blurring as tears prickled her eyes. What a whirlwind summer. She remembered the highs and lows, the excitement of young love and the desperation of not wanting to be separated from Dane. They'd spent every minute together. She'd never experienced such heart-wrenching love since then, and strangely, she was grateful. The emotions had been too intense, burning bright and extinguished too soon. She couldn't live through those ups and downs again. She knew she didn't have it in her.

She'd reserved a special place for Dane in her memories, but not in her life. Earlier tonight he promised her he'd have his say. She recognized the determined gleam in his eye. Okay, so maybe after all these years he wanted to set the record straight. She could agree with closure for both their sakes, but nothing more. She could not, would not, let Dane tear down the walls of protection she'd built around her heart.

CHAPTER THREE

DANE DIDN'T HAVE to be a savvy businessman to know Nealy would make good on her promise to avoid him. He hadn't talked to her since the tense conversation by the pool, not for lack of trying. She'd been around, helping Juliet with last-minute preparations for the parties, but although she was on the property, she managed to stay clear of him.

Each time he caught sight of her, she stole his breath away. Her take-charge attitude and the professional way she handled the staff put to rest any worries he might have had about her working here at the hotel. The themed ideas she came up with for each party were unique, yet personal to the couple. She had her finger on the pulse of the activities without coming across as overbearing. Initially he wanted to spend time with her to come clean about the past. Now he just wanted to be near her.

He straightened his tie and took one last look in the bathroom mirror before heading downstairs to oversee tonight's first engagement party. Nealy had come up with a casual Sweet Summer Nights theme meant to dazzle the guests this Friday night. Dane had to admit, he was impressed by her work so far.

Curious about her, Dane had researched Milestones by Crystal on the web. The company had an outstanding résumé of high-profile functions like movie premiers and after-parties, celebrity birthday parties and anniversaries. The sheer scale and mastery of work had built them a sterling reputation. Dane now understood why his event coordinator had been intimidated by Nealy. It wasn't Nealy herself, but the creative force behind the woman. While it explained why Angela quit, it didn't replace an important cog in hotel operations.

His general manager could have acted in the coordinator's place, but as de facto event coordinator, he mentally ran through the checklist. Canopies set up on the property for the guests to dine under. Check. A removable wood floor in place for dancing under the stars. Check. Dinner, dessert and music. Check, check and check.

Okay, one weekend of planning was fine, but he needed a new event coordinator ASAP. Nealy had been his saving grace, with the event well in hand. How did she do this all the time? He didn't have the answer, but knew things had better go off without a hitch. With the senator's presence here this weekend, the hotel's image and future were at stake here.

Since opening the refurbished hotel there had been a few scheduled holiday parties, but nothing like tonight's smaller and more subdued celebration or Saturday night's larger and more elegant affair. The Mason family involvement added a level of concern he hadn't experienced before, but he had no doubt his staff would step up to the challenge. He hired the best and expected results. If the senator was pleased with how everything went, Dane hoped he would be agreeable to booking future political events at the hotel. Dane had a lot riding on the success of this weekend.

"I'm more comfortable around bulldozers and jackhammers than dance floors and orchestras," he said under his breath. He grabbed his wallet off the bedroom dresser and slipped it into his back pocket before locking up his suite. He'd commandeered two rooms overlooking the water on the far end of the second floor and had them remodeled into executive quarters for himself. During the renovations, he'd settled into living on the property and stayed.

His cell rang as he walked down the hallway to the elevator. "Peterson."

"Tell me everything is going well."

He smiled at the voice on the other end. Uncle Hank, his business partner, out of town on another project, calling for an update. He'd been thrilled when Dane told him Senator Mason would be holding Saturday night's lavish engagement party here and wanted to make sure Dane wowed the man in order to secure more dealings with him.

"Right on schedule."

"Good. I'm glad to hear it."

"You should know better than to worry."

"Old habits."

Dane grinned. His uncle had helped Dane get his act together after high school, encouraging Dane to get a college education while giving him a job during those years. Leaving home at the height of his parents' never-ending drama had been the best move he'd ever made. The dysfunctional home had led Dane to make many rash and costly mistakes as a young man, but Hank had seen something in his nephew and mentored Dane.

For eight years now, he'd worked seven days a week learning every aspect of hotel remodeling. In the beginning, he'd gotten dirty during construction, but hard work turned to pride once he brought a struggling property back to life with his own hands. He'd always been good with finances and learned to invest wisely and make the most of his money. Now he and Hank were partners; actually, they were more than partners since Hank had done more for Dane than his own father.

"This weekend is important," his uncle continued. "Word of mouth from the senator will go a long way."

"You know I won't let anything ruin this opportunity."

"I'm counting on you, son."

Nothing like heaping on a little more pressure. "I'll call you later."

Dane signed off, a slight smile curving his lips. Uncle Hank was all about the bottom line and he'd taught Dane well.

With each new property he remodeled, Dane had become more successful and prosperous, and as a result was able to implement innovative ways to run the business efficiently and keep costs down without skimping on quality. He'd used work to fill the emptiness inside him, which he refused to examine on a deeper level. He never lacked for female company, but decided long ago never to get serious with a woman. He didn't want to end up like his parents, living in a convoluted relationship Dane never understood. Better to focus on being successful, at least in business. It might be lonely at times, but he already had one strike against him with the annulment. Between ending the marriage to Nealy and witnessing the disaster of his parents' marriage, he'd sworn off the institution. Why risk making another mistake?

But when Nealy walked back into his life, he sensed the emptiness starting to shift. Having put the past behind him, he hadn't expected his emotions to get all tangled up again. Since he knew she was coming to help Juliet, he'd anticipated an awkward first meeting. One look at her as she strode into the lobby, and a hard knot formed in his throat. Then she bumped into him and everything faded away as his attention narrowed to one thing: the love he'd lost when trying to make things right.

He locked those thoughts away as he arrived in the lobby, satisfied to find it filled with the Friday-night crowd. The main restaurant, The Rendezvous, specializing in fine cuisine, along with the more casual outdoor Sand Bar Cafe, did a brisk business. His initial profit margin for the hotel proved better than projected, a very important factor in his bid to make the Grand Cypress a destination hotel.

This property had become more than a rehab project to him. When he came back to Cypress Pointe and looked at the run-down hotel after his uncle proposed the purchase, he suddenly discovered two personal reasons for making the

Grand Cypress the most successful hotel in the Peterson Holding Group.

First, he needed to prove to others he could make sound, rational decisions based on fact, not emotion, after the impulsive marriage and subsequent annulment twelve years ago.

And second, he needed to prove to himself he was nothing like his deadbeat dad. Dane worked hard for what he now had in his life, no thanks to a father who cared more about pleasing his unhappy wife at the expense of Dane and his brother, Alex. His father never supported Dane, but never hesitated to call when he needed something or show up on Dane's doorstep when his life was sinking. Guilty of always continuing to help the old man had made Dane jaded about love and having a happily-ever-after.

So his goal was to make the Grand Cypress Hotel the place to be seen in Florida. After Juliet's much-touted engagement parties, along with the senator's connections, he hoped booking future events would allow him to build a small empire here in Cypress Pointe. But the weekend was far from over and he needed to be on his game.

He'd just checked in with the manager on duty when the Grainger clan appeared for the smaller toned-down celebration. At the tail end of the group, Nealy swept into the foyer, a wide smile on her lips, her brown eyes shining. She'd pulled her hair back in a sleek, fancy ponytail. Absolutely beautiful, she was wearing a sleeveless magenta dress and glittery black high heels.

As she passed, she caught his eye and nodded curtly. His grin spread into a full-blown smile and she stumbled in reaction. He strode to her side, taking her arm to steady her.

"Hang on there."

"The, um, floor is a little slick."

"Right." He should let go of her arm, but the softness of her skin mesmerized him. The familiar peach scent intoxicated him. He couldn't drag his gaze away from her flushed face.

She cleared her throat.

Dane reluctantly removed his hand and asked, "How is Juliet doing?"

"Nervous. Obsessing." Nealy's brow knitted in concern. "Can I ask you a question?"

Surprised Nealy would ask him anything, Dane schooled his expression. "Sure."

"Has Juliet seemed off to you?"

"I haven't seen her much. She spent most of her time with my former event coordinator."

"Right." Nealy's cheeks turned a becoming shade of pink. "When you did see her, was she acting strangely?"

"Maybe she's just preoccupied with all the preparations."

Nealy shook her head. Under the chandelier light, the diamonds in her ears flashed, just like her eyes.

"It's more. I know my sister. Something is up with her. More than the normal type of jitters."

"Your mother's been making her a little uptight. Standard operating procedure."

"What about Brandon?"

"What about him?"

"How does he seem? Like an okay guy? Even though I spoke to him last night, I couldn't get a sense of who he is. Has he been helping Juliet with the party plans?"

"The only time I see him is at his regular tennis court time on Tuesdays, here at the hotel."

Nealy tapped her foot, a contemplative look in her eyes.

"What?"

Her gaze darted to him. She parted her luscious lips to say something, but then stopped.

"Nealy…" Dane coaxed.

"I'm getting a bad feeling."

His mouth curved into a wry smile. "Since you've been in town all of three days?"

"Last night she broke into tears and I got the impression she was having second thoughts. I don't want my sister doing something she'll regret."

She started to move away, but Dane blocked her escape. She looked at him, eyebrows raised.

"Are you sure you want to make waves?" he asked.

"I need to make sure my sister isn't making a mistake."

"She's a smart woman. She can make her own choices."

"She needs to be one hundred percent sure of what she's getting into."

He ground his molars together at the obvious dig. "Unlike us?"

"I didn't say that."

"Nealy, I regret how things ended. You'll never know how much."

Nealy's rigid posture softened and turmoil eclipsed her dark eyes. "This weekend is about Juliet, not you, not me, not what we had," she said with a shaky voice, as if not believing for a second seeing each other again wasn't an issue. Her obvious struggle to keep him at bay had him hoping the aloof veneer she'd adopted could be cracked.

In this instant he suddenly realized how much he wanted her forgiveness. Needed her to say the words out loud.

"Dane, I have to go." She eased around him and with a determined stride continued across the foyer, disappearing into the fray of family and close friends.

BEFORE LONG THE GUESTS were mingling and wishing the engaged couple the best. Nealy tried everything to get her sister alone, but people interrupted or Juliet sent Nealy off on errands. Obviously Juliet didn't want to talk to her. At one point, she'd spied Juliet by the pool, having what looked like a heated conversation with a man she'd seen working in the hotel's garden the day she arrived. Strange. After that, her sister flit between family and friends, but Nealy kept an eye on her.

A light breeze picked up, carrying the briny scent of the gulf waters with it. The extreme heat of the day had passed, leaving the evening cool as the sun began its descent in the cloudless sky. As soon as Nealy could, she corralled her sister.

"Juliet, what's going on?" Nealy whispered, hoping no one overheard.

"I'm fine," she snapped. "Go have fun."

Okay, this was the last straw. Worried about her normally docile sister's sharp response, Nealy started to press Juliet when Brandon, standing in the middle of the outdoor dance floor, asked the group to quiet down while motioning for Juliet to join him. With a smile pasted on her lips, Juliet approached her future husband.

"Tonight we celebrate Juliet saying yes to my

proposal. Not that I didn't have my concerns, I might add."

Some of the guests chuckled.

"This poised, beautiful, intelligent woman has agreed to be my wife, and I am so, so lucky." He grinned sheepishly. "I know planning two parties is unusual and it has taken its toll, but I want to thank you with all my heart, Juliet."

He took her hand in his, glanced over his shoulder and nodded. On cue, music blared from the speakers and two dozen strangers ran onto the dance floor, grooving to a popular dance song Nealy recognized from online wedding videos. Chaos ensued around the bride and groom as the dancers made multiple circuits to keep the crazy number going.

Nealy took in the entire spectacle, stunned. A flash mob? Right in the middle of her sister's lovely party? Someone bumped into her and knocked her back to her senses. No, this was not happening. Not on her watch. All the hours of discussing and...

Oh, no! Juliet. Where was her sister?

Between the shaking bodies and thumping beat, Nealy sought her out. Through the frenzied crowd, she spotted Brandon trying to drag Juliet into the mob with him. Juliet fought him, her face stricken. The hours spent carefully planning this gathering had turned into a frat party. Music continued full blast while the dancers tried to encourage guests to get up and join them, including her grandmother, who danced right into the crowd with a big smile on her face, her hands up in the air swaying to the beat.

The elder Masons stood off to the side, disapproving expressions on their faces. This was more of a disaster than Nealy first feared.

Once the shock abated, Nealy stepped into the throng to aid her sister. A guy grabbed her arm and motioned for her to dance. She shook her head, but the guy didn't release her, pulling her into the frenzy. When she tried to step away again, he squeezed her arm to keep her with him. To her great relief, Dane cut in, glaring at Nealy's dance partner. The guy took the hint, releasing her arm, and moved on. Dane leaned close, lowering his mouth to her ear.

"You okay?" he yelled over the blaring music.

"Yes." She scanned the area. "Where's Juliet?"

"I don't know."

"How could this happen?"

"I'd take a wild guess and say Brandon made prior arrangements." Dane slipped his hand into hers and she followed as he led her out of the chaos. The jolt of pleasure at holding Dane's hand went beyond being grateful for his rescue. She held on as he maneuvered toward the sidelines. He was only being protective, right? So why did the connection feel so good? As soon as they cleared the crowd, Dane tugged her closer and, much to her surprise, she let him. He spoke to the man tending to the music and after a few terse words, the rowdy song abruptly ended with as much shock value as when it started.

He turned to her. "This is a disaster."

She couldn't argue. Juliet's party had been reduced to a manic free-for-all.

He tightened his grip on her hand and a memory flashed of the day they'd gone to the courthouse to get married. He'd held her hand just as tightly then. The promise of a future together had made her giddy and she stuttered when it came time to say "I do."

Standing next to Dane now, so close that she could feel his heat, made her heart race. She couldn't let Dane get to her. They'd had their moment and blew it. She would not let these jumbled feelings for him ruin years of healing the wound he'd inflicted on her heart.

She removed her hand from his. "Let's find my sister," she told him. They were no longer in the crowd; she didn't need his protection. Or the disturbingly warm, reassuring sensation of Dane's hand pressed to hers.

He looked worried and dropped his hand to his side. "I've got to do damage control. Now," he said.

She cringed. With one last fleeting look at Dane, she hurried inside. Sure enough, she found Juliet, surrounded by their family as they assured her they knew nothing about the flash mob. Nealy put an arm around her sister's shoulders as she wiped her wet eyes.

"What was that all about?"

Juliet's voice hitched as she looked at Nealy. "I don't know. Brandon loves to make every occasion memorable, but this? He knew I wanted tonight to be low-key."

"This is unacceptable," their mother announced.

Brandon rushed toward them. "Juliet, I've been looking all over for you." He stood before her. "We were… Are you crying? You're upset?"

He only noticed now? Nealy wanted to strangle him.

"What's wrong?" he asked.

"How can you ask me after that, after that mess you created out there?"

Brandon shrugged. "I wanted to surprise you.

Kick it up a little tonight. I can't do it tomorrow night with my parents' guests here."

Juliet's mouth flapped open.

"What?" Brandon asked.

Juliet's face turned red. "So it's okay to embarrass my family?"

"No, sweetie. We were having fun."

Juliet's eyes went wide. She reached for Nealy, and grabbed hold of her arm, manicured nails pressing into Nealy's flesh.

"Brandon," Nealy said. "Why don't you go tell everyone we'll be right out."

"Sure." Uncertain, as if noticing the tension in the room for the first time, he kissed his fiancée on the cheek and hurried off.

Juliet sniffed. "I can't believe he would do this tonight."

"Apparently he wanted to have fun," Nealy repeated.

"I can be fun. Hmm, maybe not like that kind of fun."

Nealy understood. She'd dealt with enough self-indulgent clients to recognize somebody who wanted things their own way and would have them, even though they'd been told no. What she really didn't like was the resulting pain she'd glimpsed in her sister's eyes when she reached the same conclusion.

"Let's get back to the party," Nealy suggested, expertly herding everyone into the banquet room. "Let's hope Brandon doesn't have any more surprises for us."

Juliet's eyes went dark. "He'd better not."

At her sister's furious expression, Nealy's concern eased.

After Brandon's impromptu flash mob, the remainder of the evening continued without a hitch. Once the party wound down, Nealy located her grandmother to drive her home. Before they could leave, Dane cornered her.

He ran a hand through his short hair. "I'm sorry this happened. I spoke to the DJ. He was sworn to secrecy and only carried out his client's wishes."

Dorinda reached up to pat Dane's shoulder. "It's over, Dane. Don't dwell on it."

His gaze tangled with Nealy's. "I don't run a slipshod hotel."

Nealy blinked, surprised at his vehemence. "I'm sure you don't."

"I didn't think there'd be any problems this evening," Dane said in a distracted tone.

"Welcome to the world of event planning. No matter how much preparation, there's always the possibility that something will go wrong. The secret is taking care of the incident as efficiently as possible and moving on. By tomorrow, Juliet will be worried about the next party."

He watched her, his expression wary. "You don't believe that, do you?"

She snorted. "No, I don't. Does Brandon even know my sister?"

A brief flash of uneasiness passed over Dane's face.

"Never mind. Let's hope there are no other surprises tomorrow."

His eyes narrowed. "The next party will run like clockwork."

"I'm going to hold you to that."

"And I'm going to hold you to a dance with me."

She should have come back with a witty retort, but instead she remained silent. Dealing with the memories of Dane was nothing like the reality of this strong, handsome man requesting a dance. Here she stood, enjoying the view of her ex-husband, not wanting to look away, even though she should. What happened to her emotional armor? Her hard-earned self-control? "Don't get ahead of yourself."

"You're in Cypress Pointe. You think I'm not going to take advantage of the close proximity?"

Just like him to think she would agree so readily. "There will be no closeness."

His wide grin elicited a shiver across her skin. Darn.

"It's a date."

"No dates. There will be no dating. No closeness and absolutely no dating."

Dorinda chuckled. "What's one dance?"

She gaped at her grandmother.

Dorinda smiled at Dane. "We'll see you tomorrow. Nealy, let's get a move on."

Dane caught Nealy's eye one last time. She didn't like the conviction in his gaze, or the self-satisfied smile on his noble face.

Minutes later she got her grandmother settled in the convertible. Stars twinkled in the sky. A perfect night for romance, if one were inclined to think in romantic terms. Which she wasn't. Under any circumstances. Especially around Dane.

She'd driven a few miles when Dorinda said, "Dane looks quite well. Very fit. Tanned."

"Grandmother, are you checking him out? You're not planning on turning into a cougar, are you?"

"Believe me, since he's been back in Cypress Pointe, the single ladies have been vying for his attention. He's kind, quite good-looking and successful. Any woman would be lucky to have him."

Nealy was instantly jealous. She tapped her thumb on the steering wheel, bothered by her grandmother's comment. She was right. Any woman would be fortunate to have this particular man in her life.

"Besides, he only has eyes for you," Dorinda added.

Nealy's face grew warm. Because Dane still had eyes for her? Or the fact she liked the idea of him still carrying a torch for her?

"Grandmother, don't go thinking Dane and I will get back together again. It's not going to happen."

"Hmm."

"You don't believe me?"

She shrugged. "Not from what I saw…."

Nealy used her warning voice. "Grandmother."

"No Dane and Nealy. Got it."

"Let's change the subject."

"Fine. Before going on my seniors' cruise I need to bring you up to date on the upgrades at the shop."

"Okay," Nealy ventured, skeptically. This sounded like trouble, pure and simple.

"I have a list of things that'll need to be upgraded."

"I'm sure it'll be a breeze."

Grandmother opened her purse and pulled out a folded piece of paper. She unfolded it, revealing a full page of work that had to be done.

Aghast when she saw the length of the list, Nealy glanced at her grandmother.

"Watch the road, dear."

Facing front and righting the steering wheel, she said, "Grandmother, I have a job in L.A. No way I'll get everything completed before I leave."

"I only have you, Nealy. Well, you and your favorite nephew, Davey, but he's too young to supervise the shop."

"Lanie lets Davey work for you? He's fourteen."

"He comes in every day, mostly to hang out, but he sweeps up for me so I slip him a few dollars. It's surprising he shows up at all, since the other family members are too busy for the shop. Not their thing."

"I'm sorry they aren't around, but—"

Her voice turned to steel. "I'm not getting any younger, Nealy. This may be my last chance to get away and have fun."

Dorinda's words affected her. She didn't like thinking about her beloved grandmother getting older. Slowing down.

"How long have you planned this?"

"Since you told me you were coming home." Dorinda shrugged, not looking one bit guilty. "I needed your help. The one person who understands what Cuppa Joe means to me."

What could she say? Dorinda had been after her for months to come home for a visit and Nealy had one excuse after another not to. After all, Nealy was the one family member who would consider fixing up the shop. For years, everyone else had been telling Dorinda to sell the place. With all the hassles she'd tolerated lately, it made sense to put it on the market. Still, Nealy hoped her grandmother would have second thoughts due to the connection the shop held for her. The shop tied her to Poppa Joe. Nealy understood how bittersweet some connections could be.

Besides, Nealy had been close to her grandmother all her life. Dorinda had accepted her for who she was without judging her. She'd found the safe haven she needed at her grandmother's place and Cuppa Joe. Growing up in a home of obsessed overachievers left Nealy lost and adrift. Her grandmother had never asked for anything in return, just loved Nealy unconditionally. How could Nealy turn her back the one time she had asked for something?

"You play dirty, Grandmother."

Dorinda crossed her arms over her chest. "A woman has to do what a woman has to do. I want to join my friends on a cruise instead of worrying about these nitpicky projects. It could very well be my last hurrah."

Nealy groaned.

"So?"

She ran scenarios through her head. After all, supervising these small but numerous projects at the shop couldn't be hard, right? She could run an event with her eyes closed.

She glanced at her grandmother and knew she never had a choice to begin with. "I'll do it."

"Splendid." Dorinda nodded as if coming to some conclusion. "I've been thinking. You're correct, the shop hasn't changed enough over the years. Still the same coffee system, as you know. So, while you're sprucing up the shop, why don't you make those coffee upgrades you've been bugging me about. Get Davey to pitch in. Then, when I get back, I'll decide if I want to sell."

"Grandmother, I hope you won't."

"Dear, I can't hold on to the place forever, hoping you'll show up and run it for me."

Great. Grandma guilt. The headache that had started forming that first afternoon she'd walked into the Grand Cypress Hotel was now upgraded to a full-blown migraine.

EVENTUALLY, NEALY MUST have fallen into a deep sleep because she never heard Juliet slip out of the bedroom the next morning. Juliet had spent the night, again, at their grandmother's and been restless the entire time. She had supposedly forgiven Brandon for the flash mob, but Nealy wasn't convinced. Meanwhile, she had an extra-long list of things to attend to today, so Nealy wasn't all that upset when she woke and discovered Juliet had already flown the coop.

Almost ten, Nealy rolled over to grab her cell phone. Now would be a good time to call Sam. Every time she'd tried since arriving in town, the call had gone straight to his voice mail. Since it was very early in L.A., she should catch him.

He answered on the second ring.

"Hey, there. How are the festivities going?"

"A few wrinkles, but for the most part we have everything under control. How's the trial going?"

"Should wrap up next week." Sam had been in court with an important case, so she hadn't seen much of him in the past few weeks. Come to think of it, she hadn't seen much of him before the trial started, either. "I promise when we win, I'll take you away to celebrate."

"I'd love to, but I may be working with Ashlee James by then. When she signs on, I'll be swamped."

"When you get back, we'll make plans. Listen, I have to run—"

She frowned. "But I need to talk to you about—"

"—to a last-minute strategy meeting. Talk to you soon."

He ended the call before she could get in another word. Had she just been dismissed? Sure, they spent more time on the phone than in person lately, but she needed to talk to him. Needed the connection, especially since she'd run into Dane, who left her confused. How could he brush her off so easily?

Annoyed, she tossed back the covers. Not the best way to start her day. Shaking off her dark mood, she hit the shower, hoping to wash away the bad feelings.

The day flew by and at 6:00 p.m., the guests had begun arriving at the Grand Cypress for engagement party number two. The Masons had been pleased with Nealy's elegant choices and raved over the details. While Nealy appreciated their response to her work, she had more pressing matters at the moment. Namely, a missing Juliet.

While the guests milled about, Nealy waited outside for Juliet. As her concern rose, she tracked down her sister Lanie, who was speaking with the waiting photographer. "Any word from Juliet?" Nealy asked.

"No. I've tried her cell, home and office

phone numbers. Nothing. When was the last time you talked to her?"

"Last night. She was gone when I woke up this morning."

Checking her watch, Nealy puffed out a breath. They'd staved off trouble since her mother was occupied elsewhere, but she'd be here any minute, demanding answers.

Pacing now, Nealy stopped before a floor-to-ceiling window. On the patio beyond the room, the guests chatted and socialized among the beautifully staged backdrop of twinkling stars draped in magnolia trees, snacking on specially made hors d'oeuvres and high-end champagne. A string quartet played in the corner. She'd created tonight's ambiance as if it was one of her elite Hollywood parties, going for all the glitz and glam she could muster. Silver tulle artfully weaved around the chairs fluttered in the gentle breeze. Glittery silver star confetti sprinkled each table. Candle flames wavered. The color scheme of white, silver and scarlet conveyed drama. Intended to impress, it delivered the effect she wanted, just as she and Juliet had envisioned.

She ran her fingers over the sheer fabric of her dress, a floating, luminous silver chiffon number with a draped neckline in the front and an open back, a wide scarlet sash at the waist fitted into a full skirt to the knees. A perfect dress for dancing, which reminded her Dane would be after her to take a turn on the dance floor with him tonight. She stopped her thoughts from wandering and switched her focus back on tonight's important event.

Where could Juliet be?

Nealy paced the room again and then her cell phone rang. She grabbed it. "Nealy Grainger."

"It's Juliet."

"Jul—" She turned her back to the room, not wanting the others to overhear. "Where are you?"

She heard a sniffle on the other end. "Not in Cypress Pointe."

"What are you talking about? The guests are all here. The Masons are holding court."

"I'm sorry, Nealy. I can't do it. I can't marry Brandon."

Nealy froze. "Wait. You said things were okay between you two."

"They were, sort of, but the more I thought about the stunt he pulled last night I knew I couldn't go through with the engagement, let alone a wedding with him."

"Hey, I don't think he meant anything by it. This is a big decision to make over one little dance number."

"It was a sign. You know, like a symptom of a bigger problem."

Oh, boy. Brandon should have thought things through. "You should come back. We'll sit down and talk this out."

"You can't be surprised. I guess I've known for a while, but after all the effort you put into the preparations, I felt guilty walking away." She paused. "I read your face, Nealy. You don't think Brandon is the one. Knowing you understood gave me the strength to do this."

Had her feelings been so obvious? Great. For sure she'd get the blame for Juliet breaking her engagement. "Juliet, please don't put this on me."

"I'd never do that. I'm just so…"

Nealy heard Juliet's sob and her heart ached for her sister. "Honey, it'll be okay."

"I'm sorry to do this, but I can't tell Mom or the others. Will you? I've already called Brandon to break it off."

Nealy bit the inside of her cheek.

"I need some time away. I'll be fine knowing you're handling things. You will handle it, right?" She sniffled. "Get Dane to help you. He's good in a crisis."

From bad to worse. The bearer of bad news *and* asking Dane for assistance? When had she become the uber-responsible one in the family?

"I'll do whatever I can."

"I need you to be the go-between until I decide what to do next."

Well, Nealy wasn't a conspiracy theorist, but there were too many people in Cypress Pointe changing the game plan on her. "You heard I'm running the shop for Grandmother? So I'll be around."

Juliet sighed. "When things die down I'll... What?" Her voice faded as if she had moved the phone from her mouth.

"What?" Nealy called back.

Her sister's voice returned. "Sorry. I wasn't talking to you."

Nealy went numb. "You're not alone?"

"I have to go. Thanks. I love you."

"Wait. What's going on? Who are you with?"

Juliet hung up. Nealy stared at the phone, feeling blindsided. Between Juliet, her grandmother and Dane, managing her time in Cypress Pointe had now turned into a major juggling act.

CHAPTER FOUR

"THIS DID NOT just happen," Nealy whispered as she lowered the phone. Juliet had bailed on her own engagement party. What was she thinking? And leaving her with the fallout? Somehow her parents would find a way to blame Nealy for this.

She needed a contingency plan. Nealy was an expert, after all, so she put her concerns aside and donned her event-planner hat. Worries about Juliet, and who she was with, would be dealt with later. Right now, Nealy had an engagement party to cancel.

"Deep breath. You can do this."

"Do what?" Lanie asked as she joined Nealy.

Hurdle number one. "Juliet isn't coming."

Lanie stared for a mere second, then playfully tapped Nealy's arm. "Super. Really, where is she?"

"I have no idea." She held up her phone. "The call I took? Juliet telling me she can't go through with the engagement."

Lanie's jaw dropped. "Oh, no. But—"

"Yes, there are at least a hundred guests out there expecting the happy couple."

"Is Juliet okay?"

"Didn't sound like it." When Lanie started to ask more questions, Nealy help up her hand. Juliet's change of heart and who she'd taken off with was her story to tell. "I don't have any more information. Right now we have to let everyone know what's happened."

Placing a hand over her heart, Lanie whispered, "I can't believe you're serious."

So serious, in fact, her stomach kicked up in rebellion at the idea. As event planner, undoing the party fell on Nealy's shoulders.

Where to start? This had happened to her once before, early in her career. A young reality-show couple had planned a blow-out event to announce their wedding plans. The party included lots of VIP guests and paparazzi. An hour before the event, the fiancé found out his intended had signed up for another show requiring her to be out of the country during all their pre-wedding activities. Needless to say, he didn't like being second choice over a television show, so he called it quits on the spot. To her credit, Nealy had put together an amazing party, so the guests stayed to wish the guy well.

Maybe today's disaster would also work out. According to Juliet, she'd already given Brandon the bad news, so his parents must also know. Yet the Masons were still here and the party outside continued in full swing. Muted music sounded in the room. Laughter and voices carrying through the glass doors. Maybe they were waiting for her to make the announcement?

Taking a breath, Nealy strode forward. Just as she was about to step outside, the doors swung open and Dane entered, his expression grim. Even in the midst of a calamity, he exuded authority, although his charcoal-gray tie hung a tad askew.

"Nealy, thank goodness. Where are your sister and Brandon?"

"I take it you haven't heard?" Nealy explained the current situation, expecting a thunderstorm, and she got one.

"What was your sister thinking?" asked the thunderstorm.

"I guess she didn't want to be engaged to a man she doesn't love?"

He sent her a "that's obvious" look. "You do realize we have a real problem here?"

"I do."

"I'm sorry, Nealy, but I really needed this party to work out. I'd hoped to secure more of the senator's business. This weekend was a test-drive to prove the Grand Cypress Hotel could handle his campaign events."

"Really? My sister just broke off her engagement and you're worried about business?"

"This is my livelihood."

"And my sister's life." She paused and looked deeply into his eyes. In a soft voice she said, "It's hard when decisions are taken out of your hands."

He grimaced, clearly aware of what she was referring to.

"Yeah, it doesn't feel great," he agreed.

The tension was broken when Lanie caught up to them. "So, what's the plan?" she asked.

Nealy figured a little lightheartedness was probably needed. "As it so happens, I'm trained to handle problems exactly like this. It's why I get paid the big bucks."

Dane's shoulders relaxed but his serious gaze never left hers. "You take the lead."

"Gee, thanks."

"Can you shut down a party without too much fuss, Nealy?" Lanie asked, glancing outside at the guests.

"Yes, I can."

"Um, I'm not sure that's going to happen." Lanie crossed her arms over her chest.

"And why not?" Dane asked as his cell phone rang.

"Because our mother is on her way over here. Things are about to get sticky."

Lanie tilted her head to one side, gesturing toward the glass doors. Sure enough, Anita was bearing down on them like a heat-seeking missile, or in her mother's case, a drama-seeking missile.

Dane pulled his still-ringing cell from his pocket and glanced at the screen. "I have to take this. Do what you can with your mother. Let me know if you need help with the rest of the party guests."

Nealy saluted him before he hot-footed it out of the room.

"You can do this," Lanie said in sisterly support.

"I'd hoped to avoid her," Nealy confessed, knowing it was impossible. The words left her mouth just as Anita halted in front of Nealy.

"We've been greeting guests for forty-five minutes without any sign of Juliet or Brandon. You said you'd have everything under control." Her gaze roamed the room. "Where is your sister and her groom?"

"About Juliet." Nealy took a bracing breath. "It seems she's made other plans."

Anita chortled, though it did sound forced. "Amusing, darling, but enough with the little jokes. Where is she?"

"Juliet won't be here. She broke off the engagement with Brandon."

"Ridiculous." Her mother's face grew pinched. "Your sister would never pull such a stunt. It's not like her."

Her mother was correct, Juliet's sudden departure was out of character for her straight-as-an-arrow sister.

"She needed some time to think," Nealy said as she used everything in her power not to squirm. "To make sure she'd made the right decision."

"You're telling me the truth? This is no joke?"

"Do you think I would make up this story?"

Anita turned pale. "What could she possibly need to think about? Brandon is a wonderful man and his parents are exactly the kind of in-laws I've dreamed of."

Indeed, this was a dream come true for Anita. Not so much for her daughter. Nealy stood taller. "Maybe Juliet had other dreams."

"She's being foolish," Anita stated as if that was the only consideration at stake here. "Get her on the phone and tell her to come over here at once."

Lanie laid a hand on her mother's arm, aware that her mother's outrage was her way of dealing with the surprise. "I think we should trust Juliet on this."

"Nonsense. There are influential people here today, celebrating her engagement."

Nealy knew she was going to regret her next words, but needed to get everything out into the open. "She's gone, Mom. Deal with it."

"Gone?" Her mother blinked at Nealy, her anger shifting to a confused daze. "What do you mean, gone?"

"As in not in Cypress Pointe." Nealy couldn't trust her mother with any more information. If she knew Juliet was with someone who was probably not Brandon, her mother would blow a gasket.

Anita turned to Lanie. "Please, go and find your father."

Lanie glanced at Nealy, who nodded in return. Once her sister left them, Anita focused on Nealy.

"What did you do?"

"Do?"

"To make your sister leave. She was fine yesterday."

Nealy silently counted to ten. She knew she'd get blamed for Juliet's decision. Ever since she'd stood up to her folks and picked her own career path, they'd taken her decision as a personal affront. Instead of fixing the relationship, they'd only grown further apart ever since. "Mom, she's a grown woman. She can make up her own mind. If Juliet has concerns, it's best she deal with them now. Not after she's gone ahead with an elaborate wedding."

The older woman shook her head. "I don't understand."

"Until Juliet decides to tell us what's going on, we should honor her wishes."

Her mother looked as if she was about to faint. "What about the guests?"

"Dane and I will handle them."

At Dane's name, color quickly returned to her mother's face. Nealy waited for her next barb, but just then, Lanie arrived with their father in tow. He went straight to his wife. "Anita?" Worry eclipsed his normally calm demeanor.

"Juliet isn't coming, Marshall. She ended the engagement to Brandon."

"But why?"

"We don't know, Dad." Nealy had always imagined what it would be like for the family to gather together in a time of crisis. United. Maybe this was the moment.

Her father frowned at her. "Why didn't you stop her?"

Or maybe not.

Nealy ignored the hurt she felt. It had been like this often, her family, especially her parents, thinking Nealy caused all the trouble. Granted, she'd been the odd man out growing up. Her parents had always tried to fit Nealy into their ideal mold, but she'd never fit. While other family members focused on what they perceived to be the "right" track, Nealy had taken a little longer to figure her life out. She couldn't help it. As a young person she'd been a free spirit, leaping before she looked. Charging headlong from one calamity to another. To gain attention? Who knew? Still, the fact her parents never saw her as an accomplished adult stung.

Nealy straightened her shoulders. Time to act like an adult. Prove her parents wrong. "This was Juliet's decision, Dad. I knew nothing about it until she called."

He stared at her as if hoping she'd change her story, then his shoulders slumped when he realized she told the truth. She remembered how powerless he'd looked during her rebellious teenage years. He wore the same expression now. She wanted to hug him, but held back.

Anita put her arms around her husband. He returned the gesture, solid in the face of diversity. Nealy could barely swallow around the lump of emotion in her throat.

Her mother pulled away and faced Nealy, her tone pure steel. "I'll take over from here."

"No, Mom. I know how to handle a situation like this. I'll do it."

"You came here to do a job and look what happened."

And just like that she was back in high school, sitting in the administration office, waiting for her mother to bail her out because she'd skipped a couple of classes or hadn't taken her studies seriously and failed to complete her assignments. She'd always been too involved with drama club, choir or breaking curfew with her friends, something more fun than focusing on the academic classes her parents stressed were so important. Unwelcome tears pricked the backs of her eyes.

She'd anticipated hearing, finally, "Job well done, Nealy. Your ideas are fabulous and the place looks amazing." But no. They wanted to take care of things. Without her.

"I'm afraid not," Dane's firm words and confidence carried from across the room. As he strode forward, he seemed to have everyone's undivided attention. Authority resonated in his voice. "Since Nealy is the event planner, she will deal with the details. Talk to the Masons."

"Dane, this is a family matter," Marshall said. "I appreciate you wanting to help, but we—"

"Mr. Grainger, I understand emotions are running high here, so I'm politely asking you to let us do our jobs while you and Mrs. Grainger take some private time to absorb the gravity of Juliet's decision."

Marshall's surprise at Dane's obvious concern rendered him speechless. Nealy felt for her father, usually he had it all together and was the one to make sense of a situation. "It'll be fine, Dad. This is a shock for everyone. Juliet asked me to take care of ending the party, so I will. Better me out there trying to explain the situation to the guests than you and Mom."

"Of course." He nodded and held his arm out for his wife. "Anita. Lanie. Come along."

Lanie glanced at Nealy, an apologetic look on her face, before following her visibly shaken parents out of the room.

"That went well," Nealy deadpanned, blinking back the moisture in her eyes.

Dane moved beside her, concern evident in his eyes. "You okay?"

Obviously, she wasn't okay. Her family had left her and were disappointed in her again. And yet for all that, her heart squeezed in admiration for Dane, who had taken a terrible situation and made it easier on them.

She brushed off the melancholy. "Fine."

"Sure?"

Yep, just like the summer they'd had each other's back. How easily they fell into old patterns. Afraid to examine that realization very closely, she said, "What do you say we get to work?"

"As you said, you're the expert. Where do you suggest we start?"

"With the Masons. Find out what they know."

Speaking with the Masons, Nealy found out they had indeed talked to Brandon. They were disappointed, too, though for different reasons, but were holding up fine. Nealy knew their poise came from years in the public eye. They knew how to rise above an unexpected development.

Since the string quartet was still playing and food and drink still flowing, Nealy called for attention and the curious guests settled down. "I'm sorry to announce the engagement has been called off. Juliet and Brandon request you respect their decision and ask for privacy at this time. Please, enjoy the refreshments before making your way out. Thank you so much for understanding."

Nealy played hostess, answering questions from the guests without giving any answers. She thanked them for coming, as if redirecting a failed engagement party happened every day in her line of work. In the meantime, Dane spoke with the caterers and his waitstaff to keep them in the loop.

Once she had a free moment, she searched out her grandmother. She found Dorinda sitting by herself, her expression drawn.

Nealy sat beside her grandmother. "What a night."

Her grandmother patted her knee. "Juliet just called. She wanted to make sure you were okay."

"Me? It wasn't my broken engagement."

"No, but she did ask you to tell the family."

"Wish she'd called Mom and Dad herself."

"I saw your parents before they disappeared. How did they take the news?"

"Well, considering they think I'm at fault—"

"Although, they're wrong...."

Nealy sighed. "They're worried about Juliet. This is very unusual behavior for her."

"I wish I'd put a stop to things before it got this far."

Nealy glanced sideways at the older woman. "How on earth would you have done so?"

Her grandmother played with the straps of her purse. "Those two weren't a good match. I should have sat Juliet down and forced her to see the truth."

"Grandmother, I sensed the same thing, but as much as I tried to talk her into rethinking her relationship with Brandon, she didn't see it until she was good and ready."

"At least I'm not the only one who had doubts."

"Try telling the folks."

Dorinda waved a hand. "They wouldn't have listened."

True. Her folks didn't listen to Dorinda any more than they listened to Nealy.

"Maybe they didn't want to know." The thought made Nealy sad. Frustrated. And a little bit angry for Juliet.

"Give them time."

"I won't be here long enough for it to make a difference. Once you get back from your cruise, I'm flying to L.A. I think I've done enough to cement my reputation in this family."

Dorinda touched Nealy's cheek affectionately. "Oh, Nealy."

The last of the guests departed. Both sets of parents exchanged uncomfortable goodbyes. Nealy noticed the senator stop to talk with Dane before leaving. Keeping busy, she signed off on a number of invoices and checked her voice mail. As she picked up a centerpiece that she intended to bring back to her grandmother's house, Mrs. Mason came up alongside her.

"Well, this didn't end as I expected."

"I'm sorry, Mrs. Mason. My sister isn't a flighty person. I'm as surprised about all of this as you are."

"Sometimes it takes a major life event to realize your best-laid plans might not be best for your future." The woman beamed at Nealy with a genuine smile, not a fake expression, which Nealy had expected. She had to hand it to Mrs. Mason. The sophisticated lady had taken the evening in stride. Must be what made her popular in her own right. "In spite of the outcome, Nealy, you did a fabulous job with the party. I've been to a great many events since we've been in politics and I have to say, I'm impressed."

"Thank you. And again, I'm sorry."

"Better to find out now, rather than after all the planning and expense of a large wedding."

Exactly. Why couldn't her family be rational like this woman?

"I know you're based in L.A., but if you ever want to make a change, let me know. I could refer you to many of my friends and political associates."

"Thank you." Surprised, and touched, Nealy thought about her clientele and said, "I'm afraid I have plenty to keep me busy, but I appreciate the offer."

Mrs. Mason pulled a business card from her purse and handed it to Nealy. "Just in case," she said before she rejoined her husband.

Nealy stared at the embossed card. She'd never worked with politicians before. How different would it be than working with celebrities? Lost in thought, she started when Dane spoke to her.

"New business?" he asked.

Nealy folded her fingers around the card. "More of a thank-you."

"You did a great job. I heard quite a few people say so."

She shrugged. "Wish things worked out better for Juliet."

"Still, people took notice. No wonder you're in demand in L.A."

Right. L.A., not Cypress Pointe. While the idea of working with the Masons intrigued her, she'd hopefully have her plate full with Ashlee James's business, once she made her decision about signing an exclusive contract with Milestones by Crystal.

"You know we could use a premier event planner in Cypress Pointe."

She shook her head. "Not interested."

"Hey, it was an idea."

"An idea you need to get out of your head."

He grinned and walked away, leaving Nealy to wrap things up.

The tables had been undressed and stored beside the stacked chairs. Decorations had gone into boxes. She put aside the special novelty keepsake items specially made for Juliet and Brandon. Juliet could decide what to do with them later. She'd made arrangements for the leftover floral arrangements to be used around the hotel and donated to some of the local churches.

The string quartet had long since left, but the dance floor remained. Under the starlit sky, Nealy kicked off her shoes and raised her arms above her head to stretch. Alone, she let out a long sigh of relief. One job down, one more to go. Please, no calamities like this when she managed Grandmother's coffee shop.

From the outdoor sound system, the up-tempo song changed to a bittersweet ballad. Nealy closed her eyes and swayed to the music. She cleared her mind of worries about Juliet and disappointing her parents. She'd take these hard-earned quiet moments to let the stress flow from her before rejoining the real world and its responsibilities. After all the excitement of the day, she deserved this downtime.

Suddenly, she sensed someone nearby. Her eyes flew open to find Dane grinning at her as he took one of her hands in his, putting his other hand around her waist, bringing her to him. "You still owe me a dance."

"Quit doing that."

"What?"

"Sneaking up on me."

"Hey, I saw a beautiful woman who promised me a dance. I couldn't resist."

"I didn't promise you a dance," she protested, but found she wasn't ready to push him away.

"Not in so many words, but I saw the yes in your eyes."

She rolled her eyes to mask her pleasure. "In your dreams."

Dane twirled her around then wrapped his arms around her as he hugged her close. With her back against his warm body, his spicy cologne enveloping her, Nealy's heart hammered out of control.

"Don't tell me you haven't dreamed of this over the years," he said in a low voice against her ear.

They swayed to the beat before he twirled her again and they came face-to-face. When he put some space between them, she exhaled with relief.

"Even though you made sure we didn't stay married?"

"Even so."

"Why?"

"You were the only girl for me?"

"You have to ask?"

He chuckled. "Yes, sweetheart, you were the only girl for me."

Now she didn't know if he was serious or

teasing her. She should leave, but her heart rebelled. For her own sake, she should run, except curiosity got the better of her.

"I've got to say, I love your choice in shoes, but seeing you barefoot like this reminds me of how we used to dance on the beach."

Immediately, Nealy was transported back to being the carefree teen she once was. How many nights had they danced on the beach in the wavering light of a bonfire? Dane had promised he'd love her forever then callously ended their marriage.

Cold reality hit her. She wasn't a teen, Dane wasn't the love of her life and she didn't live here any longer.

"It was ages ago, Dane."

"Doesn't make it any less memorable."

She stopped, looked into his eyes. "We can agree on the memories. They, you, were an important time in my life. But it's the past, Dane. Maybe it would be better if we left them there."

His eyes turned weary for a second before he sent her a sweet, secret smile she remembered. Her treacherous heart skipped a beat.

"Doesn't mean we can't make new memories," he said in a husky voice.

She halted. No. Too much, too soon. "To what end? If I wanted to spend time with you, which

I don't, I'm leaving in two weeks. I have a job, a life, in L.A."

"So you keep telling me."

"Two weeks is barely enough time to get to know each other again."

"But plenty of time for me to explain why I wanted the annulment."

Her throat grew tight. "At this point, does it matter?"

"It does. And after, maybe we could reconnect. Like old friends."

His idea felt as if he'd insulted her to her face. Nealy removed her hands from Dane's. "Friends?"

He sent her a fierce look. "We were once."

"Yes, we were. But that was before."

"Look, I'm not suggesting anything more permanent than two people who were once important to each other getting reacquainted. What could it hurt?"

It could hurt plenty. This time she had to be the strong one. The one to stop them from making another mistake. Trying to rekindle their old...friendship would bring regrets. Face it, once upon a time they'd been more than friends. Dane might have been the one to put an end to their marriage twelve years ago, but tonight she would be the one to end this...this...whatever was happening between them.

With all the willpower she could muster, she turned, snatched up her shoes and walked away from him.

LATE SUNDAY AFTERNOON, Dane entered his office to catch up on paperwork. With all the projects he had going on, he'd been on site seven days a week. The idea of turning off every device he owned and going an entire day without communicating with anyone—with the exception of Nealy—appealed to him.

After she shot down his suggestion of getting reacquainted last night, she was the last person he should want to spend time with, but still, he found himself intrigued, despite her rebuff. Yes, he understood he'd hurt her all those years ago when he filed for the annulment, but there was no denying the still-powerful spark of attraction between them. After spending just a few days with her, Dane was curious to find out more about the woman she had become. Wanted her to see he wasn't the boy she remembered but had indeed made something of his life.

His phone buzzed to announce an incoming call. He picked up the handset. "Dane Peterson."

"What happened this weekend?" Uncle Hank's voice vibrated with displeasure.

Dane stared out his window at the beach and the clear blue water beyond. A sailboat skimmed over the slight surf, heading south. Dane would love to have been onboard, enjoying an afternoon off like most nine-to-fivers. Or maybe tossing the baseball around with a few buddies to keep his arm loose for the softball game against their rivals this weekend.

"There was a slight change during the event."

"Dane, I told you this weekend needed to go well. The point was to make Senator Mason see the benefits of using the hotel in the future."

"Look, despite the canceled engagement party, the senator and his wife were more than gracious under the circumstances. Rest easy. Before everyone left, the senator told me he liked the facility. Said his staff would be calling to book a fund-raiser soon."

Hank expelled a deep breath. "I have to say, when I heard what happened, I was worried."

"Have I ever let you down?"

"Not yet."

Dane chuckled. "You taught me well, Uncle Hank. I can handle a crisis."

"I must admit, when I heard the Grainger clan was involved, I had my concerns."

At the negative tone in his uncle's voice, Dane braced himself. Due to Dane and Nealy's history, there was no love lost between the two families. "Nealy handled the upset with professional expertise. The Masons were impressed with the party and the way we took care of the situation."

"We? As in, you and Nealy? Where was Angela?"

Here came the tricky part. "Angela quit."

"Quit?"

"Yes, sir. Turned out to be a good thing. If we do work with Mason's campaign team, there will be time-consuming demands. Better to find out now she couldn't handle the pressure."

"If this goes how we hope it will, giving the senator our support will up our visibility. I want this, Dane."

Yeah, Dane knew.

"I'll be in town soon. We'll sit down and compare notes then."

"Yes, sir."

"And one last thing. Stay away from Nealy. You don't need her kind of trouble."

Dane's spine went stiff. "Excuse me?"

"She took the wind out of your sails once, son. Almost ruined your life. Don't let her get to you again."

Dane almost laughed out loud, but his uncle's warning wasn't funny. Nealy almost ruined his life? More like he'd broken her heart. He didn't blame her reaction to what he'd put in motion. Sure, he'd been down afterward, feeling all kinds of guilt about ending their marriage, and ultimately, their relationship. Once he told Nealy what he'd done, there was no going back. For all the pain, he'd never looked at the marriage and subsequent annulment as ruining his life. Just the opposite, actually. He'd gotten the annulment to save them from eventual heartache, not because he didn't love Nealy.

"Don't worry. She's only in town for a short time."

"Then steer clear. I don't want her interfering with our plans." With that, he signed off.

Dane replaced the handset in the cradle and his gaze wandered over to the window again. Yes, it sure was a beautiful, sunny day. Another boat glided by on the water. While he'd have been glad to be on that boat, taking a break from work for a few hours, his uncle's words haunted his thoughts. *Stay away from Nealy.*

As if he'd ever been able to.

She'd brought fun into his life when he'd been at his lowest point. News of losing the college scholarship had gotten him so down he didn't know what to do. But Nealy had. She'd come up to him, all smiles, her eyes flashing with mischief. He immediately lost his heart. Only to break hers.

He started to type an email on his computer, but his memory drifted back to an earlier time...

Standing on Nealy's front porch, ready to shatter her dreams after coming from the courthouse. Taking a shaky breath, he rang the doorbell. He heard running from the other side, then the door burst open. Nealy vaulted herself at him, her arms circling his neck.

"I'm Mrs. Dane Peterson," she said, followed by a giggle. "Can you believe it?"

He eased her arms away to set her away from him. "Nealy, we have to talk."

"I know I promised not to tell my folks until you were here, but I couldn't wait. I spilled the news to Juliet after I got home last night and before I knew it, we told the entire family. My dad isn't even mad we took his car."

"Stole his car."

Nealy waved her hand in dismissal, as if taking her father's car was a minor point. Since Dane had been on the police chief's radar all summer for causing mischief with Nealy or his buddies, using the car could have landed him in hot water if Nealy's dad decided to make it an issue. "We said we wanted to be together and we made it happen." She giggled again. "The lady helping us at the courthouse must have thought we were crazy."

"We were." After finishing their shifts at the hotel, Nealy had been upset about an ongoing argument with her parents. He found her sitting under one of the magnolia trees, crying her eyes out. His heart broke for her. He gathered her in his arms, whispering sweet promises to make things better. She suggested on a half chuckle they run off and get married. Sure, they'd joked about getting hitched a couple of times since they'd started dating, but it had always been just that, a joke.

He'd pulled away, glimpsed her tear-stained face and told her he wanted to take care of her. Forever. Before he had time to think it through, he'd convinced her to go through with the idea. She agreed and they'd gone to Nealy's house. She snuck inside, grabbed the keys to her father's car, and they drove to the courthouse.

"They aren't thrilled. Dad wanted to storm over to your place, but I begged him not to." Her eyes went big and round, pleading. "Forgive me?"

"About the marriage, Nealy. I...I did something."

Her grin faded. "Are you okay? Did your family kick you out?"

"No. They don't know. It's me. I changed my mind."

"About telling your parents?"

"No. About being married. I filed for an annulment."

"What?" Her face grew pale. "Why?"

After they'd driven her dad's car back late last night, he left Nealy on her doorstep with a searing kiss, promising forever and an enduring love. Crazy about her, he went home, slipped in the back door to make his way to his room. Before he could get there, the loud arguing from his parents' bedroom stopped him in his tracks. They tossed accusations at each other, debating money, questioning each other's commitment to the marriage, to the family.

"I didn't sign up for this mess," his father raged.

"And I never wanted marriage. Kids. You ruined my life."

His blood froze.

Yeah, his parents' marriage was not the best, but his mother never wanted him or his brother?

For as long as Dane could remember he, and his younger brother, Alex, escaped when their parents started in on each other. Dane had protected Alex. Together they'd forged a bond of shared pain, united in hiding the scars inflicted by their mom and dad's loveless marriage. Their parents had tried to use the boys whenever they were on the outs. All they cared about was getting back at each other, never once considering the harm inflicted on their children. Still, the damage of living in a dysfunctional family had taken its toll.

Had he run off with Nealy thinking her love was enough to heal him? He'd done exactly as his parents had, agreeing on the spur of the moment to get married, never thinking about the consequences they'd set in motion.

Dane shut himself in his room and crawled into bed. He didn't sleep while his parents' argument continued on the other side of the wall. When the gravity of what he and Nealy had done hit him full force, he knew he couldn't sentence both of them to the same fate as his parents. Getting caught up in an instant of craziness was one thing, but they'd made a decision affecting each other's future. He had a minimum-wage job. No college education. How did he expect to take care of her? And what about her plans for college? He couldn't go with her. And when she hinted about reconsidering college so they could start their lives together, he didn't want her dropping out because of him.

He'd tossed and turned. His chest ached when he finally came to the logical conclusion. He couldn't stay married to Nealy. As much as he loved her, he couldn't tie her down. Didn't want her resenting him one day. Didn't want her to feel like his mother, weighed down in an unhappy marriage. At this point, he couldn't promise her a bright future. Not when he didn't know where his own life was headed. He needed to figure out his life path before he could take care of a wife. Nealy deserved better. They both did.

By dawn, he'd convinced himself he would do the right thing and followed through with the only answer he could come up with.

"Nealy, I don't know what we were thinking, but we can't stay married."

"Why not? We love each other. We'll make do." She reached for him but he backed away.

"Love isn't enough. It can't find us better jobs. We don't have a place to live, even."

"We'll find somewhere we can afford. We can get second jobs." The desperation in her voice grew. "We'll figure this out together, Dane."

"What about college? You're enrolled. Ready to go."

"I can go later."

He shook his head. "No way. I've already lost my ride. I won't let you miss out, too."

"It's my choice."

"And it's my choice to get an annulment."

When she saw the determined look on his face, realized he wasn't backing down from his decision, the hope in her eyes extinguished. "You're serious."

"I am."

Tears rolled down her flushed cheeks. He

reached out to thumb them away but she ducked her head.

"I'll never forgive you for this," she whispered before stepping through the threshold and closing the door in his face.

"No, I don't suppose you will."

He waited a few tense moments, hoping she'd return.

She never did.

The buzz from the telephone snapped his attention to the present. No, Nealy hadn't forgotten or forgiven.

Amazingly, through years of fighting and bitterness, his parents had stayed together. Dane had come to understand their relationship was an addiction neither could live without, even though the marriage was unhealthy. He'd seen his parents inflict enough hurt on each other to make him run from the altar. No, he'd decided marriage wasn't in the cards for him, but maybe, in the short time Nealy was in Cypress Pointe, he could convince her to at least forgive him. He didn't want their shared past making her any more wary of him than she already was. He couldn't change the past, but with the two of them in Cypress Pointe, maybe fate was giving him a chance to make amends. The question remained, would she listen to an apology?

He pictured her shock when she'd run into

him in the lobby. Recalled watching the shock turn to anger. Yet in the four days she'd been here, she'd softened a tiny bit towards him. Could he wear her down enough to change her mind about him?

He had to try to find out.

CHAPTER FIVE

THE SUN HAD just peeked over the horizon Monday morning when Nealy unlocked the old half-glass, half-wooden front door of Cuppa Joe. After seeing Dorinda off on her cruise, she arrived at six o'clock to get started. Excitement and wariness wrestled within her. Years had passed since she'd crossed the threshold, yet she couldn't wait to get the place up and running with her new ideas.

She'd dressed for comfort this morning, in a sleeveless loose-fitting tank top in a swirling black, blue and beige pattern, worn jeans and ballet flats. She left her hair loose. Not her usual L.A. style, but for a Cypress Pointe coffee shop, she was good to go.

The tote bag she carried slipped down her arm as she removed the key from the lock and stepped inside. The scent of coffee lingered in the air, along with the familiar feeling of home, something she'd only ever experienced here. Nealy found the switch on the wall beside the door and flipped it on, the buzzing of the fluorescent overhead lights filling the silence. Nealy perused the room. Not much had changed over the years.

She walked through the main area of the shop, past tables and chairs on either side, to a tall freestanding counter farther in the back. On it sat the cash register and along the wall ran a long counter holding two coffee machines, a three-compartment sink and beneath it a built-in refrigerator. Dorinda had even added a dishwasher, as Nealy had suggested. A hallway led to the restrooms and rear exit.

The half dozen small tables and chairs scattered around the customer area were the same ones Nealy remembered from her childhood. To her shock, Nealy noticed a couch tucked in a far corner. She wanted to thank whoever convinced her grandmother to add the homey touch. For years, everyone had called the coffee shop Dorinda's living room. Now it looked like one.

Finished surveying the place, Nealy went behind the counter. She tucked away her tote and purse and opened the cabinet doors to take inventory. The storage space held everything from stirrers to sugar packets to jars of cinnamon and nutmeg. Coffee and filters were located next to the coffeemakers. Grandmother had two brewers, both with two lower warmers and one raised warmer to keep multiple pots of hot coffee ready while another brewed.

"Let's get this party started."

Nealy pulled out filters and beans and proceeded to get the coffee brewing. Once she had that going, she searched for the ceramic mugs, as well as paper to-go cups and lids. Right where she remembered them. As the aroma of coffee began to fill the room, she rounded the side of the counter to check the condiment station. It looked as if Sierra, her grandmother's one employee, had restocked the supplies before closing the shop yesterday.

Thinking about the weekend, an image of dancing with Dane popped into her head. What was wrong with her? She hadn't slept well last night, unable to get him, or the scent of his spicy cologne, out of her mind. She'd vowed to avoid him, yet there he'd been at every turn.

Out of the blue, Nealy heard, "Excuse me, dear. Is the coffee ready?"

Nealy nearly jumped out of her skin. With a hand over her heart, Nealy spun around to find a well-dressed elderly lady standing by the counter.

"Sorry. I didn't hear you come in." Because she was too busy thinking about Dane.

With a slow gait, the woman crossed the room. "You probably don't remember me. I'm a friend of your grandmother's." The elderly lady stuck out her hand. "Terri Simmons."

Nealy shook the woman's hand, noticing her weathered skin. As she studied the woman with the lovely snow-white hair and pretty features, her memory kicked in. "Mrs. Simmons, hello. How is the hip doing?"

"Please, call me Terri." The older woman's face softened. "I'm so pleased you remember."

"Grandmother keeps me up-to-date with the happenings in Cypress Pointe." Frowning, she asked, "Why aren't you on the cruise with the other ladies?"

"Since the hip surgery I haven't been steady on my feet. The idea of all that walking on a cruise ship made me nervous. Instead of joining the ladies, I promised Dorinda I'd keep an eye on you and the shop."

Nealy thought wryly, leave it to her grandmother to send help when she'd insisted Nealy take over. Nealy always liked her grandmother's stories about her group of ladies.

These women had been friends for as long as anyone could remember. Cuppa Joe had always been the place they got together, especially when times were hard. If the ladies needed support or a shoulder to cry on, Dorinda always welcomed them. Marriage, raising children, adjusting to life's changes, friendship, loss, were all discussed over the years, and they became a support group, too, when one of their husbands passed away. Dear friends who had been by each other's sides and still remained close allies. Nealy took another glimpse at Terri, noticing how frail the woman was. Now Nealy understood. Her grandmother had given Terri the job of watching out for Nealy in order to give her friend something to occupy herself with, since she couldn't go on the cruise.

"Let's hope there's not much to keep an eye on," Nealy said.

Terri winked. "Oh, with you back in town, I'm sure I'll be busy. I can't wait to see what scrapes you get yourself into."

Nealy pressed her lips in a tight smile. Looked as if her reputation as a wild child still preceded her. Even her long absence hadn't quelled the prevailing view. Before heading back to L.A., everyone in Cypress Pointe would see her as the smart, accomplished career woman she'd grown into, not as the girl who'd draped toilet paper on the trees in front of the mayor's house on a dare. She'd become a woman who could plan major events, run a coffee shop and stay out of any public bouts of high jinks.

"No scrapes, Terri. Just hard work."

Having made her point, a point Nealy would

stick by or die trying, Nealy turned as the door opened and her nephew walked in.

"Davey. What are you doing here so early?"

The fourteen-year-old scuffled across the room and hoisted his backpack onto the counter. "I always come in before school to help Great-Gram."

"Wouldn't you rather sleep in?"

"Nah. Besides, Mom makes me get up so we can all eat breakfast together." He wrinkled his nose. "I'd rather be here."

"What's wrong with eating with your family?"

He shot her a look conveying how dense she was.

"Point taken. When I was in high school I didn't spend much time at home, either."

"School is out for summer pretty soon and Great-Gram said I could work here. She has me sweep up in the morning. Take out the trash sometimes." He walked to the closet located just down the hallway and removed a broom. "Better than hanging out at home."

Okay, two references about not wanting to be home. Problems or teenage angst? Thinking about her nearly perfect sister Lanie, Nealy went with the angst angle.

As Davey headed outside to sweep the entrance of the shop, he passed an elderly man coming in. Walking with military precision, his sparse hair combed and his clothes pressed neatly, a folded newspaper tucked under his arm, the elderly man nodded to the women and strode up to the counter.

Nealy glanced at Terri. "Time to get to work."

Nealy rounded the corner and addressed the man. "May I help you?"

"Where's Dorinda?"

"She's away. I'm Nealy, her granddaughter, filling in."

"Dorinda always gets my coffee."

"Well, today you get me."

The man scowled at her. Nealy ramped up her smile. Perhaps someone got up on the wrong side of the bed?

Terri stood next to the man. "Ed, behave. Nealy here can pour a cup of coffee as well as Dorinda."

He nodded to the collection of pictures featuring Nealy on the wall. "They do things different in California."

Oh, good grief. Nealy upped the wattage of her smile, even as her cheek muscles grew tight. "Coffee is coffee, no matter where you brew it."

"You haven't snuck in any of them newfangled drinks, have you? I like mine black and hot."

"Black and hot coming up."

Nealy got busy with the order. When she returned with the cup, Ed held out two one-dollar bills. "Oh, you're ready to pay? I haven't rung you up yet."

"I pay the same every day."

After Nealy took his money, Ed chose a table in the corner by the front glass window. With the money in hand, she rang up the transaction on the small register. Not a fancy POS computer system, but it sufficed for her grandmother.

"You know," Terri said, "you should get to the bakery for the pastries."

"I was going to have the order delivered."

"Dorinda usually stops there first before opening the coffee shop. She likes to pick out a different selection every day."

Seemed like a lot of extra work when she could just call the order in.

"Do you want me to go over and choose?" Terri asked.

Nealy nodded. "I'd appreciate it."

Terri held out her hand. Nealy looked at Terri's empty palm.

"Money, dear. I can't shell it out. Fixed income, you know."

Nealy blinked at the older woman. Tapping a few keys, she opened the drawer and pulled out two twenties. She hoped more customers stopped by soon or her drawer would turn up empty very soon.

Terri left on her errand. Ed sat in the corner reading his paper and a few customers strolled in. Nealy filled orders and finished familiarizing herself with the shop, although so much was still the same. She'd loved this place when she was growing up, loved spending time with her grandmother. From the looks of it, Davey did, too. As customers came in, he greeted each by name. Nealy grinned. Maybe Cuppa Joe's would stay in the family after all.

As the residents of Cypress Pointe began to venture out, more folks stopped in for a coffee run. Some lingered and chatted, others took their to-go cups and hurried off to work or errands. Nealy stayed busy. When Terri returned with the bakery treats, she helped take people's orders. Together, they made a good team.

Davey rounded the counter to collect his backpack. "Gotta go. Not sure if I can come back this afternoon, I have a thing after school."

"A thing?" Nealy laughed. She remembered the vague wording being code for trouble.

"Yeah." He fiddled with the strap on the pack. "Sierra will be here tomorrow, right? She promised to help me with a...um...project."

Sierra, a college student, worked part-time for Dorinda. Nealy didn't miss Davy's pink cheeks or the way he wouldn't meet her eyes. Hmm. "As far as I know."

"Cool. See you later, Auntie."

"You know I hate it when you call me auntie."

Davey started calling her auntie when he and his folks came to L.A. for a visit a few years ago. It started out in teasing, but when Nealy balked, saying the name made her sound like a spinster, he wouldn't let go.

He grinned and sprinted out the door.

"Brat," she called after him and laughed. She had a lot of love for her nephew.

The morning rush lasted for a good two hours. Taking advantage of a lull in traffic, Nealy cleaned the tables. She'd just finished when a familiar voice spoke her name.

"Nealy Grainger. Heard you were in town."

She looked up to find her friend Lilli Barclay hurrying over for a hug.

Nealy grabbed hold of her friend and squeezed hard, then pulled back to take a good look at Lilli. They'd seen each other last year when Nealy came home for a long weekend to celebrate Davey's birthday, but something about her friend looked different. "I'm sorry I haven't talked to you lately. How are you?"

"Busy." She glanced up at the tall, rugged man who joined her and smiled. "Happy."

The man held out his hand. "Max Sanders."

"Oh, my gosh, Max. I remember you. You and Dane hung out together."

"Still do. We're friends and business associates."

"Small world." Her gaze went back and forth between the two of them as realization struck. "You and Lilli are together?"

Max took Lilli's hand in his. "Yes."

Nealy raised a brow at her friend.

"It's a long story. We'll have to catch up."

"Right now we need coffee," Max informed her. "Lilli has to get to the marketing agency and I've got a conference call with a new client about installing a security system."

"Coming up." Nealy got busy preparing their order.

"I just heard about Juliet," Lilli said. "We were supposed to attend the engagement party, but Max had to go out of town on business so I tagged along. How is she doing?"

"When she gets back in town I'll let you know."

"She left?"

"Right before the party."

"Wow. I don't leave town often but the one time I do, there's all kinds of drama. How is Brandon taking it?"

"I don't know. Juliet called him before the party to break the news."

"And your parents?"

"You know my parents."

"Yes, I suppose they aren't happy, but still, Juliet must have had a good reason."

Max dropped a five on the counter. "Keep the change." He glanced at Lilli and smiled. "I recognize the look on your face, babe. It'll take you an entire day to catch up, but we've got to get a move on."

Lilli checked her watch. "He's right. Nealy, we'll catch up later."

"Sounds great."

She watched the couple stroll out of the shop. She was happy for her friend, but wondered how those two had gotten together. She remembered Max from the whirlwind summer she and Dane had eloped. He'd been good friends with Dane, even though they'd gone their separate ways when Max enlisted in the navy.

Just thinking about Dane again brought back bittersweet memories. She needed to let go. In a couple of weeks she'd be back in L.A., back to her life. Usually when she thought of Milestones by Crystal, and her apartment, and even Sam for that matter, she got a warm feeling, but this time…not so much.

By midmorning she had a chance to sit down and look at the to-do list her grandmother had left her. Most of the items were straightforward, like requests to spruce up the inside with some fresh paint, updating the furnishings and connecting the shop with Wi-Fi. But the storefront? A different matter altogether.

In keeping with the town ambiance, the Merchants' Association asked for the entire storefront to be improved. Though the inside jobs were easy for her, she had no idea how to tackle the exterior, except to call a contractor.

Notebook and pencil in hand, she went out to the sidewalk, taking a few steps back to get a complete view of the entire storefront. Faded and peeling brown paint covered the building. The siding around the windows needed to be refreshed and new signage would go a long way in pulling Cuppa Joe into the current theme. Easy enough, right?

Not for Dorinda. And Nealy understood why. Her grandmother might have made a few interior changes to the shop, but for the most part, the place was exactly the same as when Grandpa Joe died. Her grandmother didn't have the heart to make any changes. Dorinda may not be emotionally able to make changes, but Nealy could and her grandmother was counting on it.

The easiest fix would be to paint the current stucco siding, but all the other stores on Main Street had new facades built around the windows and doors. The colors varied, from bright hues to sedate neutral colors, but anyone could see the buildings were well maintained. Some had stucco finishing, others a wooden or brick front. Big store windows displayed merchandise, or in the case of the candy and ice cream shop, stenciled lettering covered the glass in a whimsical pattern sure to draw a tourist's attention. Spaced along the sidewalk, there were neatly trimmed potted plants, as well as ornate steel streetlights with large frosted globes on top. Very quaint and charming. And, to top it all off, each store sported a canopy. Right now, Cuppa Joe was the one store without one. How much would one cost to buy and install?

Next door had a new tenant who was busy getting the space ready for a clothing store. She'd seen electricians and other workmen disappear inside, heard the buzz of saws and banging against the communal wall. The owner probably had a plan ready for the outside look of the place, which put her way behind the curve. She had to generate some ideas, fast.

Her grandmother's reluctance for change had gone on long enough. The Merchants' Association was making her life miserable with visits and reprimanding letters. These officials were like bill collectors on steroids, hounding her grandmother, who couldn't let go of the wonderful memories connected to the shop. Grandpa Joe was a ghost Dorinda could not overcome.

Her grandmother had said she'd rather close, that is, until longtime customers spoke up and Dorinda swore she wouldn't let the town down. If her grandmother didn't make the proposed changes, the Merchants' Association promised her a "meeting" to discuss the situation. And do what after the meeting, they didn't say. It just seemed threatening. Knowing how much her grandmother didn't like to be told what to do, Nealy knew this was a real issue for her. Cuppa Joe had been one of Cypress Pointe's first businesses, the only surviving original shop, but still, who needed this kind of pressure? Not Grandmother. No wonder she was thinking about selling the place. She didn't need this kind of headache at her age.

Studying the building, Nealy started sketching as an idea began to take shape. It might be good for all involved, if the evil MA would go along with her plan. In the end, the idea didn't pan out; she didn't like the results. She envisioned a trendy, streamlined look carried throughout, but to her own eye, the drawing looked lame. She finished the drawing anyway, grimaced and closed the notebook. No, she needed to get in touch with a contractor.

She took a step back toward the shop, noticing Dane in her peripheral vision. His steady stride and confident posture made her heart pick up a beat. Definitely not what she needed this morning.

He stopped in front of her, his gaze taking her in, not missing any part of her casual outfit, her loose hairstyle or, she figured, her frustration. A slight smile hovered on his lips. "So, how did the first shift go?"

"Fine. Did you expect otherwise?"

"No. You always liked working here. And at the hotel." He glanced at the shop and back to her. "Shouldn't you be inside, waiting on customers?"

"Actually, my helper is doing the job."

"Helper?"

"One of my grandmother's friends. She showed up to…help me." Nealy made finger quotes in the air.

Dane chuckled. "You aren't a needing-help kind of woman."

"I think Terri would appreciate having something to do."

"Nice of you to accommodate her."

Nealy shrugged. "I do what I can."

"You didn't answer my question."

"Why I'm not inside? Just trying to come up

with a new idea for the front of the shop. The evil MA is giving Grandmother a hard time."

"Evil?"

"Her name for them."

"I don't think they're evil. Overzealous, maybe."

"Whatever they are, she can't please them. They're calling her or stopping in to bother her all the time."

His brow wrinkled. "Bother her?"

She pulled the list from her back pocket and handed it to him. He scanned the paper. "Yeah. I knew about this."

"You did? How?"

His gaze met hers. "I'm the president of the association."

Nealy gaped at him. "Excuse me?"

"Guilty as charged."

"Why would you do this to my grand-mother?"

"I'm not involved with the day-to-day running of the organization. I'm more of a figure-head. They asked me to join a while back due to their mission to revitalize downtown. Since I have experience rehabbing buildings and I have strong ties to this community, I accepted."

Nealy fumbled for words, so taken aback by Dane's admission. "You go along with their tactics?"

"I didn't know they were strong-arming Dorinda. She didn't say anything."

"You know her. She wouldn't make a fuss."

"Still. This place is in sad shape." He scanned the building from top to bottom. "I get how your grandmother feels about Cuppa Joe, I'm not surprised she hasn't listened."

She narrowed her eyes at him. "So if you didn't come to give Grandmother grief, what are you doing here?"

"I came to check on your new neighbor and see how the clothing store is shaping up." A slow smile spread across his face. "You thought I came to visit you?"

She ignored his comment. "Maybe you can ask the construction workers to keep the noise down?"

He raised an eyebrow. "Right."

Nealy noticed a crowd beginning to gather around them. No arguing on the sidewalk and causing a scene. Decorum was her middle name now. She grasped Dane's arm and steered him toward the shop, just in time to catch Terri step away from the window.

Just what she needed. An audience inside and out.

"I'll speak to the association and get the members to tone down their approach with Dorinda."

"I'd appreciate it," Nealy said, still miffed that Dane had a part in causing her grandmother so much worry.

"Maybe there's something more I can do to help Dorinda." Dane trailed after her. "To make up for the way the association has treated her. I can handle some of the work on the list."

"No way."

No way could she be here day in and out with this man nearby. She might be getting used to being around him because he lived in Cypress Pointe now, could maybe handle this new adult relationship they had, but it didn't alter the facts. Their history didn't need repeating. The less she had to deal with Dane Peterson, the less she had to be concerned about the unwelcome, and equally hard to dispel, excitement inundating her whenever he looked her way.

"Listen, Nealy. The association isn't all bad. They want to make the town attractive for tourism. Face it, without changes and improvements, most of the businesses would dry up."

"Not Cuppa Joe. The locals support my grandmother."

"Of course they do, but you have to agree, fixing the place up isn't a bad thing."

She wished he wasn't right. Or so sure of himself. Or still so darn good-looking.

"I'll take care of any upgrades." The mirth in

his eyes made him even more attractive, which only annoyed her more.

She angled her chin at him. "I'm an intelligent woman, Dane. I can figure it out."

"Maybe, but this isn't like planning an event." He sobered. "Would working with me be so bad?"

Yes, yes, yes, because then she'd never get him off her mind.

She had to give herself time to cover her convoluted feelings for him. Grabbing hold of a nearly empty pot of coffee, she dumped the dregs into the sink, and kept her back to him.

"Nealy, would you risk messing up the existence of Cuppa Joe just to make a point?"

She froze, considering his words. If it meant she wouldn't have to be around him? Maybe. She couldn't help but be honest about it, at least with herself.

She refilled the decanter with water and busied filling another filter with fresh grounds. "Do you want a cup of coffee before you stop by to check on next door?"

"Getting rid of me so soon?"

"I'd hate to hold you up."

He chuckled. "I'll take a cup to go."

She poured a cup from a fresh pot and handed it to him. When Dane fished in his pocket to collect his money, she held up her hand. "It's on the house."

"Thanks." He gave her one last long look. He didn't bother hiding his interest, or his frustration. She could still read him after all these years. "I'm serious, Nealy. Think about my offer. It makes sense."

He turned from the counter and passed several customers to get to the door.

Nealy blew out a breath. Terri rounded the counter to stand beside her. They both watched Dane leave.

"You know, dear, at your age you shouldn't be scaring off eligible men like Dane. He'd make a fine husband. Just ask the other single women in town."

Nealy looked at the older woman's serious face. "Thanks for the advice, but I tried that once with him and things didn't go so well."

In her heart, Nealy knew she had to scare Dane off. Nothing could happen between them. They were two different people living very different lives, and as far as she was concerned, the two would never overlap.

LATER THAT AFTERNOON, her grandmother's employee, Sierra, came to work after school until the shop closed at four o'clock. If Nealy ran things, she'd extend operating hours until at least nine or ten at night. But she wasn't in charge, so she settled for reviewing her notes on transforming Cuppa Joe while here in Cypress Pointe.

Her cell rang. She glanced at the caller ID. Her boss.

"Hey, Crystal. How are things going?"

"I can't find the Rocket Fuel sports drink promotion file. Did you send it to me before you left?"

"Yes. Look under Rocket Promotions. I also wrote the file name down and left a sticky note on your desk, remember?"

She'd made a point of telling Crystal about the file the day before she left, anticipating that her busy boss with her fingers in so many projects would forget the details.

"My desk? Why didn't I… Oh, here it is."

"Just where I left it."

"Sorry. It's been nonstop crazy."

"I understand. I'm neck deep in family obligations here."

"Right. Family." A slight pause. "Nealy, sweetie, I need a go-to person to liaise with the people from Rocket Fuel. I'll bring Felicia in on the project."

"Felicia? She just joined Milestones by Crystal."

"True, but she's come up with plenty of ideas."

Nealy thought about the note on Crystal's desk. She'd covered every contingency so the Rocket Fuel event would run smoothly. Still, should Nealy be worried? Her coworkers weren't sharks, but they would grab any opportunity to move up in the company. What could she do about her boss's decision when she was on the other side of the country? "I'm sure Felicia will be an asset."

"That's just what she said."

Nealy rubbed her forehead. "Any word from Ashlee James?"

"Not yet. Her advisors said we won't get a firm answer about a contract until she's considered every event planning company in town."

"If anything changes, let me know."

"Darling, I have you on speed dial. Once I hear, I expect you on a plane back to L.A."

"Okay. Thanks for the update."

"Talk to you soon."

Sighing, Nealy returned to the task at hand. She'd managed to squeeze in calling two contractors to get an idea of the cost of updating the front of the building. Neither would give her an estimate over the phone. She scheduled on-site appointments for the next day.

Switching gears, she pulled out information

on new coffee systems. She had just started to analyze her choices when her sister hurried into the shop.

LANIE DROPPED INTO the seat opposite Nealy, masking her usually sunny disposition with a dejected look. "I hate my life."

"Good to see you, too. I'm fine. Thanks for asking." When she didn't offer the desired effect of a smile, Nealy frowned. "What's the problem?"

Lanie fidgeted with her purse. "I didn't realize I was holding so much inside until I sat down."

"Come on, what kind of problems could you have? Great husband, great kid, great job and you're the one in the family Mom most approves of."

"Because I always do her bidding. Trust me, inside I'm rebellious."

Nealy grinned. "Coulda fooled me."

"I could be rebellious if I wanted."

"Sure you could, but why would you?"

"I'll tell you why. My great husband? He'd rather work or play golf than spend time with me. Davey is wonderful, but he's a teenage boy. I try, but his world is foreign to me. I miss my little boy and the fun times we spent together. And the job…?"

"The job?" Nealy prompted.

Lanie felt her face flush. "I want to make a change but the people in my life won't agree to it."

Nealy straightened her stack of papers.

"Listen, I know everyone thinks of me as the sensible sister, but I'm long overdue for a meltdown." She nodded toward Nealy's paperwork. "Cuppa Joe business is finished for the day. I need you to be the voice of calm and reason before I lose it."

"Let's get some coffee to go. I have a feeling this conversation will last awhile. The beach will give us some privacy."

The tension in Lanie's shoulders eased. "Thanks."

Nealy filled two to-go cups and hooked arms with Lanie to walk the few blocks to the beach. They soon found an empty bench and settled in. Though it was late in the afternoon, the June sun was still warm, a precursor to the hot, sticky summer drawing closer each day. The greenish-blue water lapped the sand in a gentle rhythm. Children's laughter mingled with the screech of seagulls.

Inhaling the salty air, Lanie leaned back against the back of the wooden bench, taking solace in the familiar scene before her. "We have so many memories here. Remember when we were little and Grandmother decided to have a beach day and brought us without any help from Mom and Dad or Grandpa?"

Nealy's eyes lit up. "We ran her ragged. Going from the water to the pier and hours building sand castles, she swore she'd never do it again."

"But she did. Many times."

They sat in companionable silence for a few moments.

"You must love the beaches in California," Lanie said. "We drove by when we came out to visit you, but from what I saw, the coastline is stunning."

"I've been to the beach a total of two times since I've lived out there." Nealy frowned. "I work too much. Sad, isn't it."

"No. Grown-up. Once we get out of college and start our lives, reality invades."

Nealy put a hand over hers. "Okay, what's going on? You've never been Miss Gloom and Doom before."

Lanie took a sip from her cup and peered out over the water. A few seconds passed and she said softly, "I don't think David loves me anymore."

Nealy coughed. "Why would you think that?"

"It's the little things. We used to talk all the time, but now we almost have to schedule appointments to see each other. I thought after all these years together we'd get closer, but now I'm not so sure. We used to be the couple with this wonderful marriage from day one, who couldn't stand to be apart." She paused. "What went wrong?"

"You do realize I'm not the person to come to with romance problems. I told Juliet the same thing."

Lanie wiped the tears from her eyes. "I don't expect you to solve my problems, not that you couldn't. What happened between you and Dane was…"

"A debacle?"

"I wouldn't go that far. You two were just a little overly enthusiastic."

Nealy laughed. "Okay, we'll go with that."

"He wasn't all bad."

"No, he wasn't. Up until the moment he broke my heart." She sighed. "You and David made being married look so easy. I guess I wanted the same thing with Dane."

"Nothing is easy. Getting married in college and having a baby a year later? Hard work." Lanie hesitated. "Not everyone should marry young."

"True. I'm the poster girl of bad decisions. But you did it. You and David have always been happy."

"We were, for a long time. But lately, I'm not sure and I don't know what to do." Her tone turned to pleading. "I know you have two weeks left to visit. I'm sorry to burden you more. It's that, well, I don't really have anyone I can talk to about this. No one I trust, anyway."

"First Juliet asking romance advice, now you revealing secrets. I feel like I've been thrust into an alternative universe." Nealy looked as if she was considering something. "You've been married what, fifteen years?"

Lanie nodded.

"And somewhere along the way the magic sorta died?"

Lanie blinked rapidly, devastated by that thought.

"Sorry. Not the best word choice."

She nodded again, still unable to speak.

"If you want things to be better, like they were in the old days, maybe shake your marriage up? Be spontaneous. Mysterious. Totally unpredictable, unlike good-girl Lanie."

"I…" Confusion, then interest, spurred her to ask, "How would I do that?"

Lanie knew her sister had spent years keeping the impulsive side of herself under control and helping Lanie now would be a conflict.

"I could give you a pointer or two."

Relief flooded her. "Really?"

"Sure, I would. I love you."

"I love you, too." She angled her brows at Nealy. "Sure you wouldn't consider moving back here? Think of the mischief we could get into. We've missed out on so many years together, you, Juliet and me."

"Speaking of Juliet, she called me last night. She's still pretty mum about what's going on with her, but she assured me she's fine."

"Do you believe her?"

"She didn't sound nearly as upset as when she left town. Hopefully she's figuring things out."

"When she gets back, we'll have a girls' night out."

"I love the idea of being closer to you both, but right now staying in Cypress Pointe doesn't fit into my life. I have a job in L.A., remember?"

Yeah, she did. "Then I'm thankful for whatever you can do to help me."

"Hey, that's what sisters do." Nealy stood and dropped her empty cup in a nearby trash can. "And speaking of jobs, are you still thinking of running for mayor?"

Lanie threw her cup away and the two started walking down Main Street. "I haven't dismissed the idea."

"Even if David doesn't want you to?"

She nodded.

Nealy shrugged, her eyes wide as she stared at her. "That'll get his attention for sure."

"Especially since I'd be running against one of the partners in his law firm."

"Ha! That's definitely one way to shake up your marriage. Not sure it's the best, but…"

Lanie grinned. "Sometimes I can think out of the box."

Nealy threw an arm around Lanie and hugged her close. "At last, another Grainger who sees the appeal of drawing outside the lines. Welcome to the club."

CHAPTER SIX

THE NEXT MORNING, Nealy stared at an estimate to update the storefront and swallowed hard.

"Call me when you've made your decision," the contractor said as he gathered up his papers.

"Sure," she said, taking the business card the man offered. "Not gonna happen," she grumbled as he walked away.

Both estimates were more than Nealy expected. Grandmother had left her a budget, one that now squeaked. Nealy dealt with events going over budget all the time and still managed to whittle down the expenses to make the client happy. She could do the same for Grandmother, even if it meant cutting into the nest egg she'd squirreled away over the years.

She wandered back into the shop and was greeted by the rich aroma of coffee. Time to try her hand at some of the smaller projects around here. See what happened. If she could take care of some of these indoor jobs, she'd keep costs down. She executed major events, how hard could a few repairs be? Like any job, all she needed was a well-thought-out plan. Since planning happened to be her bread and butter, she decided it was now or never.

She found a small toolbox pushed way back under the counter filled with the basics: hammer, screwdriver, tape measure. She'd seen a ladder in the closet. All the tools she needed. When Sierra arrived for her shift, Nealy went out front to replace the blown bulb in one of the overhead light fixtures. Easy peasy.

Five minutes later, Nealy walked to the counter, a broken fixture in her hand.

Sierra, attending to an empty coffeepot, looked over her shoulder at Nealy. Her eyes went wide at the mangled piece of metal. "I don't think the fixture is supposed to come off the wall."

"Ya think?" Nealy tossed the mess into the garbage. "You should see the wires hanging out of the wall."

"Call the electrician?"

Nealy cringed, mentally tallying the expense. "Yep."

Sierra pointed to the hallway. "The toilet paper holder in the restroom is loose. Shouldn't be hard to fix."

Determined to make up for the light fixture, Nealy grabbed the screwdriver and strode to the bathroom. The toilet paper holder hung at a forty-five-degree angle, as if the screws were barely secured to the wall. All she had to do was tighten a few screws, right? She tightened one side, but had trouble getting the screws to stay put on the other. The more she turned the screwdriver, the bigger the holes got. The bigger the holes got, the looser the holder became until the entire thing fell from the wall.

"You have got to be kidding me."

Conceding defeat, she set the roll of toilet paper on top of the toilet tank. The holder needed to be positioned in a new spot on the wall and the holes needed to be spackled and painted. Since today's track record pretty much stank, she decided to fight this battle another day. Or hire someone else to do the job.

In her head, she heard a great big ka-ching as more money slipped away.

"How'd it go?" Sierra asked when Nealy returned to the front of the shop.

Nealy held up the holder. "Don't ask."

"Should I call a plumber?"

"No. I'll get my brother-in-law or someone to fix it."

"Okay." Sierra glanced around the room. "What now?"

Nealy marched over to the counter. "You know what? I'll take the pictures off the wall. I think I can handle this."

She crossed to where her grandmother had hung the framed photographs Nealy sent her, a little embarrassed at how prominently they were featured. She'd meant for only her grandmother to enjoy the pictures, not framed for all of the whole of Cypress Pointe to see. As she took each one off the wall, she smiled at the memories.

When she started doing small, niche events, never in a million years had she imagined she'd meet Hollywood legends, let alone work with some of them. She'd met one of her closest friends this way, celebrity chef Jenna Monroe. During a fund-raising event for a cancer research charity, Jenna was scheduled to do a private cooking session for a select group who had pledged extra-large donations. Nealy was tasked as her gofer for the day. They'd worked well together, and continued their conversation long after Jenna's demonstration was over. Hungry after the hours spent at the event, they went for sushi and became fast friends.

Once she removed the photos from the wall, Nealy took the hammer and began removing the nails. She'd gotten a few out when Sierra squealed. Thinking Sierra might have hurt herself, Nealy jumped. Consequently, the hammer shifted in her hand and chipped a huge chunk of paint from the drywall.

"What's wrong?" Nealy blurted.

"Huh?" Sierra looked up from her phone. "My boyfriend texted me. He has a surprise for me tonight. I guess I got excited."

"Sierra, seriously, put the phone away. I can understand the lure of true love, but the boy can wait till you finish your shift."

"Fine." Sierra dropped her phone into her purse.

Nealy stood with her hands on her hips, examining the rather noticeable paint chip. Good thing she planned on painting anyway. As she removed the last nail from the wall without mishap, she turned to find Dane and Max Sanders standing behind her, arms crossed, grinning ear to ear.

A warm flush covered her cheeks. "What?"

"I liked the pictures," Max informed her. "Especially the one with you and the tall blond guy. I got the impression you two were engaged until your grandmother corrected me."

She scoffed. "Engaged? To a famous movie star? Wow. So not me."

Dane's smile grew wider.

She looked at Max. "You thought I was engaged?"

"That's what it looked like."

A while back, she'd been talking to her grandmother about Sam, and she mentioned she hoped they might get serious, maybe even engaged. Wishful thinking. She and Sam couldn't even find time to have dinner, let alone decide to get married.

Max shrugged. Then he focused on the wall. "Why is there a hole?"

"It's not a hole. And, um, the hammer slipped."

Dane grinned. "You're kidding, right?"

"You should see the bathroom."

The corner of Dane's mouth quirked.

She scowled at him.

"The Grainger family's strong suit isn't manual labor," Dane explained to Max.

"Gotta give it to Nealy, though. At least she tried," Max said.

Nealy wagged a finger at Dane. "I'll have you know the Graingers are good at plenty of other things."

"Like jumping in feetfirst without looking? Oh, wait, that's your talent. Still, a little impulsive there, Nealy?"

She bristled. "Not anymore."

A knowing grin curved his lips.

Her stomach flipped at the "yeah, right" look on his face. Who was she kidding? He knew her reckless streak better than anyone, considering he'd been by her side most of those times. Staying out after curfew. Spray painting graffiti on a seawall down by the beach. Borrowing her dad's car without his permission—borrowing, since she refused to believe it was actual theft. They hadn't always thought things through.

"So what are you guys doing here?"

"I had a meeting scheduled with Max at his office, but he suggested we move to Cuppa Joe." Dane nodded at the wall. "We didn't expect to be entertained."

She noticed the briefcases both men were carrying. She blinked, having a hard time reconciling these two serious businessmen with the two teenage scoundrels she remembered. They had all pulled their lives together, which made her wonder if she and Dane would have been successful if they'd stayed married. Sure, it would have been tough, holding down a job while going to college and maintaining a home, but she'd been determined to put her heart and soul into that marriage. Since Dane had destroyed the dream, she could only imagine and speculate as to how things would have ended up. Would they have rallied together? Or would the pressure have been too much to bear? She'd never know since Dane had taken the decision out of her hands.

Would she ever get over his doing so? She glanced at his mischievous smile and wondered.

Maybe it was time to try. Although she still didn't trust herself around him.

"Looks like you should stick to making coffee. I have to ask, though," Dane said as a puzzled look crossed his face. "Why are there wires hanging out where the light fixture used to be?"

Nealy's face flushed again.

"Ah. Another DIY."

"A mishap."

"Just like the bathroom," Sierra chirped as she brought the men their coffee.

Nealy sent the girl a death stare.

"Well, you didn't finish," Sierra huffed.

Gently placing the hammer on the counter, Nealy said, "I may be a teensy bit over my head."

Dane and Max exchanged amused glances.

"I told you I'd be happy to help you," Dane reminded her.

"And as much as I don't appreciate your offer, I decline. Again."

"He does know what he's doing," Max told her.

"I don't doubt his ability. It's the principle. His connection to the Merchants' Association makes him a traitor—going against my grandmother, the way he did."

"You don't trust me? I'm wounded."

She made a point of ignoring him. "Max, I

understand you sometimes do handy jobs for my grandmother. Any chance I can get you to help me? Besides the minor things inside the shop, I still have to do something about the outside appearance."

"Nealy, I'm afraid I don't have time right now. I'm in and out of town on a big security job."

"Okay. Then can I ask your opinion?" She handed him the estimate from the contractor. "Do these figures look right?"

Dane leaned over to glance at the piece of paper. "No kidding you want Max's help."

"Looks a little high to me," Max told her, handing back the paper.

Her stomach sank.

Max's cell rang and he took the call, leaning away from Nealy and Dane to get some privacy.

"You know," Dane told her, coming to stand beside her, "I have an idea."

As he moved closer, a hint of intimacy deepened in his voice. Sparks arched between them with an urgency Nealy couldn't ignore. But what happened if you played with fire? You got burned. Yet she couldn't leave his side.

"I know you're temporarily filling in until Dorinda gets back, but a responsible business owner would take measures to assure a positive outcome to a problem. You need work done.

Work you can't handle alone or spend a lot of money on. I have the means and ability to do the work at a price you can't refuse."

She regarded him with a wary expression. "Which is?"

"An exchange for services rendered."

"Interesting." She tapped her finger against her chin. "What are you proposing?"

"You help me with the events booked at the hotel, since I have no coordinator, and I'll make sure the storefront is what the Merchants' Association wants without you having to shell out a dime."

"Barter our services?"

"Hey, I'm not too proud to admit planning parties and ceremonies is not *my* strong suit. But construction is. In my capacity as president of the MA, I can pull permits pretty quickly since they're after you to get this done."

A customer walked in. Nealy took a few minutes to pour a cup of coffee and chat up the lady before returning to him. The offer was out of the blue, but she wasn't one to refuse a good deal. But work with Dane? The ultimate clincher.

"So?" he asked. "What do you say to my offer?"

She hesitated. His heartfelt request had her conscience reeling. Could she do this? With him?

"Don't make a rash decision here, Nealy. Working with me shouldn't stop you from getting Cuppa Joe in shape and it will keep the Merchants' Association out of your grandmother's hair."

It sounded good, but… "Give me a day to think about it."

He nodded before joining Max, who had taken a seat at an empty table after finishing his call.

To be honest, there was only one answer. Was she ready to deal with the consequences?

DANE WALKED TO his car, his business with Max concluded and his mind on Nealy and her reluctance to accept his offer. He didn't blame her. The trust between them had been shattered. Now he had a way to show her he had her best interests at heart. For all he knew, his gesture might go toward finally healing the past.

He pulled car keys from his pocket, noticing a man lounging against the front bumper of his BMW. Not just any man. His father, Rich Peterson.

Even though his folks still lived in Cypress Pointe, Dane didn't see them very often. Last time he'd talked to his dad, he'd told Dane he had a job at the marina. Dane hoped his father hadn't lost his job. Again.

"Dad. What are you doing here?"

"Nice way to greet your old man."

Dane kept silent. The look on his father's face said the man was spoiling for a fight.

"What do you want?"

"Who says I want anything? Can't a man visit his son?"

Sure he could, if visiting was the real reason behind the visit. Dane knew better.

"Just get to the point."

"You're exactly like your mother. Always have an attitude."

"I assume this is about Mom?"

"I need a loan. She wants one of those new electronic tablets and I'm short on cash right now."

What else was new? Short on cash and wanting something. Typical. Every time his mother made a request, his dad snapped to, hoping she might love him because he met her demands. Trouble was, no matter what his father did, she was never happy, always pushing him for more. And his dad always went along with her whims. So he came to Dane, asking for a loan, which he never repaid, or to crab about the pitfalls of his marriage.

Deep down Dane resented how his father used him, but who was he to balk? From the time he was a teenager he'd done whatever he could to keep the family peace. First, by shielding Alex from the ugliness, then later, by allowing himself to be a pawn in his parents' game. When he was younger, he thought he was helping to keep them all together. Now he realized the enabling had gone on too long. Just like the annulment of his marriage, he'd thought he'd come up with the right decision by mediating for his parents. Now he questioned his actions.

"Dad, she'll survive without a tablet."

"You know how she gets."

Yeah, Dane knew.

"Not right now."

His father stared at him before his eyes got mean. "You're saying no?"

"Look, if you want to get Mom a gift, use your money. I can't give you any more."

"Since when?"

"Since I'm tired of you coming to me when you want a handout. I'm not responsible for you two."

His father looked confused. "You always help."

"And that's a problem. Maybe it's time you took a good hard look at your life and make some changes."

"Why would I?"

That was the sad part. His father didn't see

the circular path he was on as anything but normal. And Dane had contributed to his delusions.

"Buying Mom stuff isn't going to make her any happier."

"What do you know about being married?"

Nothing. He didn't plan on finding out anytime soon, either.

"I need to get to work." He rounded his father to unlock the car door.

"That's it?"

"I'm sorry, Dad."

Red fury covered his father's face. "No son of mine would turn on me like this," he spat and stomped away.

That was a new twist. Most of the time, his father couldn't keep from fawning all over Dane until he got what he wanted. First time Dane says no and he's the bad guy? Dane had no idea how long his father's tantrum would last, but he knew one thing for sure. He couldn't continue to play into his father's manipulations, even if it meant not having the man in his life.

Sad, but necessary.

He drove to the hotel. The day was warm and sunny, not a good match for his dark mood.

Once at the hotel, he circumvented his staff and headed straight to his office. When he opened the door, he stepped in to find his uncle seated in one of the matching armchairs situated in the corner of Dane's office, reading papers from a file spread open on the coffee table.

"Uncle Hank." He crossed the room as Hank rose from the chair. "Good to see you," he said as they shook hands.

"Likewise. The Sarasota property took longer to get up and running than we projected."

"I heard you were gone so long because Aunt Sonia likes it down there."

Hank grinned. "That, too."

Dane placed his briefcase on his desk and took a seat in the vacant armchair. "What brings you by this afternoon?"

"Checking in with my favorite partner."

"Your only partner."

Hank nodded at the briefcase. "New business I don't know about?"

"I'm making a change in security for the hotel. Omega wasn't working out."

"I'm surprised. They came highly recommended."

"But didn't deliver. I found a new firm. We'll be working with Max Sanders."

"Max Sanders? Are you sure his small firm can take care of our needs?"

"I like his ideas and implementation for a new system. The more high-end clients come to the hotel, the greater our need for top-flight security."

"Are you sure you can trust him?"

"Yes. He's been in the navy and spent time as a cop in Atlanta. I did enough research to find out he knows what he's doing."

"I'll have to take your word." Hank stood and walked to the window, staring out over the gulf vista.

The man had a razor-sharp mind, always processing information. Dane waited until his uncle gathered his thoughts to get to the gist of his visit.

"Seems like old home week for you. Sanders. Nealy."

"Tends to happen when you come back to your old hometown. The past catches up."

"So long as you keep it at a distance."

"I'm afraid that's not possible. I'll be working with both of my old buddies."

Hank turned. "I get Sanders. But Nealy?"

"Since Angela quit unexpectedly. I talked to Nealy about an exchange of services. I'll do some fixing for her at the coffee shop. She'll look after planned events here, until I can hire a replacement."

"Can Nealy handle the events here?"

"She's very professional. Even though Juliet and Brandon's engagement ended, the parties were quite a hit."

"You know you're playing with fire, son."

Impatience flashed through Dane. He didn't need his uncle reminding him this might not be the best idea he'd ever had, but Hank showed the stubborn glint Dane remembered from the summer he'd dated Nealy. He hadn't approved then; he clearly didn't now.

"I get it, Dane. The past is the past and you're an adult."

"I think I've proven I can handle myself."

"I'd say you have."

The result of Dane's hard work included fifteen properties with two more projected for the future. Together they had enlarged Peterson Holdings at a rate Dane hadn't imagined possible.

"Have you gone over the report for the Pensacola property?" his uncle asked.

"I'm glad you brought up the subject." Dane rose to cross the room, pulled open a desk drawer to remove a thick file. "I went over the numbers."

"What do you think?" his uncle asked as he took a seat again. "Pretty solid?"

"I have to disagree."

Hank didn't hide his surprise. "On what grounds?"

Dane joined his uncle. "First of all, with all the properties we've acquired in such a short length of time, I'm afraid we'll overextend ourselves. The projections are not as stable as you first assumed."

"The property has potential."

"Yes and no. We shouldn't jump yet, since we already have two new projects starting soon."

Hank rubbed his thumb and forefinger over his chin. "Have you been up there to see the property?"

"No. These conclusions are from the preliminary information you gave me."

"It can't be all bad. Why don't you go up there and see for yourself."

"I can't go out of town right now. I have too much going on here."

"Because of your events with Nealy?" Hank aimed a keen glance at Dane. "You have staff for a reason."

"Yes, the staff is excellent, but I'm hoping to work with Nealy."

Hank stared him down.

"There are two interviews for event coordinator set up for next week, but in the meantime I need to be here to make sure the schedule runs smoothly."

"How many weddings have we booked?"

"Two, as of today. Mary in marketing has been calling wedding planners and is getting the news about our wide range of services to the local market, as well as national bridal magazines."

"Good. I have to admit, I was leery when you came up with the idea, but now I see the potential. We should profit quite well."

"Also, the restaurants are making money." Dane passed a spreadsheet to Hank. "As you can see, we've appealed to the locals and the wider region since there are few options for an upscale restaurant in the area. The café is doing well, too."

"Fine, fine, but getting back to Nealy. If she's as good as everyone says, you don't need to be here."

"I want to be here."

Hank went quiet for a moment. "Do you think that's wise?"

Dane met his direct gaze. "Look, Uncle Hank, it's not all about Nealy being in town. I've grown…attached to this property. Like I have more at stake here. I like being in Cypress Pointe. It feels good to reconnect with old friends and stay put in one place for a while.

"Peterson Holdings is strong right now. I don't want to see us rush to expand at the expense of being cash poor. Let's work with what we have because we're making money."

"It's not like you to be so conservative."

"And it's not like you to take unnecessary risks."

The two men stared at each other, at an impasse.

"I'm not giving up on the Pensacola property," his uncle announced, "but we'll put the idea on the back burner for now. In the meantime, hire an event coordinator. Your time is too valuable to hang out at parties. I need your mind focused on the future of Peterson Holdings."

"Yes, sir."

"And, Dane?"

Dane raised an eyebrow.

"You have two weeks to find a suitable replacement. If you have no success, I'll take the hiring duties out of your hands."

Dane's first reaction was to argue with his uncle, until he realized the man expected a knee-jerk reaction from Dane to prove his point. "Yes, sir."

"Now, on to family matters. Spoken to Alex?"

"He's undercover, so, no."

"Your folks?"

Dane's mood plummeted even more. "I ran into Dad before I came here. Seems he's short on money."

Hank winced. "Sorry."

"Same old. I don't want to talk about him." If

he did, Dane would have to revisit the mistakes he'd made in the relationship with his father.

"Okay, then. Get on with your work. Your aunt and I expect you to stop by for dinner soon. She misses you."

Dane stood and showed him to the door. "I'll be there whenever she sets a time."

Hank turned to look at Dane. "You know we love you, son. Want the best for you."

Dane's taut expression eased. "You have been out of town too long. You're getting maudlin on me."

"It's my age. Don't pay me any mind." He paused. "I know you've sworn off marriage. Can't say I blame you. Your parents soured you to the idea, but, Dane, the right woman is out there."

Dane opened the door. "Time to go."

Hank slapped him on the back, recognizing the subject as closed, and strode away.

Once his uncle left, Dane walked back to his desk and pulled the schematics Max had given him from his briefcase. Despite his relationship with his folks, Dane knew Uncle Hank wanted him settled and happy. He could be unmarried and happy; after all, he'd been single for twelve years and counting. What were a few more?

Still, his uncle's push to get him to Pensacola couldn't have been more obvious than if he'd just come right out and told Dane to leave town because of Nealy.

Dane knew his uncle meant well, but as a grown man, he'd make his own decisions and accept the consequences. Especially with Nealy here. He didn't need any posturing from his uncle, since his personal life had never before affected business decisions.

Unrolling the plans, Dane spread them over the desktop, knocking a baseball cap from the corner of his desk. His old high school cap. A wry smile curved his lips. He retrieved it from the carpet and replaced it on the credenza behind him with the rest of his collection.

After his dreams to play college baseball fell apart, a new door opened. His uncle showed him the possibilities of life after baseball. Taught him about hard work and dedication. Since he'd let Nealy down, he'd needed a new passion. A career to immerse himself in. Dane knew he'd never have gotten this far in business without his uncle's help and confidence that Dane would indeed make something of himself.

He returned his attention to the security system proposal. Max had delivered on the ideas they'd discussed. He pored over the details until his mind wandered off. Wandered to Nealy, to be exact.

What was it about her? She'd captured his

heart when they were kids and he'd never been able to shake it. He thought he'd never see her again, until fate intervened. He'd been so mired in regrets and what-ifs, he'd never taken romantic chances. Then Nealy appeared again in his life.

Sure, he was curious about her. Curious about his reaction to her.

But did her coming exit from Cypress Pointe make anything between them seem safe? Certainly she'd have a say in the matter of them revisiting their relationship and so far he figured her response would be a big, fat, resounding no. So why complicate things?

Shaking his head, he thought about seeing her at the coffee shop earlier. Even dressed in more casual attire, she didn't lose her take-charge attitude. Her cheeks may have become a shade of appealing pink when he teased her about her unsuccessful attempt at repairs, but she'd stood up to him. When she did, his blood pumped with excitement. All he knew for sure was he wanted more face-to-face time with her.

He had to admire her. She might be over her head with repairs, but when Nealy was in, she was all in. And improving Cuppa Joe had her full attention.

On a whim, he pulled out a blank sheet of paper to start recording ideas for the Cuppa

Joe storefront. The Merchants' Association had developed a small beach-town flavor for Main Street. Lots of beaded board, neat trim and crisp eye-catching colors dominated the style. Dorinda's shop still sported a dingy stucco exterior, old tarnished light fixtures and a faded, worn-out sign.

As he sketched, something Dorinda mentioned about a vacation in New England came to mind. Using distressed clapboard shingles on the outer walls and brightening the look by framing out the window with fresh, clean white trim, Cuppa Joe would have a brand-new storefront. He envisioned white shutters and a beveled glass door. He sketched a logo for the new sign, perhaps to hang over the door if Dorinda agreed.

Satisfied, he set down the pencil and stretched out the kinks in his shoulders. He couldn't wait to see if Nealy would go for his design. She definitely didn't want to work with him, but he hoped she'd agree with his vision.

Lilting laughter floated through the window as Dane slipped the papers into his briefcase. He peered outside. A young, pretty, blonde girl ran backward across the grass as a tall, dark-haired boy her age chased after her. He recognized her from the coffee shop. Sierra? Yes, that was her name. He also recognized Bobby, one of his employees in ground maintenance.

Sierra slowed down. Bobby caught her hand, pulling her into his embrace. As they began to kiss, Dane moved from the window, giving the young couple privacy.

He remembered how he'd chased Nealy around this property. He'd been crazy about her. He'd went along with every goofy reason she gave their bosses so that they could work, or rather, be together. He'd recognized that time spent with her on the job might take his attention away from serving customers, but it was something he was willing to risk.

He'd loved running around town with her, loved her free spirit. Loved her.

Had he been too hasty in ending their marriage all those years ago? Never one to second-guess his decisions, Dane didn't like the direction his thoughts took.

Problem was, he could be crazy about Nealy again if he allowed himself. Not wedding crazy, but close enough. Even if he decided to give in to the feelings simmering close to the surface, she was still angry with him. A lot of pain had passed, but he knew he'd done the right thing by getting an annulment. While the grown-up Nealy piqued his interest, he was glad to see a bit of the old spirit in her. Maybe what they'd had was the closest he'd ever have to getting married. So why the hitch in his heart whenever she was around?

He hoped, for the sake of Cuppa Joe at least, that she'd let her guard down a bit. Didn't mean she'd ever want to trust her heart with him again. Smart, since he didn't do serious. But still, he could not deny the strong attraction, the pure longing he could recall at a second's notice.

He ran a hand over his face. "Pull yourself together."

He might be foolish for contemplating spending time with her while she was home, but each time he met up with her, their spark burned brighter. More meaningful.

Anything between them was a long shot for sure.

She was home for two more weeks. How hard could maintaining control be?

CHAPTER SEVEN

"I STILL CAN'T believe Great-Gram said you could update the shop. Are you sure you heard her right?"

Nealy glanced up at her nephew, who had plopped down in the chair across from her. She laughed at the confusion on Davey's boyish features. "Yes, she gave me permission."

He picked through the brochures and papers scattered atop the table. She'd made copious notes on a yellow legal pad in between waiting on the morning coffee crowd. If she went along with Dane's proposal, she'd be able to complete her entire to-do list.

"And you're seriously going ahead with the idea?"

"Yes. Before Grandmother changes her mind."

He picked up a glossy brochure featuring a shiny, new espresso maker, along with the manufacturing specs. He wrinkled his nose. "Looks complicated to me."

"These new models practically run themselves. Just push a button and you get an espresso, cappuccino or latte. It's pretty cool."

"What about plain old coffee?"

"We'll keep the original brewers." She laid down her pen. "I know Grandmother has mixed feelings about changing the shop. But if we want to stay competitive with other coffee places, we have to get with the times, otherwise people will go elsewhere. Or a savvy entrepreneur will visit Cypress Pointe and realize what a great opportunity it would be to open a competing coffee shop, one offering a variety of coffee drinks and stays open late. If that happens, Cuppa Joe is sunk for sure."

He looked dubious. "You keep saying *we*. This is your third day here and you'll be leaving in a couple of weeks."

Nealy ran her hands over her jeans. How did she explain her actions to Davey without sounding hypocritical? "You know I've always had a soft spot for this place. I want to see it successful, keep the shop in the family. Updating makes the most sense to ensure the future."

"But who will run it? Great-Gram can't do it forever. She wants to retire."

"I hear she's been talking to you."

He shrugged. "We talk about a lot of stuff. She's tired of running the shop and wants a break."

"I'm sure she wants a break, but Cuppa Joe holds a lot of memories for her. She deserves to slow down, but I don't think selling the shop is the right move."

So far, Nealy hadn't come up with an alternative everyone could work with. She noticed the time on the clock on the wall. "Don't you need to get to school?"

"Yeah." He rose, shuffled across the shop and tugged his backpack, covered with stickers of all colors and shapes, over his arms.

"What's with the stickers?" Nealy pointed to a large orange circle on the front of the pack.

"Different stuff from school. Clubs. Sports. You know, for support." He stared at Nealy, so serious for someone so young. "I don't want Great-Gram to be disappointed."

"Me neither." She ruffled his hair. "When did you get so grown-up?"

He ducked, brushing his hair back into place as he hurried out the door, almost running into Dane.

"Someone's late," Dane said as he came inside.

"School," she told him, annoyed to find herself tongue-tied. Wearing a dark blue T-shirt, worn jeans and scuffed work boots, he kept his *GQ* air about him by holding his leather briefcase. Why did he have to be so gorgeous?

A smile tugged at his lips, his eyes remained steady on hers. With both of them dressed so casually, it made things between them less professional and more personal. It wasn't what she wanted. Nor did she want him looking at her as if she were the only woman on earth.

She gestured at his attire. "Day off?"

"No. Don't normally take days off," he stated. "Need some measurements to finish up my designs for the storefront. Then I'll get started."

"Even though I asked you to give me a day?"

He set his briefcase on a nearby table and crossed his arms over his chest. His wide, toned chest. "Have you thought about it?"

"All night."

"And…"

"You're way too demanding."

"When I decide on a project, I like to get right to it."

She knew all about diving right into a job. She'd been guilty of doing it more times than she could count.

"So?" he queried.

"I agree."

"You could have given me your answer to begin with."

"What's the fun in that?"

He grinned and looked at the tabletop. "What're you up to?"

"Deciding on which equipment to buy for the shop."

"I'm glad Dorinda's on board. This place is special to her."

Nealy's heart skipped a beat. Not everyone got that about her grandmother. "Things should be in motion before she gets back from vacation and changes her mind."

"Speaking of vacations, have you heard from Juliet?"

"She texted me a couple times. Said not to worry."

"But you are."

A note of melancholy tinged her voice. "Yes, I am. A little. She's an adult and seems safe, but I still don't know where she went or who she's with."

"I might know who."

"Tell me."

"Josh Hamilton, head of landscaping and jack-of-all-trades at the hotel. He asked for vacation leave about the time Juliet disappeared."

"Why would she… Is she safe with him?"

"Josh is a great guy. I've known him awhile. His work here is second to none and he's well liked among the other staff. I got the impression he has real feelings for her, so I'm sure he'll take care of her."

"Well, at least that mystery is solved."

She glanced at him, trying to reconcile this Dane with the boy he once was. She never would have pegged him to be concerned enough about Dorinda's livelihood to base a business decision on her. Nealy didn't like this glimpse of the caring side of Dane. It made him human, not the hard-hearted guy she'd purposely stayed away from all these years. "Thanks for thinking about my grandmother. You could have had an agenda and just gone ahead and opened a coffee place if you wanted."

"See, I'm not all bad."

True. He might have been a heartbreaker once, but the man Dane had become didn't seem to trounce on other people's feelings. Just hers.

"So," Dane said. "Let me show you what I've come up with for the storefront." He withdrew sketches from his briefcase and motioned for her to follow him outside.

"I want to cover the stucco with treated shingles. Make it more beachy-looking. Reframe the windows, add shutters. New light fixtures and a new sign."

She glanced at the faded plaque on the wall. It read Cuppa Joe in all capitals with a small carving of a coffee mug under the letters.

"I hate to see the sign go."

"Don't worry, we can hang it in the shop."

His crooked smile had her stomach in knots. "Hey, we'll place it over the hole you made in the wall."

"It's not a hole. And I planned on painting the shop anyway."

"Since you took all your pictures down, Dorinda needs something to replace the memories. Your granddad's sign fits the bill."

She had to agree. The gesture was thoughtful and just plain nice. It was becoming more difficult to remember Dane was the bad guy.

"To replace the current sign, I've made a few drawings for you to choose from. We can either hang the sign from the canopy like the other shops or place it over the door."

"Either sounds good."

She studied the sketches he offered her. "How'd you come up with this idea?"

"Your grandmother once told me about a vacation she and your granddad took to New England. She admired the rustic architecture so I took the inspiration from her own descriptions."

"I'm impressed."

"Good. You can help me." He pulled a tape measure from his back pocket. "Mind jotting down the numbers as I call them out?"

"Sure." She ran inside to get a paper and pencil then rejoined Dane. "Go ahead."

Dane measured and Nealy scribbled down the figures. A sense of déjà vu overtook her. When they'd been dating, they did everything together. They'd worked plenty of overtime at the hotel, for instance, just to be with one another. Whenever they handled the snack bar, they always made more sales than any of the other employees. If she had lifeguard duty, he would show up and play with the little kids, keeping them from the deep end. She'd helped him bus tables if it meant they could take off a few minutes early. Once, they'd made a good team. Been best friends. Now…she wasn't sure what they were.

"So, when did you get interested in building?"

"After we went our separate ways." He was focused on Nealy. Waiting for a response? She kept her mouth shut. "I went to live with my uncle and he introduced me to construction and remodeling and how to do it profitably. You remember Uncle Hank, right?"

How could she forget? He never approved of Dane and Nealy getting serious so fast and made his displeasure known.

"I remember. He's the reason we always met at Swindler's Ice Cream Shop."

"He's still as opinionated as ever."

"Good to know." She didn't plan on engaging him in conversation while in town.

"Anyway, I went to live with him and my aunt. They helped me straighten out my life. I needed a job before I started college, so I did grunt work for my uncle's business. I loved it and learned every aspect of rehabbing and saving old structures."

"And now you're the boss."

"Part owner."

"An impressive climb for a guy who didn't know what he wanted to do when he grew up."

"You're one to talk. You had no clue what to do after high school, either."

"As long as I didn't have to go to law school, anything would do."

He chuckled. She'd shared her aversion to anything law-related when they were dating.

"So how'd you end up planning events?"

"I sort of fell into marketing in school. Got a few gigs pushing new products and got hired by a beverage company. The company moved to L.A., I followed. I had a friend who needed help with a party and I did such a good job she asked me for help again. Soon after, I discovered I had a natural talent for coordinating events. Fast-forward to Milestones by Crystal, where I work now."

"I'm going to have to return the impressive

compliment. I researched you online. You've done some amazing stuff."

"Thanks. It took a while, but once I found something I loved, I went all in. You know me, no half measures once I commit."

After she said the words, she realized Dane might think she meant him. She had, years ago, but not now.

He called out the last number. "Finished here."

"Thanks, Dane."

"Don't thank me until after I tell you about the events scheduled at the hotel."

As much as she didn't want to spend long hours with Dane, fixing the shop would keep them in close proximity and the events at his hotel would also throw them together. He was right, with his background and experience he would make the to-do list at the shop disappear quickly. And deep down, she did feel a little guilty about Angela quitting as the hotel's event coordinator. Since a teensy part of the reason Angela left might have been her fault, in good conscience, Nealy couldn't turn him down. She'd always prided herself on her commitment. Loyalty. And while she didn't work for Dane, her involvement had put him in this bind.

"Two events?"

"A ladies' tea and a wedding rehearsal."

She cringed when he said wedding.

"I know you said weddings aren't your thing, but the wedding is pretty much under control."

"Then why do you need me for the rehearsal?"

"I explained the current situation to the bride and she wasn't overjoyed. She didn't hire a wedding planner because she and Angela were so in sync. I got the feeling she'd prefer to deal with a female coordinator more than she would me, so I wanted you to fill in."

"What about the wedding? Won't she expect me to be there?"

He looked down at his feet, then back to her. "It's right before you head for L.A. I figured you'd have a lot to do."

"Oh." Awkward. "When is the tea party?"

"Noon this Saturday. Most of the planning is finished, but if you wouldn't mind swinging by the hotel later today, we can go over the particulars to see if we need to make changes. Saturday we'll simply have to stand by to make sure the tea runs smoothly."

"Sounds like you have everything under control. You need me why?"

He grinned. "You aren't getting out of this."

"Oh, all right," she grumbled, trying to ignore the pleasure she felt at the thought of them working together again.

Why couldn't he have felt the same about their marriage? That there was no way of getting out of it.

When they first were flirting, then dating, she'd been the one to push the issue of getting serious. When they'd gotten married, she never looked back because, let's face it, she took their relationship to heart. Enough to commit to forever. But if Dane had concerns, she never gave him time to think them through. If they'd taken their relationship slower, maybe he wouldn't have ended up taking matters into his own hands.

She'd never know for sure.

Nealy took a step backward on the sidewalk to take in the building. "Poor Cuppa Joe. This place has no idea what we have lined up."

Dane chuckled. "Times change, Nealy. We have to go with the flow or get left behind."

She glanced at him. "You're also a wise man?"

"It's funny how life experience can shape the decisions we now make as adults."

"Like an annulment?"

"Not necessarily, but that's part of our past."

"And we've moved into the future."

"Does that mean you forgive me?"

She pondered his question. At the mention of the annulment, her anger level hadn't gone off the charts. So maybe Dane was right. The future did change how we looked at things. Dane wasn't the horrible villain she'd typecast him. He'd grown up. Become successful. Thoughtful. A good guy. If Dane could get over the past, she should, too.

"Yes. I do."

Relief flickered in his eyes. "You don't know how much hearing you say those words means to me."

"We were kids. You were right when you said we rushed into marriage. We hadn't been thinking."

"No, but we had good times together."

Yes, they had.

That magical summer Dane had been all hers. As much as the summer had ended in pain, there were still lots of good times to remember. Nights at the bonfire. Sneaking into the hotel pool after hours. She hadn't allowed herself to think about those times. Maybe the healing had started by coming home. Seeing Dane again. She'd needed to get over herself and now was as good a time as any.

He stared back, and to her dismay, they were standing mere inches apart. She caught a whiff of his spicy cologne. His vibrant whiskey-colored eyes still caught and held her attention. Dane had grown up. So had Nealy. And if she could be here, have a decent conversation with him, maybe she could put all her animosity behind her, once and for all.

But that didn't mean anything else should happen between them. "Don't get any ideas, Dane. Our relationship ended a long time ago. This is solely business."

Dane's intent expression closed and the edge in his voice brought them back to reality. "I'll see you at my office later?"

"Yes, I'll stop by."

"Excellent." His hard gaze relented a bit. "Maybe afterward I'll take you for an ice cream."

She laughed. "Nice try, but I think those days are over."

He winked and walked away.

LANIE TOOK A deep breath as she stood outside her husband's office. Her impromptu lunch surprise would catch him off guard since he always ate in the office. Not today.

She rapped her knuckles on the door and swung it open. "Knock. Knock."

David's surprised expression quickly morphed into full-blown concern. "Lanie. What's wrong?"

"Nothing is wrong. I came by to take you to lunch."

He blinked. "Lunch?"

"Yes. The meal we eat at noon."

"But I brought my lunch. You watched me make it this morning."

She tried to contain her exasperation. "And it looked boring so I decided to shake things up."

He didn't say a word.

"Well?"

"I have work to do."

"And work will still be here when we get back." She came forward into his office and took hold of his arm to tug him to his feet. "Just say, 'Thank you, Lanie.'"

"Wait. Let me get my jacket."

"No need. It's a lovely day. You'll be fine."

She dragged him down the hall and through the reception area, waving at the puzzled receptionist. "David will return after lunch."

Once outside, Lanie led David to her car. She opened the passenger door to remove a large wicker basket and held it up. "Lunch."

"This is unusual," David said.

"It shouldn't be," she answered, taking his hand in hers. "Let's go to the park."

Eating lunch with her husband should be a normal occurrence, but she and David were at different law firms and rarely saw each other until after hours. She handled mostly estates and wills for a small firm, while David handled higher-profile cases like workplace compensation claims and companies suing each other. They'd both established a clientele and worked crazy hours, which Lanie had grown tired of. She wanted to quit the mundane lifestyle they'd transitioned into and go back to the exciting time when their love had been new.

They stopped a few blocks away at a small, well-tended grassy nook not far from the marina. She claimed an empty picnic table and put down the basket, inhaling the fresh sea air. A young woman jogged by, pushing a sleek stroller with a sleeping infant inside. Squirrels darted across the branches of the large oak providing them shade. Why didn't they come here more often?

Lanie laid out the food she'd ordered from the Pointe Cafe. "Go ahead. Eat," she instructed her husband as he stared at the spread before them. "I got some of our favorites." Warm pressed Cuban sandwiches, savory potato salad and fresh baklava awaited them.

David filled his plate and started eating. Lanie smiled. Getting David out of the office was a first step. He did have a tendency to be preoccupied with what was happening at the office, which left precious little time to spend with family.

They ate in silence for a few moments until David put down his fork, wariness in his eyes. "I can't stand it any longer. What's going on?"

"Nothing? Can't a wife take her husband to lunch?"

"We haven't gone to lunch since... I can't remember. When we first started working?"

"Probably. Then we had Davey and you were building your practice. We've gotten so busy, we've forgotten what a good time we had those first years of marriage."

The muscles tightened along his jaw, a sure sign Lanie had hit a sore point. "Are you saying I'm not fun?"

"No. I'm saying we've let our marriage fall into a rut. We don't do things together, just to be together. When was the last time we got in the car and drove along the coast to stop at a restaurant or spent a lazy afternoon together?"

"Since we acquired a mortgage, two cars and a son who is growing so fast we spend all our money on food and clothing."

"Not all of it." She pouted. "See, this is what I mean. What happened to spontaneity? We have good jobs, but you worry about finances and we never see each other long enough to talk about our day. We've gotten to the point in our careers where we are stable and secure, yet we never do anything for just the two of us."

"It's called growing up, Lanie. We aren't kids anymore."

"I don't want to be a kid again, but I do miss the way we couldn't stand to be apart. In college, we were always together. We couldn't wait to get married and start our lives. What happened to those people?"

"Like I said, we took on responsibilities. Maybe getting married young kept us from sowing our wild oats." He looked out over the boats swaying in the water. "Something we both missed out on."

"I didn't want to sow oats. I wanted to be with you." She paused and took a breath. "The other night, at dinner with the senator's family, you seemed interested in what living in California could offer. I know I shut you down right away, but would you want to start over somewhere new?"

"It was just conversation."

"But if you had the opportunity?"

He hesitated long enough to cause Lanie worry. "I don't know."

Her stomach twisted. He hadn't come right out and said no. Could he be wishing for a different life? And when did they get so polite with each other? When was the last time they'd shared their feelings? She couldn't recall.

"Be honest with me. Has our marriage gotten stale? Are you unhappy?"

David threw up his hands. "Where is all this coming from?"

"I feel as though we're strangers sharing the same house."

"You're overreacting."

"Am I? What about the stranger part? You work, you play golf, you and Davey sometimes play ball. When we do eat dinner together, you're quiet or distracted."

"You didn't answer my question. Where is this coming from?"

Tears pricked the backs of her eyes. "I miss you, David. We've lost our connection." She pushed at the food on her plate with her fork. "I was talking to Nealy the other day—"

"Oh, great. The voice of reason in your family."

"Hey, don't pick on her. She had some wise things to say."

"Like?"

Anger started boiling in her, adding to the turmoil twisting in her belly. "Like making sure to spend time with my husband. Putting a little excitement in our lives."

"And what would she do? Plan a big party? Make some coffee?"

She didn't dignify his outburst by responding. Instead, she went right to the crux of the matter. "What about romance?"

"I don't think your sister is the role model for successful relationships."

"Maybe not, but at least her life hasn't lost its spark."

David took the napkin from his lap, balled it up and threw it on his plate. "We don't need sparks. Work and home is enough."

Lanie wanted to cry. Is this all they had left between them? Standing, she tossed the remainder of lunch back into the basket.

"Don't you think you're looking for problems where there are none?" David tried to reason. "We have a good life, Lanie. We've been together a long time. We have a terrific family and extended family. What more do you want?"

She stopped cleaning up and stared at her husband. "*Sparks,* David. I want us to be so antsy to see each other we can't get through the day. I want us to take off for a romantic getaway whenever we feel like it."

"Lanie, I don't know."

"Let's go away this weekend," she pleaded. "My folks will watch Davey. We can drive to the other coast. I'll find a B and B. It'll be romantic, just the two of us."

"I can't. I have a big case I'm dealing with and I have to file important papers next week. I planned on working this weekend."

She looked at him, numb. "I've just finished telling you that unless we do something our marriage is in jeopardy and you want to work?"

"Hey, wait a minute. You didn't say anything about our marriage being in jeopardy."

She scoffed. "What do you think I've been talking about?"

"I don't know. I figured talking to Nealy has got you all riled up."

"Don't blame this on Nealy. This is between us."

"Lanie, calm down. Things are fine the way they are."

No, things were far from fine.

"If you don't see that things need to change," she threatened, "then I'm going to go ahead with running for mayor."

He winced and then shook his head. It was the most emotion she'd seen in him in a long time. "You're complaining because we don't spend enough time together. If you become mayor, how do you propose that will help?"

"You don't want to spend time with me now, so what difference does it make?"

"That's not what I said." He ran a hand through his neat hair, clearly frustrated. "This conversation has gotten out of control."

Lanie stood firm. She believed every word she'd said.

"Lanie, please don't do this. There's no point to your starting a campaign."

"Give me one good reason why."

"You'll be running against my partner. You can't possibly win."

"Wrong answer." She picked up the basket and stomped away.

David hurried to catch up to her.

"Have you thought this through?"

"Yes."

"Lanie, this is insane."

"No. What's insane it to keep going on like we are. I'll let you know when my first rally is."

CHAPTER EIGHT

DANE DROPPED THE REPORT on his desk then rubbed his eyes. No matter how much his uncle tried to convince him to agree to the Pensacola job, the numbers didn't make sense. With a sinking sensation, he realized he might have to drive up there and talk to the potential contractor himself. Hank wanted what he wanted and Dane had to be sure he had everything in line to talk his uncle out of making a mistake.

His phone buzzed. Grateful for the distraction, he answered quickly. "Dane Peterson."

"Dane, please tell your father to come get his things." His mother sounded almost hysterical. "I put everything on the front porch."

His anger and frustration rose immediately. "I'm working, Mom."

"I'm on my lunch hour. I don't have time to hunt him down."

"Neither do I."

"I want your father gone."

For the hundredth time, that is. Until she changed her mind and wanted him back.

"I have no idea where he is."

"Check the marina. He's managed to keep his job."

"Mom—"

"Please, Dane." Her voice wobbled. "This is the last time."

He imagined her crying and gave in, yet again. "Fine."

He hung up, regretting the job ahead. When he'd become the middleman, it was to keep his brother, Alex, out of all the dysfunction. His parents had latched onto Dane's willingness and look at him now. Still the errand boy.

He grabbed his keys and sunglasses, locked the office and let the general manager know he'd be gone for a while. He drove to the marina, white-knuckling the steering wheel the entire way.

He parked and stopped at the marina office, inquiring about his father's whereabouts.

"He's on Wyatt Hamilton's boat. Slip fifteen."

"Thanks."

His footsteps thumped on the wooden pier as he strode toward the boat. Water lapped the pilings, deceptively calm, much like his outer expression. His emotions, however, were anything but. He found his father sitting on a low post, paper bag in one hand, a sandwich in the other.

"Mom wants you to come get your stuff," he said, forgoing polite greetings.

"Uh-huh. She screamed at me before I left for work." He took a bite of his sandwich, chewed and swallowed. "I'll get to it."

"You two sort this out on your own. Don't call me anymore."

A pained expression pulled at his father's once-handsome features. "Giving up on me?"

"I don't want to be in the middle any longer."

"Ah. Taking your mother's side now?"

"I'm not taking sides here." Dane stuffed his hands in his pants pockets and glanced up at the sun. Seagulls played in the sky and he wished he could fly away, too. "I'm done."

His father peeled a piece of crust from the sandwich and tossed it into the water. Seagulls dive-bombed, fighting over the scrap of food. Appropriate imagery, considering his parents' relationship.

"Where am I supposed to go?" his father asked.

"Anywhere." Dane took a breath. "I gave you the message. I'm out of here."

His father's brittle laugh carried over the water. "Word of advice, son. Never let a woman get a hold of your heart."

As if Dane hadn't been privy to his father's wisdom all his life. He turned, walking away from the pain and constant battle of being involved with his parents at their worst. Angry with himself for wishing they'd be different. Thankful for the stark reminder of a life he'd avoided. "Don't worry," he muttered. "Not gonna happen."

BEFORE THE MEETING with Dane at the hotel, Nealy hurried back to her grandmother's house. She'd closed the shop at exactly four and had just enough time to change from her casual coffee-shop outfit into a raspberry-colored blouse, black pencil skirt and black pumps. She might not work for Dane, but she felt more comfortable dressing in a professional manner for this occasion. In her mind, being professional made their interaction less personal. Around Dane, she found she had to keep personal out of the equation.

Yes, she'd agree to barter her services. And to be honest, after two days spent mulling over coffee machine systems and handling the regular crowd, she looked forward to taking on a creative type of endeavor. Since Dane had gone above and beyond what she would have expected for the storefront's face-lift, the least she could do was lend her expertise in throwing a tea party. How difficult could that be?

She parked and reached for her briefcase. Just

as she stepped onto the hotel's veranda, her cell phone dinged, alerting her to a text.

"Not again."

Crystal had texted Nealy five times this afternoon about an L.A. event Friday night. While Nealy appreciated her boss's faith in her skills and commitment to the company, Nealy had left detailed notes about the party. All Crystal had to do was sit still and read the list Nealy had compiled.

Crystal: Time of flower delivery?

Nealy tapped out her response: Three p.m. at main house.

She hit Send, hoping Crystal would quit bothering her for the rest of the day, but with the three-hour time difference, Nealy doubted it. Tempted to turn the cell off, she hesitated, afraid she might miss an important development if she did so. After all, the call from Ashlee James's people might come at any time. She needed to know the minute that happened, so she dropped the cell in her purse and pulled open the door to the hotel, running into Dane's uncle Hank Peterson.

"Oh, excuse me."

Hank stepped back and motioned for Nealy to enter.

He'd aged well, still fit and healthy. His dark hair had become a distinguished gray. He was frowning though, so Nealy assumed his negative opinion of her had also remained the same.

She swallowed. "Mr. Peterson. How are you?"

"Doing quite well. And you?"

"Busy."

"And being in Cypress Pointe is part of being busy?"

"Yes. I'm sure you heard about my sister's engagement party."

"And its cancellation."

"Yes, unfortunately the relationship didn't work out."

"Seems to run in your family."

She felt her face flush.

"And you are here today because?"

"I have an appointment with Dane."

He eyed her suspiciously. "My nephew mentioned you'd be working with him. I can't say I approve."

Regardless of what she did or did not do, it seemed he was as disapproving as ever, and so she wouldn't be cowed by him.

"It didn't take long for you to insert yourself into Dane's life."

"If anything, Dane came to me. I didn't ask for his help at the coffee shop, he offered."

"Just like you didn't hesitate to fill in for the hotel's event coordinator?"

"We're exchanging services, nothing more."

His shrewd eyes narrowed. "I don't want your short time in Cypress Pointe ruining Dane's hard work. Please don't let memories of *your* youthful mistake take his eyes off of important business matters."

"My mistake?"

"Dane had a difficult time getting over you. I don't want you hurting him again."

Dane had a hard time getting over her? He was the one who had wanted the annulment to begin with. She was the one who'd spent years getting over him—her first love. So maybe they both hadn't used their best judgment and had jumped into something neither of them had a clue how to handle. "I assure you, Mr. Peterson, I'm only in town for a short while before heading back to L.A. I'm assisting your nephew, nothing more."

"Glad to hear it. Dane has a lot to offer someone. He's at the age where he should be thinking about settling down. He needs to find a good woman."

Wait. Was it because she didn't fall into the "good woman" category? She shouldn't be surprised. Hank had never liked her dating Dane. He always thought of Nealy as Dane's downfall. Funny how people could see things so differently. Dane's uncle hadn't been upset over the annulment; he'd looked at it as fortune smiling on his nephew. Dane would be able to find a good woman to start over with. Some woman right here in Cypress Pointe.

Who? And what would she have to offer Dane?

Would she touch his heart the way Nealy had? Understand him the way she had?

Nealy knew she was being ridiculous. She and Dane had no place as a couple. Too many years had gone by. They'd both changed. Grown up. Still, she couldn't ignore the flare of jealousy flickering in her heart—maybe because deep down she always pictured herself with Dane.

She did not want to go there. Besides, her guilty conscience reminded her, she had Sam waiting for her back in L.A. He might not be her first love, but she should be thinking about him, not Dane.

Glancing at Hank, she saw the censure in his eyes. She'd never measure up to the kind of person he wanted Dane to marry. And therein was the problem. When Dane left her, she thought it was because she didn't measure up. Piled on top of her heartache had been uncertainty and disappointment. A tough combination to overcome for anyone, let alone a teen girl longing to be with the boy she loved.

Hank continued to watch her, waiting for a response. Nealy got it—don't mess with Dane's heart. She almost laughed because it was the last thing she wanted to do. And frankly, she didn't need Hank bullying her. Dane was capable of making his own decisions. "If you'll excuse me, I'm running late."

"I'm sure we'll see each other again before you leave town."

She hoped not, but nodded. "Have a nice evening."

She strode across the foyer, head held high. No way would she let Hank Peterson reduce her to the insecure girl she'd once been. A lot of soul-searching had gone into becoming the woman she was today. She wouldn't let Hank destroy her confidence with a few critical comments.

Once she reached Dane's office door, she took a deep breath and knocked.

"It's open."

Nealy walked in, pushing her conversation with Hank out of her mind. "Hi. Sorry I'm late."

He stood and rounded his desk, the consummate professional. "No problem. I was reading over a proposal my uncle dropped off."

Good. Business right away. "Your company keeps pretty busy?"

"Yes. Can't complain. In light of the economy, things could be worse."

"I understand. With money being tight for many people, we still manage a steady calendar of events. I'm grateful."

"And I'm grateful for your help." He twisted around to retrieve a clipboard from his desk. "Tea parties aren't really my expertise."

"Sorry to hear that."

He chuckled.

"So, what is the tea party for?"

He glanced down at the papers he was holding. "Myra Hendricks, head of the Cypress Pointe Junior League, scheduled the party to acknowledge volunteers. From what I understand, it's a mix of ages, but you should know most of the women attending."

Nealy scrunched her brows together. "I remember Myra. Went to school with her daughter." If she remembered from her grandmother's updates about life in Cypress Pointe, Myra's daughter was still single. "Lovely."

At her sharp tone, he glanced at her questioningly.

"So, um, what had Angela come up with?" she said.

"Why don't we go over to the room where it'll take place. I had one of the waitstaff deliver some of the supplies there already."

"Your hotel has plenty of multipurpose rooms."

"I planned it that way, hoping to take advantage of groups with special events to book, like Saturday's tea party."

She smiled her professional smile. "Lead the way."

Minutes later, they were in the room as Dane told her, "Thirty women signed up for the party. This room has the space needed while still maintaining privacy from the hotel guests."

"Budget?"

Dane flipped the top paper on the clipboard and called out a number. Tight, but she'd make it work.

Nealy scanned the space. Tables had been set up with cloth coverings draped over top.

"White tablecloths? A bit dull, don't you think?"

"Looks fine to me."

"Didn't Myra have any input in what she wanted for decorations?"

Dane shrugged. "I wasn't part of the conversation."

She snapped her fingers and put out her hand. "Clipboard, please."

He handed it over.

"Spring flower mix? What kinds of flowers?"

"Does it matter?"

"Absolutely. If I know the flower types I can

pick a colorful tablecloth." She continued going down the list. "As far as dishes and flatware go, is it restaurant grade?"

"The restaurant inventory is more formal than the café so we'll use it. We also have a choice of glassware you can look over."

She nodded. "Teacups?"

"We have them. But just to warn you, they're plain white ceramic. Like our coffee mugs."

"Hmm. Not…great. Are the ladies bringing their own cups?"

"Not that I'm aware of."

She glanced at her watch. "Hmm." Too late to call any rental places or antiques stores around town to find vintage teacups and saucers. Tomorrow would have to do.

"What's with all the hmming?"

She glanced up. "Oh. Nothing. Just thinking."

"Why do I get the feeling this is going to cost me?"

"Because it is. I'll call around to find some pretty teacups." She flipped the page to read the next one on the clipboard. "Menu?"

"Traditional. Finger sandwiches, fruits and desserts."

She smiled at him. "Hey, you got one thing right."

"Yay for me."

She chuckled. "Trust me, it takes time and

imagination to nail the ambiance of certain events."

"Seems you do."

"I've been at this awhile."

He met her gaze with just enough heat that her skin tingled.

"I do appreciate you doing this," he said.

"Just like I appreciate what you're doing at the coffee shop. We're even."

"I was kind of hoping for more."

Uh-oh. "More than being even?"

He leaned against the wall and crossed his arms over his chest. "I know you've forgiven me for the annulment, but I'd still like to explain why I did it."

Oh, boy. Guess she couldn't hide from the past no matter how much she wanted to. "Is this necessary?"

"Yes."

Nealy realized part of being an adult meant dealing with unpleasant conversations. Like the one they were going to have if the determined expression on Dane's face was any indication.

"What is there to say?"

"I'm sorry."

Oh. Her heart squeezed at his admission, throwing her emotional equilibrium off.

"Um, thank you. Now, about the flowers—"

"Not so fast." He stared at her hard, as if

searching her expression. "I know I tried to explain at the time, but you never got the entire story."

She sighed. "What story?"

"After we got married, I went home to hear my parents in the middle of one of their worst fights. Not unusual, but the weight of what we'd done settled on my shoulders. We were kids, Nealy. How was I going to take care of you? Where and how would we live? How would we survive?"

She remembered him expressing those concerns then, but she'd been too shocked to think rationally.

His voice went flat. "Listening to my parents gave me a glimpse of what our future might be like and I didn't want that for us. Filing for an annulment at least gave us a chance."

"But not together."

"No." Regret made his expression somber. "I don't know what I expected you to do, but walking away afterward didn't occur to me."

"You'd just broken my heart."

"I understand now. At the time, I thought we'd talk it out. Make plans to get remarried after we both finished college."

She reflected on her conversation with Hank Peterson. "Your uncle seems to be under the impression you took our breakup badly."

His brow creased. "When did you speak to my uncle?"

"Doesn't matter. Please answer the question."

He pushed away from the wall and paced the room. "Yes, I was upset. I thought we loved each other enough to figure out our next move. Didn't think you'd move away for good."

"Is that why you never called or looked for me?"

"You made it clear you were done with me. After a while, total separation seemed the best option for us. We both moved on with our lives."

At last, the bottom line. Yes, they'd both moved on.

Seeing how successful Dane had become made her heart hurt, because he'd indeed gone on with his life. Without her. She'd taken her broken heart and moved far away, making a good life for herself in California. Time had separated the bond they'd forged, but maybe now they could have some kind of friendship, as they'd had as kids. Friendship only, because falling in love again would be too dangerous for her.

"As much as I hated it then, you probably did us both a favor," she admitted. "The only thing worse than breaking up after a few hours would have been calling it quits after a few years."

He stopped pacing and stood before her,

much too close for comfort. A strange look crossed his face, as if he wanted to confess something to her, but it quickly disappeared. "So we act like adults now. Work together without any problems, right?"

"It's the only alternative."

Nealy had no doubt she could be professional around Dane. After all, she wouldn't be in town forever. Soon she'd be back to her job. Back to her life, with the reminder of how much Dane had changed. How much she was still attracted to him.

For now, trying to ignore the fact that he'd turned into a caring, responsible man made the present difficult. His smile held the same hint of mischief that drew her to him in the beginning. The same tightness in her chest she always experienced around Dane had grown more intense. Her reaction to him had not waned with time and past hurt. If anything, seeing him again made her reaction stronger.

He came forward, moved into her space. She did everything in her power not to lean into him and yet she failed.

His gaze fell to her lips and she nervously licked them. A flame lit in the depths of his eyes. Nealy's heart rate was pounding as she waited for his next move. She felt spellbound, unable to move.

The spark between them developed into a full-blown flame. He lifted his hand, hesitating for a mere second before brushing calloused fingers over her cheek with a soft stroke. His familiar touch was like an awakening to her. He seemed to have every intention of moving this new relationship back to a place she had kept locked in her heart. As much as her body longed to be held in his arms again, as much as she reveled in anticipation of his kiss, reason lingered on the edges of her mind. She grabbed hold of it and took a step back.

"This isn't right."

"Sure feels right to me."

"Dane, you didn't want to stay married to me all those years ago. Why would I want to start something with you now?"

"Because there is an undeniable connection between us."

"Was. Was a connection. The only thing between us now are memories. Regrets." She frowned. "Besides, I don't think Sam would approve of me kissing another man."

His eyes shadowed.

Nealy moved farther away from temptation. The urge to kiss Dane was calling to her but she couldn't go there. They had no future together. She couldn't trust her heart with him again. "You said no problems. I think kissing would constitute a problem between us. Not to mention ruining our working relationship."

He made space between them, his eyes dark and brooding. He might try to hide his emotions from her, but she knew he was trying to come up with a new angle.

"Fine. At least say you'll come cheer for me Friday night."

"Cheer for you?"

"At softball. I'm on a city league and we have a tough game this weekend."

"You're still playing?"

"Yeah. I might not have been good enough for the big leagues after my injury, but I play whenever I'm in town. Could never give it up completely."

Baseball had been Dane's passion and when he'd lost his scholarship and a shot at becoming a pro, he was down on himself. But Nealy had been there to pick up the pieces and their bond had grown even stronger.

"We used to play catch, remember?"

How could she forget? The memories had been seared into her mind, never fully exorcised. He'd seemed larger than life on the field, at command with a ball and glove in his hand. Not even the loss of a scholarship could take away his drive for the game.

"So, you'll come out Friday night?"

Why not? While she was home she might as well hang out with the locals. See if Dane was still as top-notch as he used to be. Besides, she never could resist a challenge involving Dane and he knew it.

"We'll see."

CHAPTER NINE

FRIDAY EVENING, NEALY climbed the sun-warmed metal bleachers to take a seat beside Lanie. She'd debated showing up, but curiosity had gotten the better of her. Small-town Friday night meant a softball game and besides, she didn't have anything else to do. Why not join in? She should catch up with the good folks of Cypress Pointe. And oh yeah, Dane would be in action again.

The past two days had been productive. She'd decided on an espresso machine her grandmother could operate without much fuss and placed the order, receiving a quick delivery date of Monday. To get ready for the new machine, she'd ordered additional bags of coffee beans, a new grinder and a variety of flavored syrups to accompany the new drink menu. With the new drink selections in mind, she also rented a small ice machine and a blender to make cold drinks. Caught up in the excitement, she'd stayed up late one night to design new coffee cups with the Cuppa Joe logo. Now all she had to do was recruit help to paint the inside of the shop on Sunday, make up the new menu board to hang on the wall, call the local cable company to connect Wi-Fi, and next week she'd be ready to unveil the new shop.

Just in time for Grandmother's return.

In between making all these plans, she'd learned from the regulars at the coffee shop about the importance of tonight's game. A strong rivalry between Cypress Pointe and the other team, the city of Clearwater, had gained momentum. Clearwater had trounced Cypress Pointe for two years running and held the number one spot in the league. The boys from Cypress Pointe had recruited as many stellar players as they could find, maintained a strict practice schedule and swore tonight would be the night they regained victory. Competition had stirred up this town and, as indicated by the crowded stands, folks had shown up in large numbers to support their boys.

The late-evening sun shined brightly. The scent of hot dogs and greasy French fries wafted from the concession stand. At another game happening a few fields over, the clang of a ball hitting the metal fence echoed her way. The excited crowd milled about, waiting for the opening pitch.

Nealy shaded her eyes with her hand to peer

at the field. Dane stood on the pitcher's mound, working out the kinks in his shoulder. She recognized a few of his teammates. "Where's David?"

Lanie pointed to home base. "Catcher."

"Since when?"

"Since Marty Fellows tore up his knees in a motorcycle accident."

"Ouch."

"So now I sit here worried the ball will give David a concussion."

"Not with all the gear he's wearing. He's safe."

Lanie cocked her head. "Although, a good hit to the head might wake him up enough to realize where our marriage is headed."

Nealy glanced around and lowered her voice. "Are you sure you want to discuss your marital problems here?"

Lanie shrugged. "At this point I've given up."

"Hey, don't be like that. I have faith you two will work things out."

"Like you and Dane?"

Nealy jerked sideways to look at her sister. "What?"

"You two are spending time together. I just thought…"

"Well, you thought wrong. We're two old friends helping each other while I'm in town."

"Right. Tell that to your face. Every time you see him you get all mushy."

"Mushy? No way. I'm a professional."

"Professionally lovesick."

"Lanie, I have a boyfriend. Remember?"

"Oh, yes. Whom you haven't talked about since you came home. What's his name again?"

"Ha-ha, you're such a comedian. His name is Sam."

"Have you talked to *Sam* lately?"

"We keep missing each other." True. But why hadn't she called him more? Or vice versa. She disliked being put off, as he had a habit of doing, but she could have found the time if she wanted to. "He's got a case and I'm busy at Cuppa Joe."

"Davey told me you're serious about upgrading the shop."

"I am." She leaned back, enjoying the last warm rays of sun on her face. "He's a good worker."

Lanie sighed. "He knows something is up between David and me. Finds excuses to stay out late."

"Kids aren't dumb. They know when things aren't right at home."

"I don't know what to tell him."

"Nothing. There's nothing to say right now." A commotion stole Nealy's attention away from her sister as her old friend Lilli climbed through the throngs to make her way up the bleachers to take a seat next to Nealy.

"Hey, girls. Am I late?"

"The game is about to start," Nealy informed her.

"Good." Lilli looked out at the field. "There's Max on first base." She waved with wild abandon at her boyfriend. He nodded his head in response.

"You two make a cute couple."

She sighed dreamily. "I know."

Nealy and Lanie exchanged amused glances. "What?"

"The first stages of love," Lanie stated. "I'm jealous and revolted at the same time."

"The beginning stages are fun," Nealy agreed. She and Dane had been intense from day one, and after he ended the marriage, the strength of her love for him had taken years to fade.

Lilli teased, "Hold on to your jealousy, girls, because Max and I plan on a long, happy, nauseatingly in love relationship."

Lanie threw her a "you'll see" look, which Lilli ignored.

The game started. For the next few hours Nealy sat back and watched Dane play. He still filled out a uniform with his athlete's physique, which she tried not to notice. Okay, she was human. He looked good. He hadn't lost his graceful moves. The ball still flew from his fingers with precision and speed. In the first five innings he'd kept the batters from scoring, while Cypress Pointe had scored two runs.

The next time he went up to bat, Nealy admired how focused he was on the ball, as if his life depended on it. Just as he'd focused on her once.

"Hit a home run, Dane," a woman a few rows down yelled.

"Show us what you've got," shouted another.

Nealy looked over the crowd to see who cheered for Dane. "Candy Thomas? Isn't she married?"

"Nope," Lanie informed her. "Second divorce six months ago. On the prowl. Has Dane in her sights."

Nealy shuddered.

"And the other woman?"

"Callie Simmons," Lilli said.

Nealy's brows rose. "No way." She remembered Callie from high school as a mousy, timid girl. Not the bombshell in the tight T-shirt with eyes on Dane.

"Yup. Slow bloomer."

"Let me guess. She's after Dane, too?"

"Well, they aren't technically after him,"

Lanie told her, humor lacing her tone, "but they show a lot of interest whenever he's around."

Nealy shouldn't ask the next question, but wasn't able to stop herself. "Has he shown an interest in anyone in particular?"

Lanie smirked and nudged her elbow. "Why, thinking of dumping Sam?"

"Funny. No, just curious."

"Who's Sam?" Lilli asked.

"My boyfriend."

"Back in L.A?"

"Yes, back In L.A."

Lilli pressed in close, her shoulder touching Nealy's. "Do you miss him?"

"Of course."

"Then why didn't he come with you?"

"He's busy on a case. He's an attorney."

Lilli's brow furrowed.

"What? We both have demanding careers. We date when we can."

"Doesn't sound very romantic."

Lanie chuckled and held out her palm to high-five Lilli in front of Nealy's face.

"What is this, pick-on-Nealy's-relationship night?"

Lilli nodded toward Dane. "When he's around, you bet."

Nealy rolled her eyes. "Okay. Fine. My dating life is sad. But you didn't answer my question about Dane's dating life."

"He dates here and there." Lanie looked over at Lilli. "I've never heard of any serious relationship, have you?"

"No," Lilli replied. "Doesn't mean he's never had one. Well, besides Nealy."

Nealy shifted on the suddenly uncomfortable bleacher.

"He travels a lot. Maybe he has a girlfriend in another town," Lanie suggested.

"If he does he hasn't brought her around Cypress Pointe," Lilli said. "Trust me, the rumor mill would be all over it in no time."

True. Cypress Pointe had a very healthy, active gossip system.

So a couple women had a thing for Dane. Why not? He was available. Successful. More handsome than a man had a right to be. He could date whomever he wanted. They'd broken up a long time ago. Moved on. So why did the idea of another woman loving Dane bother Nealy so much?

She tried desperately to put thoughts of Dane with another woman out of her mind. She had no claim on the man. She'd walked away. Left with a broken heart. A teenager's heart. What about her adult heart right now? Okay, she still harbored feelings for Dane but she'd be crazy to imagine them being together. She'd always be waiting for the day he would betray her trust in him. Not a great foundation on which to build a relationship.

"And anyways," Lanie blithely chatted on, despite Nealy's inner debate, "after what he's been through with his parents, I'm sure he's gun-shy."

"His parents? What are you talking about?"

"I never told you this, since you didn't like hearing about Dane. They're still married, but determined to use Dane as some sort of whipping post in their relationship. I don't know why he bothers."

When they were kids, he never spoke about what went on at home. If she asked, he clammed up, so she didn't bug him about it. Maybe she should have, especially given what he'd told her recently about the arguing he overheard when he went home after they were married.

"I think that's why he shies away from serious relationships." Lilli added her opinion. "Trust me, I understand. My folks never got along when I was growing up, but Dane's parents are the worst."

She stared at Dane standing on the pitcher's mound, tall and proud, her heart softening.

In the next two innings, Clearwater managed to gain two runs to tie the game. Dusk had descended and the spotlights switched on, illuminating the field. In the last inning, Clearwater batted first. Nealy watched Dane intently as he pitched. Before the third strike, Clearwater had managed to score another run to gain the lead. As the Cypress Pointe players filed into the dugout, the home crowd jumped to their feet, cheering and shouting support to the players as they got ready to bat. All they needed were two runs to win the game.

Max was up to bat first. Lilli dug her fingers into Nealy's denim-clad leg. "Oh, my gosh. I'm so nervous."

Nealy pried her friend's fingers from her leg. "Chill."

Lilli clasped her hands together over her heart and closed her eyes. "I'm afraid to watch."

Nealy poked her. "Open your eyes, silly. You don't want to miss any of this."

Lilli squinted. "You're right."

On the third pitch, Max hit the ball. The outfielder scooped up the grounder and threw it to first base, but Max made it safely. Lilli screamed, then jumped up, clapping and yelling.

Nealy rubbed her ear.

Two more batters came up, one walked and the other struck out. Dane took his position, bat in hand as he waited for the pitcher to send him the hit to win the game.

Nealy held her breath. It had been his dream to play professional ball and although his plans had changed, he still took the sport seriously.

Strike one.

Nealy's stomach turned.

The next pitch came at him and Dane slammed the ball. As the outfielders scrambled to collect the fly ball, they missed as it landed and bounced away. Everyone in the stands stood to shout, Nealy included. When Max crossed home plate, Lilli grabbed Nealy's arm, hopping up and down. The next player also crossed home plate safely.

Dane rounded the bases. He raced to home plate as the outfielder threw the ball to the catcher. He slid as the catcher caught the ball. Nealy's heart pounded. Had he made it? Dane stood, wiping dirt from his pants as the umpire called him out. The crowd yelled. Even though he hadn't made it, his hit gave Cypress Pointe the winning home runs. The team rushed out of the dugout, high-fiving and hugging as the home-team fans clapped and cheered.

"I'm going to find Max," Lilli yelled and bounded down the bleachers, disappearing into a group of exiting fans.

Nealy glanced at her sister. "How about you?"

Lanie gathered her purse. "I'll meet David at home."

"Party pooper."

Lanie shrugged and made her way down the bleachers.

Nealy stayed seated, watching the pandemonium die down.

The two teams exchanged well wishes before returning to their respective dugouts to gather their equipment. Friends and family surrounded their winning heroes as they headed to the parking lot. A few women waited by the dugout. Dane exited a few moments later, his equipment bag thrown over his shoulder. He greeted the women, laughing and chatting, until he looked up and his gaze met Nealy's. Excusing himself, he headed in her direction. When the women realized he wasn't interested in what they had to offer, they wandered off, leaving Dane and Nealy the only people left at the ballpark.

She carefully stepped down the bleachers, her shoes echoing on the metal. He waited at the bottom, his smile wide as she reached him.

She ignored the flutter of nerves inside her as she stepped onto the concrete walkway. "Congratulations. Looks like you haven't lost your touch," she told him.

"It was a team effort."

"Yeah, but c'mon, you're still good. You rallied the team."

"Tonight was different."

"How's that?"

"We wanted to win the title back. The other team kept ragging on us about what losers we were. A guy can only take so much ribbing before it becomes personal."

"Well, you guys did Cypress Pointe proud."

"And you always were my good-luck charm."

In a quick motion, he dropped his bag, slid his hand around her lower back and pulled her in for a celebratory kiss.

Surprised by his move, it took a few seconds to sink in that Dane's lips were on hers. Dane. Her first love. The one man she could never forget.

And just like that, the heartache of twelve years melted into pleasure.

Her arms circled around his neck. She leaned into him, swept up in the dizzying sensation of Dane's mouth on hers. Not a soft brushing motion or a hard press, just the right pressure to show her this kiss meant business. A wave of tenderness flooded her as she stood enveloped in the arms of the man she'd never gotten over. The man she never thought she'd have the chance to kiss again.

Dane hugged her closer, nipping at her lips. She pulled away, cradling his face between her hands, studying his expression. Yep, it was there. The passion burning in the depths of his gaze. She brought her face close to his, his breath warm on her lips before they met again.

The kiss seemed to last forever before the bright lights switched off with a loud electrical boom and startled Nealy, bringing her to her senses. Shrouded in darkness, she lowered her arms and stepped away, her breath ragged and her face hot. They stared at each other in the moonlight until a distant car horn broke the spell.

He ran a finger over her arm, eliciting goose bumps she didn't bother hiding. "They say you can't go back. If I wasn't standing here right now, I'd have believed them."

"Maybe going back isn't what it's cracked up to be. Maybe they, whoever they are, know the secret is moving forward."

"Is that what you've done, Nealy? Moved forward?"

"I had to and I'm glad I did."

"I guess we both did."

"Dane, let's move on. You apologized. I accepted. You have a hotel empire to run. I have events to plan in L.A. This moment is romantic and exciting, but if I were here for a few more months, we'd find a way to get on each other's nerves." Sure, by trying not to snag him for another toe-curling kiss. "Let's leave tonight where it belongs, in the memory books. A nice place marker to replace the past."

He scooped up his equipment bag. "When did you become a philosopher?"

"When you decided to cross the line. We talked about not kissing, remember?"

"You have a problem with kissing?"

"No, but we aren't supposed to be doing this."

"Fun stealer."

Her lips quivered, but she refused to let him see that his humor had relieved the tension between them.

The sprinklers switched on in a sputter, hissing a steady beat over the field.

"Thanks for tonight," Dane said, his husky tone causing more goose bumps on her skin.

"You did the work, throwing strikes most of the night."

He chuckled. "I meant for the kiss."

"Oh." *Duh*.

"Though it meant a lot to see you in the stands."

"Despite my newly crowned title of fun

stealer, I did enjoy it. Sitting in the stands with Lanie and Lilli was like old times."

"Care to join me for a victory burger? The team is meeting to celebrate."

Oh, how she wanted to celebrate with him, wanted to arrive at the restaurant on his arm. But the history between them made her wary. She couldn't get in too deep here or she'd surely regret it. "Um, thanks, but I'll pass. I plan on being at the hotel early tomorrow to make sure everything is in place for the tea party, so I should turn in."

"Maybe you should, but you don't have to. How about a swim in the hotel pool? The owner won't mind if we sneak in after hours."

She swallowed hard, keeping her mind focused on the correct answer. "No. I'll see you tomorrow."

He escorted her to her rental car. She paused before getting inside. "I'm glad you kept up with the game, Dane. You're still talented."

He shrugged. "It's more of a hobby now."

In the faint lighting of the parking lot, she saw his gaze lower to her lips.

She didn't dare move as the tension around them grew.

"Okay, then. Tomorrow," she croaked. Could she sound any more nervous? she wondered.

His grin sent her heartbeat racing again. "To-morrow," he said.

He slung his equipment bag over his shoulder and walked to his car, leaving Nealy to recognize how unsatisfying being cautious actually was.

CHAPTER TEN

NEALY TOOK AN appraising view of the decorated tea-party room before checking her watch. The ladies would be arriving any minute. That meant Dane would put in an appearance, as well. Honestly, she was more concerned about facing Dane than anything else at this moment.

She'd tossed and turned the night before, unable to stop thinking about Dane's spontaneous kiss. Her lips still tingled at the memory of the sizzling exchange.

Not only had she not expected to see Dane while in Cypress Pointe, she never imagined she'd be working with him. Work she could deal with. Kissing? Oh, no. And yet for all her griping about spending so much time with him again, she hadn't stopped him from kissing her. She'd enjoyed it, in fact.

She was so conflicted.

The changes in him had been such a revelation, and his kiss mesmerizing as ever. *Stop,* the wise section of her brain admonished. *Go for it,* the free spirit encouraged. Yikes. Her mind was no help whatsoever.

All night she went back and forth between the two suggestions, resulting in no sleep. Confused, and a little annoyed Dane would put her in such a situation when she asked him not to, she called Sam when she got out of bed. The call went straight to voice mail. Aggravated, since she knew he'd be up, she tossed the phone on the bed. Is this what she had to look forward to with Sam? A hit-and-miss kind of relationship? Before this trip, playing tag with Sam hadn't bothered her. Now she had plenty of questions and no answers. Compared to Dane, and his serious pursuit of her, Sam's lack of interest had finally made an impression on her. Maybe it was time to rethink her relationship with Sam.

She had to admit, Dane's attention was flattering, but she still held back, for more than one reason. Her job required she live across the country. A job she liked. A job she excelled in. There were only so many weddings and tea parties she could plan in Cypress Pointe, so even if she considered moving back home, she'd have to start a business from the ground floor. Did she want to invest the time and energy in that process when she was at the top of her game in L.A.?

As much as she couldn't deny the strong attraction between them, she'd always be wondering if she could trust her heart to him. Afraid he'd hurt her again. She admired the man Dane had become, but to take a chance with her heart when she wasn't sure of what he wanted? Not a smart move.

Which put her back at square one. Dane still intrigued her, but she didn't want a long-distance relationship. Look how well things had turned out with Sam and they lived in the same city. No, long-distance was out.

After her first cup of coffee and plenty of arguing with herself, she dressed in a pale pink sheath dress and high sparkly pink pumps, her hair piled on her head in a stylish updo, ready for the event at the hotel.

Nealy rubbed her aching temples. She should have taken a walk along the beach to clear her head, but duty called. Myra Hendricks entered the room, trailed by her daughter Briana, dressed to the nines, already scoping out the place in search of someone. Dane? Probably. He was one of the most eligible guys in Cypress Pointe.

Nealy strode forward to greet the women. "Mrs. Hendricks. Briana. So glad to see you both."

"Call me Myra," the older woman said, surveying the room. "My goodness, Nealy, you transformed this into a proper English garden."

Nealy smiled, proud of her accomplishment completed in a few short days and a tight budget.

Once Dane explained the tea-party idea, an English garden theme lingered in her mind. With a blank slate to start from, she'd made a call to a local flower shop. Working with the talented florist, they'd come up with a mixture of lilies, daisy poms, carnations and heather in shades of white, pink and purple, arranged in a rustic basket to create cheerful table centerpieces. On the recommendation of the florist, she visited a lawn-and-garden nursery and purchased potted hydrangea, in deep wine and bright pink, as well as baskets of sunny gerbera daisies to scatter on the floor around the room. While there, she discovered a display of pink roses on a white wooden arbor. How could she have a garden tea party without roses? Once positioned around the room, the glorious aroma of blooming buds scented the air and the English tea party was made official.

"I had no idea," Myra said as she wandered around the room.

Side tables draped in pale green cloth had been set up to accommodate the tiered plates of dainty sandwiches, desserts and fruit. Pink lemonade punch, as well as an assorted tea collection, would be the beverages of choice. There were eight round tables with seating for the same number. China teacups, which Nealy managed to find after scouring all the antiques shops in town, were placed at all the settings. There weren't enough matching sets to go around, but she liked the diversity of different colors and shapes on each table. As a gift for attending, the women were each going to leave with their very own cup.

"Great job," Briana commented, coming up beside Nealy. "Dane hasn't arrived yet?"

Nealy blinked. Yep, another smitten woman. "Not yet."

Suddenly Briana's eyes grew wide and a predatory smile crossed her lips. Nealy turned to spot Dane talking to his aunt as they entered the room.

"Excuse me. I need to touch up my lipstick."

"Of course," Nealy replied to empty air.

Dane and his aunt approached. He smiled at Nealy, the same self-satisfied smile after the searing kiss from the night before. She had to downplay the kiss's affect on her. Not a big deal. Happened all the time. *Liar.*

"Nealy, you remember my aunt Sonia?"

"Yes. Mrs. Peterson. Nice to see you again."

The woman peered around the room with a critical eye. "Lovely job, Dane."

Dane shifted. "Thanks, but I had nothing to do with the decorations."

"Still, it is your hotel," his aunt stated.

His tone conveyed all business. "This is a group effort."

Mrs. Peterson looked everywhere before she acknowledged Nealy. "Beautiful."

"Thanks, but Dane should get the credit. I merely took his ideas and ran with them."

Dane's brows rose up. "Don't let her fool you, Aunt Sonia. Nealy is a genius."

Nealy remained silent, but her gaze tangled with Dane's. A flashback of last night's kiss came to mind again and her cheeks grew warm. Dane, recognizing her blush for what it was, sent her a wolfish grin.

Watching them closely, Mrs. Peterson seized Dane's arm and pulled his attention away from Nealy. "Remember, dinner tonight at seven. Don't be late."

A wrinkle creased his forehead. "I'll be honest, Aunt Sonia, with everything I've got going on, I totally forgot."

She glared openly at Nealy. "I see."

"Don't worry, I'll be there."

Nealy could hear the resignation in his voice. No way was he getting out of dinner.

His aunt turned back to Dane. "I invited a friend to join us. Just to even out the dinner table."

Awkward. Could his aunt be any more obvious?

"Um, thanks, I think."

"Come greet the ladies at my table."

Dragging him off to where she would be sitting, Dane went along with his aunt as more ladies filed in, oohing and ahhing at the transformed room. As Nealy basked in their pleasure, she heard her sister's voice in her ear.

"Nice way to show off."

She spun around to see Lanie, who was smiling, and her mother, her face a blank mask.

"If you got it, flaunt it. That's my motto."

Her sister laughed. Her mother cringed.

"So…Junior League?" Nealy said to Lanie.

"You know the Graingers. We're all about volunteerism and civic duty."

"Some of us," her mother pointed out.

"Well, Mom, you'll be glad to know I'm part of the time-honored tradition. Today's work is pro bono."

"I thought you and Da—" Nealy elbowed her sister in the side before she could spill the beans.

"Just give me this one," Nealy whispered in Lanie's ear.

"Gotcha." She rubbed her side. "Looks like the ladies are out in full force."

A group of women had formed around Dane. Taking pity on him, although she couldn't imagine why, Nealy moved to her purse to remove her phone to send Dane a text: Now you owe me.

When his phone alerted him to a text, Dane excused himself from the group. He pressed a button and read the message. Looking up, he met her gaze across the room and mouthed a silent "thank you."

"Smooth," Lanie complimented.

"I do what I can."

"About what?" her mother asked, joining the conversation.

"Helping the community," Nealy answered.

Lanie snorted.

"Good, good," Anita said and nodded, a distracted smile forming on her lips. "You decorated this room very nicely, Nealy. Very appropriate."

Appropriate? What on earth had she expected? Male dancers?

"Thanks, Mom."

Her mother caught her gaze. "I mean it. The decorations are very tasteful. And I must admit, despite your sister's departure, the engagement parties were also beautiful. You handled the guests wonderfully when Juliet canceled."

Wow. Kudos from her mother. She and Lanie exchanged amused glances.

"Now you have an idea of what my job entails."

"Hmm," her mother responded and moved to amble around the room.

"High praise," Lanie commented. "She's a tough audience."

Even though Nealy knew she and her sister were joking, the fact that her mother had something nice to say about her work warmed her heart. For the first time ever, her mother had a glimpse into Nealy's world. Maybe now she'd reconsider her opinion of Nealy's life being anything but frivolous and shallow.

As the ladies mingled, Dane returned to her side.

"Things are under control?" he asked in his serious tone.

Nealy frowned. What happened to the easygoing guy from last night? "So far."

He eyed her from head to toe. "You okay?"

"Peachy."

He opened his mouth, but before he could say anything, Briana sashayed over to engage him in conversation. Leaving him to fend for himself, she crossed the room to give final instructions to the waitstaff. Once finished with her task, she noted Dane had left. Good. She didn't need him second-guessing her every move. Or making her aware of him on every level.

As she performed her last-minute checks, Lilli and her mother, Celeste, arrived. Lilli hurried over to give her a hug. "Coffee shop to tea party? You're a master."

"I wouldn't go that far."

Lilli laughed. "You remember my mother?"

"Certainly." Nealy held out her hand. "A pleasure seeing you again, Mrs. Barclay."

Celeste Barclay shook Nealy's hand, but like everyone when they first arrived, her attention centered on the room. "Lilli told me you were a premier event planner. She wasn't kidding."

"I never kid about my friends," Lilli said.

Celeste took a step back and placed a hand on her hip. "I thought we did a wonderful job decorating and preparing our last charity fundraiser, but, Nealy, you seem to take event planning to the next level. Between the engagement party for your sister and this, I'm going to give you a call when I come up with next year's fund-raiser's theme."

"Thank you, but I'm filling in here. Pretty soon I'll be back in L.A."

Celeste smiled. "You'll help."

Nealy glanced at Lilli.

"She never takes no for an answer."

"Wow."

"Yeah, I've heard the same response a time or two." Lilli grinned. "It would be good to have you back home."

At the sincere expression on her friend's face, Nealy tamped down her regret. As much as she enjoyed being home, she had to look forward to the Ashlee James account. The famous designer would elevate Nealy's stature in the company. If her mother thought she'd done a good job here today, think how impressed she'd be when her daughter worked with someone as well-known as Ashlee. Nealy's path might not have been law, like the rest of her family, but maybe now her parents would see the success she'd garnered in a highly competitive, lucrative industry. Besides, she had too much up in the air to make a major life change. Too many things to think about. The best place to figure her life out would be in California. Away from Dane's romancing ways and hot kisses.

Myra clapped her hands and brought the tea party to order. The chatting, laugher and smiles went a long way to easing Nealy's concerns about taking over at the last minute. She always worried before an event, hoping she executed the plan according to the client's expectations. Today was no different, but the added pressure of knowing Dane was busy somewhere in the building kept her on edge.

Don't worry about Dane.

All of Nealy's personal concerns took second place when Myra began her speech thanking the volunteers. When she finished, Myra enlisted Nealy's help to raffle off the floral arrangements and potted plants. When Myra announced the women would be going home with the teacup at their place setting, everyone clapped in delight. All in all, a good day.

While the guests visited the buffet to fill their plates with luncheon goodies, Nealy's gaze moved about the room, checking for any potential problems. So far, so good. Until she noticed Mrs. Peterson's table and the older lady's triumphant expression. Nealy coughed as she realized all the women seated at the table were single. Mrs. Peterson nodded smugly. Nealy imagined she was holding court, with Dane—the prize—that one lucky lady would receive by the good graces of his dear aunt.

"It's sad," Lanie remarked as she stopped beside Nealy, taking a strawberry from her plate. "Ever since you came back to town, the singles have been mobilizing against the competition." Lanie bit into the fruit.

"Competition?" Nealy glanced at her sister. "Me?"

"Who else? You're the only one Dane has ever gotten serious with."

Nealy shook her head. "I'm not getting back with him so all this posturing is for nothing."

"They're single. Maybe they think they have to at least try."

Nealy winced. "Please tell me Dane isn't desperate."

"He's not. He's not a monk either, but like I said, nothing serious."

Lanie left to take her seat at the table. Nealy watched the women at Mrs. Peterson's table with a mixture of jealousy and sadness. While she might not like these women targeting Dane, she had no right to feel like this. She'd walked away from him years ago. Yes, she had a good reason not to stay with him, which brought up the sadness.

Since she'd been back in town, much of the hurt had abated. She could talk to Dane without the heavy pain in her chest. She could appreciate what he'd accomplished in the time they'd been apart. Even admire him for his success. And while she couldn't trust her heart to him again, the kiss he'd laid on her the night before made the simmering attraction stronger. She could enjoy his company as a friend, but not romantically, right?

To make the point to herself, she went to her

purse to find her phone. She bit her lip, then texted Sam, asking him to call her. They were still missing each other's calls, which would have worried Nealy if she believed in fate. She knew Sam was busy. They'd connect soon and things would go back to normal.

Don't count on it, the not-so-fun part of her brain scoffed.

One more week in Cypress Pointe. Once the new account came through, she'd be completely preoccupied and worry about Dane would disappear. And her visit would have been but a pleasant memory.

Soon, the tea party ended. Many of the women stopped to compliment Nealy before leaving. She glanced at her watch. Sierra had agreed to cover Cuppa Joe until Nealy finished here. At the rate the women were going, she'd get there just in time to close the shop. She looked up to find a friend from high school standing in front of her. A very pregnant friend.

"Nealy, it's been ages."

"Marianne." Nealy hugged her. "Look at you."

Marianne rubbed her belly. "Two months to go. I am so ready to deliver."

"Congratulations."

The woman sighed with contentment. "I'm so excited. Phil and I have been trying and trying and almost gave up, but this little miracle baby is all we hoped for."

Nealy smiled. She'd never thought about starting a family, because first, you had to be in a devoted, committed relationship. Seeing Marianne glow made her think about internal alarm clocks, which had never been on her radar before.

"Your sister says you're here on vacation?"

"Yes. I'll be headed back for a big job in L.A."

"What a shame. If you were going to be around, I'd try to convince you to plan my baby shower." Marianne grimaced. "My mother-in-law is in charge."

"I would have loved it."

"Oh well. I guess I'll have to settle for stork cutouts, clothespin games and cake with pink and blue frosting."

"A very traditional theme."

"Also a very nice way of saying boring."

"There's only so much you can do with a baby theme."

"Yes, but storks? Really?"

Nealy laughed. "You'll have a good time."

"As long as the baby is healthy, I can put up with anything." She grinned. "Good to see you again, Nealy. Don't be a stranger."

Marianne moved on. Nealy checked her watch again.

"Plans?" Lanie asked as she sidled up beside her.

"I promised Sierra I'd be back to take over for her."

"You finish up here. I'll go to Cuppa Joe."

Nealy was shocked.

"Look, you came all the way from California to help Grandmother." She grew sheepish. "None of us here have chipped in to help. It's about time."

"Thanks. I shouldn't be too long."

"Take your time. You've been working nonstop since you got home. Not much of a vacation."

"I would like to take a walk along the beach."

"Then do it. Besides, Davey said he'd be at the coffee shop. I can spend time with him."

"Is he still finding escape routes away from you guys?"

"Yes. David asked him to play golf today, but Davey insisted on doing his shift at the coffee shop. Do you know of any reason he'd pick working over hanging out with his father?"

"Sure. Sierra."

"Sierra?" Lanie's eyes widened. "He has a crush?"

"I'm pretty sure."

"My baby?"

"No. Your teenage son."

"He didn't say anything."

Nealy chuckled. "Did you expect him to?"

"I… We…"

"Your son is growing up, Lanie."

She opened her purse to remove her car keys. "Like I said, take your time. I have some important reconnaissance work."

"Yeah. Davey's gonna love you for interfering."

Lanie took off, and before long, the last of the stragglers exited the room. The staff came in to finish cleaning up and tearing down the room. Duties complete, Nealy was ready to call it a day when Dane entered the room, all smiles.

"Hey, you got great reviews."

She attributed his compliment to her rush of excitement, not the fact that Dane had kissed her last night.

"It turned out well."

"Well? From what I heard, you wowed them."

Nealy shrugged.

"Cypress Pointe could use an event planner like you." He held up his hand. "Wait. I could use an event planner like you. Any way I can talk you into staying?"

"You know I can't."

"I have two interviews set up for next week

but you'd save me the trouble of searching if you stayed."

Is that why he wanted to hire her? For the sake of expedience?

She turned away to collect her bag. "Sorry to put you to all the trouble."

"Wait." He touched her arm. She jerked away. "What's with you?"

When she faced him, he took one look at her face and took a step back. "Uh-oh."

She hadn't planned on giving him what for, but between the kiss and trying to maneuver her to make his life easier, just as he'd done in the past, she snapped.

"You do realize you probably can't afford me. And if you could, what makes you think I'd work for you?"

"Nealy, calm down. I was kidding."

"Kidding? You consider trying to manipulate me a joke?"

His humor faded. "Manipulate? Whoa. It never crossed my mind. You're good at what you do. I couldn't have put such a polished event together this last-minute and then have everyone rave over it."

Okay, maybe she had overreacted. She blew out a breath. "Thanks."

He crossed his arms over his chest. "Let's go get some ice cream. I have no idea what kinds of things to look for in a competent event coordinator. You can give me a few pointers."

"Sounds like you're trying to be my boss, again."

"Again?"

"Well, since I've been back, but more so right now."

He grinned. "Sorry."

"No, you're not."

He held his arm out, motioning her to leave the room first. She took the lead with Dane following close behind. Awareness danced over her skin. Instead of putting the past with Dane behind her, his presence proved how much of a hold he still had over her, which was exciting and scary at the same time.

CHAPTER ELEVEN

"LET'S TAKE MY CAR," Dane said as he led her to his white, sporty BMW, opening the door so she could slide in, onto the smooth leather seat. He jogged around the front of the car and joined her, started the car and eased it out of the hotel's parking lot.

"So, you're not running over to the coffee shop?"

"Lanie is covering for me."

"Lanie?"

"Yes, she wanted to help. Needs something to do."

"Because?"

"She and David are going through a rough patch."

Lanie and David? They'd been married for as long as Dane could remember. If they couldn't make a marriage work, could anyone?

As he drove downtown, his thoughts went to the recent phone calls from his parents. His dad had called to complain about his belongings scattered all over the front porch. His mother had called Dane to have him relay a message to his father, *Stay away.* Again, he was thankful he'd ended the brief marriage to Nealy. Who knew where they'd be today? Unhappy? Always bickering like his folks? No, thank you. Since she'd forgiven him, the tension between them had eased, for which he was grateful. Maybe now they'd have a chance to get to know each other again.

"I think today will be the first time we don't have to sneak into Swindler's to enjoy an ice cream together," he said.

"We used to sneak because everyone in Cypress Pointe likes to talk about who saw whom where. It's annoying."

"Can't fight it." He knew full well once people saw them today, the rumor mill would be working overtime.

"This isn't a date," she reminded him.

"Never said it was."

"Good. I don't need the hassle of explaining us to anyone."

"You've made it very clear there is no 'us.'"

"And yet you kissed me last night."

So she was affected by his kiss. He hadn't planned it, but when she stood there in front of him, a soft smile on her face, he couldn't help himself. And while he should be kicking himself for giving in to impulse, he couldn't deny the chemistry they had.

"I explained why I kissed you."

"Good-luck charm? You can do better."

"It's the truth. I've wanted to kiss you since the first day you showed up at my hotel."

When she kept silent, he glanced over at her with an unrepentant grin on his face. "You can't tell me you weren't curious."

"I wasn't curious."

"C'mon. We'd have to be dead not to wonder what it would be like."

"After how things ended between us, what made you think I'd kiss you in return?"

The surrender in her eyes, but he wouldn't tell her that. She'd figure it out soon enough. "A guy can hope. And judging by your response, it was worth taking a chance."

"I responded out of shock, not any unresolved feelings for you."

"Then I'll have to keep trying to convince you otherwise."

"Dane, it's pointless."

"If I thought trying to prove I'm a changed man was pointless, I wouldn't have asked you to the game."

"What are you up to?"

He tightened his hands on the steering wheel. "Nealy, I've apologized for my colossal stupidity. We were kids, for Pete's sake. Entitled to make mistakes. In fact, I think it's required as a rite of passage."

"Okay. I understand why you ended the marriage. With years of hindsight, I can appreciate you trying to protect both of us." She ran her hands over her skirt. "But I don't see how kissing me now will change anything."

"I don't, either. I just know I had to."

He had to. Those three words made his stomach clench as he waited for her response. He still believed he'd done the right thing for both of them by getting an annulment, but the kiss last night reminded him of everything they'd shared in the past. He wasn't the kid she remembered. Nor was she still the same girl whose heart he'd broken.

Before he had a chance to remind her of all the facts, they'd reached their destination. He escorted her into the ice cream shop. The sugary confectionary scent greeted them, pleasant memories from their past.

He led her across the scarred wooden floor to the display case. "Let me guess, still a vanilla girl?"

"My taste has graduated." She scanned the ice cream selection. "How about Rocky Road?"

"Got it. Why don't you get us a table outside while I take care of the order."

He watched Nealy head to the door, almost getting run down as Sierra and her boyfriend barged into the shop.

"Nealy. How was the tea party?"

"Turned out great."

"Cool. This is my boyfriend, Bobby."

He stuck out his hand. "Nice to meet you, ma'am."

She glanced at Dane, a rueful smile on her lips. She didn't look like a ma'am. More like a gorgeous woman of just the right age for him.

"We came to get some ice cream before we go out on Bobby's brother's boat," Sierra announced.

"Everything okay at Cuppa Joe?"

"Yes. Your sister is there. And don't worry, Davey has everything under control." Sierra took Bobby's hand. "See you later."

The couple moved to the counter to discuss their choices. Dane watched Nealy step out into the warm afternoon sun, searching for an empty table. A family got up to leave and she hurried over to save a white, iron bistro table under a canopy. Dane joined her a few minutes later, handing her a cone.

"Thanks."

He sat across from her. "So, Sierra and her boyfriend. Remind you of anyone?"

She wrinkled her brow as she secured a napkin around the wafer cone.

"Us," he told her.

"I don't see it," she replied, having a lick of her ice cream.

Ever since he'd seen the young couple on the hotel grounds the other day, more and more memories of the summer with Nealy bombarded him. Some mingled with regret, others about the good times they'd made together. "C'mon. You have to remember how crazy we were about each other."

"No, I really don't have to."

"We thought we had the world in our hands."

"Until we didn't. It took me a long time to get over you, Dane."

"You think I had it any easier?"

"All I know is one minute we were married, the next we weren't."

"And I explained."

"Still, you're determined to take us down memory lane."

He shrugged. Why was he pushing the issue? To get a response out of Nealy? Sure. But beyond the banter? He just couldn't stop.

"It would never work between us, you know. I'm going back to L.A."

"Did I say anything about getting together?"

How easy it was to mess with her. "But if we did, ever heard of Skype?"

"I'm going back to my life. My boyfriend."

"How is old…what's his name?"

"Sam. He's fine."

"If I were your boyfriend, I'd have come with you."

"You aren't, so it doesn't matter."

"What's his excuse?"

"He's working."

"So am I, but I still make time to see you."

"You're being ridiculous."

"Just calling it like I see it."

A glob of ice cream dribbled over the side of the cone onto her finger. Without even thinking, he handed her a napkin and she used it to wipe her hand. It was a small gesture, but they seemed in tune, connected still to one another. Was it so effortless with Sam? he wondered. He met Nealy's gaze. All sound and movement around him faded as he focused on her. How could he have believed they could take up where they left off, as if nothing monumental had happened between them? Not good. Not good at all. Especially when the longing in her eyes told him she wanted another kiss.

Breaking the heated connection, Nealy rose to throw the paper napkin in the trash. A Beach Boys song rang out from her cell phone. She retrieved the phone from her bag and smiled when she read the caller ID. Holding up the phone in triumph, she said, "It's Sam. I need to take this."

She stepped away from the table, chatting, with a big smile on her face. A forced smile? It seemed forced to him, but what did he know? He might not like her connection to some other guy, but he couldn't ignore the reality right in front of him. *Back off, Peterson,* is what it said.

She approached the table. "Yes. I'll call you the second I land at LAX." She sent ol' Sam smoochy kisses before hanging up.

"Air-kisses over the phone are not as good as the real thing," he crabbed, not at all pleased with the images running through his brain, of her back in L.A., walking on the beach, her windswept hair and beautiful smile aimed at this Sam guy. He didn't deserve this loyal, generous woman. "Sam would know that if he were here."

"And I'm pretty sure he wouldn't appreciate you kissing his girl."

His girl, huh. "Point taken. But, Nealy, all I'm asking is to get to know each other again."

"I don't think it's a good idea."

"It's not like I'm asking you to get married again."

Nealy went white. She momentarily froze before dropping her phone into her bag. "I should go."

"I didn't mean it like that." He ran a hand through his hair. What was wrong with him? Picking a fight because he didn't like the fact she had a guy waiting for her while he was sitting right here, wishing for something with her? Man, he was turning into his father, lashing out and on edge. Why? Because Nealy wasn't a permanent fixture in his life?

"No wedding bells. I get it, Dane," she said, hooking her purse strap over her shoulder.

In his frustration, he'd said the one thing to make her run. On purpose?

"Don't take off," he said.

"It's okay, Dane. I need to get to Cuppa Joe anyway."

He stood. "Let me take you back to the hotel to get your car."

She waved him off. "I'll have someone bring me over later." Without another word, she turned on her heel and left.

Dane watched her walk away.

Maybe it was better if she went back to L.A. Back to Sam. Anywhere, so she wouldn't get him thinking about what life would be like if she were his.

LANIE RAN A damp cloth over a table as David came rushing into the coffee shop.

"Is Davey okay?" he asked, out of breath.

Lanie straightened up. "Yes. He's taking the garbage out." She eyed him from head to toe. David, always neatly combed and pressed, looked a bit...rumpled. "What's up with you?"

"You called to tell me we have an emergency with our son. What do you think?"

"I think I told you not to rush home."

"I did and neither of you were there."

"We're working."

He glanced down at the apron she'd tied on over her skirt. "I can see. Care to tell me why?"

"To keep an eye on Davey."

David ran a hand through his hair. She hid a smile. She'd noticed David reverting back to the nervous habit he hadn't exhibited since college. Was she getting to him? "Lanie—"

She shushed him as Davey slammed the back door. "Quiet."

Their son strolled into the main area, stopping short. "Dad. I thought you were playing golf."

Lanie shot him a quelling look.

"I, um, came home early," he said.

"Cool." Davey took a spot behind the counter. "Hey, Mom, you rang up the last purchase without making a mistake."

"I figured out your instructions."

"It's not rocket science."

"He said to the technologically illiterate."

Davey grinned. "You're picking it up fast."

"I am, aren't I?" Lanie had come to the shop with the intention of spying on her son. Instead, she'd ended up working beside him, learning about the shop and enjoying every minute.

"Why is Mr. Hollings always so crotchety?" Davey asked in a low voice while viewing the elderly man at his usual table. Their only customer this late in the afternoon.

"I think he misses his wife."

Her son was knowledgeable about running the shop and he knew the customers by name. He had more than a little bit of Dorinda's way with people.

David walked up to the counter. "While I'm here I might as well get a cup."

"You're up, Mom."

Davey stepped aside to let Lanie take care of the order. She poured a cup and set it on the counter. "Condiments are on the side."

As David went to doctor his coffee, Davey said, "You know, you two should talk."

Lanie blinked at her son. "What?"

"I don't know what's going on, but you guys are acting weird." He retrieved his baseball cap from under the counter. "I have an errand to run, but since the shop is about to close, maybe this would be a good time to figure stuff out."

So her son knew all along? How had she overlooked it? Because she'd been consumed by regaining the old magic with her husband? "I don't know what to say."

Davey bussed her cheek. "I love you, Mom."

Her eyes watered. "I love you, too, kiddo."

He hurried out the door. David came to lean against the counter to watch their son leave. "Where's he off to?"

"I don't know, but it has something to do with a girl. A much older girl."

David stared at her. "Our son?"

"Nealy thinks he has a crush on Sierra."

"Sierra?"

"The college girl who works for Grandmother." She sighed. "We'd know all about her if we were engaged in Grandmother's business."

"Explains why you're wearing an apron."

Lanie poured herself a cup and motioned for them to take a seat at an empty table. The afternoon crowd had grown slack, giving them some privacy.

"Have you had 'the talk' with Davey?"

David turned pink. "Yes. Turns out they have a class about relationships in school. He filled me in on a few things he shouldn't know about."

"At least you talked to him. He knows we care."

"So, this girl?"

"Cute. Older. Pays attention to Davey. Has a boyfriend."

"Does he know?"

"Yes. When the boy came in to pick Sierra up after her shift ended, he and Davey high-fived. Is that some kind of guy code I'm not privy to?"

"Not if Davey likes this girl and her boyfriend knows about it."

"Then I'm confused."

David took a sip of his coffee. "This is pretty good."

"Which we'd all have known if we got our coffee here." She stared into her cup. "What must Grandmother think of us?"

"She knows we have busy careers."

"Yes, but after spending one afternoon here, I can understand why she's thinking of giving the place up. It's a lot of work and she is getting older."

"I thought she had help?"

"She does, but we both know working long hours can be stressful. Plus, she has the added burden of worrying about the finances and running the operation all by herself."

"A burden she should be sharing with her family."

"You know she doesn't want to be a burden." Lanie relaxed and peered around the shop. "With the new coffee system coming Monday, we have lots to do tomorrow."

"We?" His brow went up. "What kind of work?"

"Nealy asked if we'd help paint the inside of the shop. Dane is doing the outside work and when Grandmother gets back, she'll have a whole new place."

David looked around. "It has grown a bit shabby."

"Davey told me there's been pressure from the Merchants' Association to fix it up. Grandmother had almost given up, until Nealy came home."

"Despite her stubbornness, we should have insisted on taking a part in running this place."

"She probably would have shooed us off."

"Yet she let Nealy come in and take care of some things."

"From what I understand, Grandmother asked her to look after the place while she was on the cruise, then dropped the remodeling idea in her lap once Nealy got here."

"Still, Nealy seems invested."

"Even given a surprise to-do list, she always loved this shop." Lanie stared into her coffee. "My grandparents opened it together, ran it for years together. They were totally committed, to each other and their business."

David wrapped his hands around his cup. "It wasn't hard to miss how much they loved each other."

Lanie felt a pang of remorse. She always thought she and David had that kind of love. Now she wasn't so sure.

"So, will you help paint tomorrow?"

"Will you stop thinking about running for mayor?"

"If it means we'll spend time together, then yes. And Davey will be here." She stood. "He knows something is up between us, by the way."

David grimaced.

"I'm going to call my folks, too. We should make sprucing up Cuppa Joe a family affair."

David stared up at her, angled his head. His eyes flashed with a look she hadn't seen in a long time. Interest.

Cheeks flushed, Lanie covered her surprise by glancing down at her clothes as if she'd spilled something on herself. "What?"

"It's good to see you excited."

She reached across the table to take hold of his hand. Grew light-headed at the familiar rush she always experienced when touching her husband. "It's good to be excited for a change."

David rose, carrying his cup to the trash. A

customer walked in. Lanie took an order from the customer, not bothering to hide her smile when David came behind the counter to pour the cup. When he smiled and spoke to the customer with easy camaraderie, her heart went haywire.

She loved this man. Taking the reins to recharge their marriage had to be done. They were worth it.

She grinned. David's brow rose in return. *Oh, you poor, unsuspecting man.* She would come up with a plan to make him remember when they first fell in love, even if it meant shaking him out of his staid, predictable world.

CHAPTER TWELVE

SUNDAY MORNING, NEALY took a step back, tilting her head as she got some perspective of the accent wall behind the counter painted in a dark café au lait, a nice contrast to the other three walls painted in French vanilla.

Davey came up beside her and threw an arm over her shoulders. "Great job, Auntie. Great-Gram will love it."

"I sure hope so."

"It looks awesome. The shop looks better than I thought it would."

She sent him a sideways glance. "You doubted me? I'm crushed."

He chuckled. "Nah. Just wasn't sure about your choice of colors, but it looks like a real coffee hangout now."

"As long as you're happy," she said drily.

"It only matters what Great-Gram thinks."

"Yes. It does."

With the shop temporarily closed, the Grainger clan had come out in full force to paint the shop and spruce up the place. Nealy was surprised, but pleased, her parents had donned old clothes to work without complaining. Lanie and David painted side by side. Davey supervised.

The morning had flown by in a flurry of activity. While she enjoyed freshening up the interior of the shop, she hadn't ventured outside to inspect the progress of the storefront. If she did, she'd have bumped into Dane, who was busy at work tackling the proposed changes.

He'd shown up earlier than the family, already at work with two helpers, removing the current stucco finish. By late morning, they'd started adding the weathered shingles. She'd kept her eyes averted from the maddening man. Given the scene at the ice cream shop yesterday, she wasn't ready to face him.

And last night, she'd walked away, after he'd made his point. No wedding bells for Dane. Didn't matter, really. She had no intention of getting back together with him anyway, so the whole idea was moot.

Since she'd been angry and upset, she changed course. Rather than go to the coffee shop, she detoured to the beach instead. She'd slipped off her high heels and sank her toes into the wet, gritty sand as she strolled along the shore. How she'd missed the unmistakable scent of the gulf. Her heart squeezed as she dodged children tossing a ball in the surf and others building a sand castle. After spending a week in town, she'd realized she was homesick for the place. Coming back to visit a few times seemed okay, but now? Twelve years had passed since she'd last seen Dane. A long time to hold a grudge, or grudges, actually.

The continuity of small-town living was appealing versus the hustle and bustle of the big city. Here, folks may move at a slower pace than in L.A., but they seemed truly content with what they had and their future. To be honest, apart from her job, Nealy wasn't as content with her life as she thought. Why try to convince herself otherwise?

She'd missed spending time with her sisters. Missed watching Davey grow up. Realized good friends like Lilli were few and far between. And before Dane ruined the moment, she'd rather enjoyed bantering with him again.

Swinging her shoes beside her as she walked, she'd expelled a heavy sigh. Any notion of settling down here would be years down the road. Her career was in high gear. She intended on making a name for herself in the industry. In order to accomplish her goal, she had to return to L.A.

The steady waves washed over her ankles. Late-afternoon sun warmed her face and the wind ruffled her hair. While walking along the water had always brought her solace, now her insides churned.

Dane's words echoed in her head. *It's not like I'm asking you to get married again.* It shouldn't come as a surprise. He hadn't wanted to stay married to her before, so why would he consider it now? Plenty of women in Cypress Pointe were interested in dating him. He had his pick. So why did he go out of his way to spend time with her? Why kiss her? What was up with him?

And so her thoughts had cycled, over and over, with no answer in sight. Even though she'd talked to Sam, they were still in limbo. She'd played up the phone call in front of Dane, not wanting him to know things were falling apart. By the end of her walk, she'd decided to make an effort to fix things with Sam, mostly as an excuse to get Dane off her mind.

The sudden banging on the wall knocked her out of her musings.

"They're making even more of a racket than we are," her father remarked.

"That's the new clothing store. At least it's just hammering today. Last week, the fire alarm went off a couple of times. I heard one of the workers say something about electrical issues."

"Some of these buildings are getting old,"

he said. "I imagine a new tenant would have to bring the wiring up to code."

The whine of a power saw cut into the conversation, followed by the clunk of wood falling on concrete.

Nealy cringed. "I hope they finish up soon."

"Since we're almost finished," Lanie announced, "I'll put on a pot of coffee. David ordered lunch from Pointe Cafe. It should be here soon. We can sit down for a family meal. Won't that be fun?"

Nealy sent her sister an "oh, please" look.

The group worked as a team to clean up the empty buckets, wash off the brushes and put the tables and chairs back in place. Nealy still had some decorating to do once the walls dried. She'd visited a couple of the antiques shops in town to find colorful prints to hang on the walls. The menu board listing the new specialty coffee drinks would arrive in a few days. All in all, the transformation had been painless. The end result better than she had envisioned.

The door opened as a delivery guy carried in three large bags of food. Her father and David argued over who would pay the bill; Dad won, as usual. Her mother and Lanie set out the meal. Much to her chagrin, Lanie invited Dane and his helpers to join them.

"We ordered plenty," Lanie told him, giving

Nealy a smug smile. Oh, they were so going to have words later.

As everyone got started, Dane came up beside Nealy. She went stiff, held her breath until she realized her reaction was stupid. Maybe if she didn't acknowledge Dane he'd leave her alone.

"Hey," he said.

Okay, no luck on the ignoring part.

"I'm sorry about yesterday. It was a bone-headed thing to say."

She glanced at him and noticed he looked as if he hadn't slept well.

Join the club. "Can't argue with you."

"Chalk it up to a hit on my male ego when you started air-kissing Sammy."

He was jealous? How had she missed that part? "Sam. And there's no need to get all weird. The more I spend time with you the more I realize I dodged a bullet."

A shadow flickered in the depths of his eyes. "Yeah. Okay. I deserved that."

"Just eat your lunch."

She took her plate to join her family. Her mother seemed to be casting an evil eye at Dane, but otherwise her parents were cordial. She didn't have to worry about them warning her away from Dane. He'd done a good job all by himself.

"Your father and I were commenting on what a change you've made in this place," Anita told her.

"Good or bad?"

Marshall sent her a sheepish grin. "I guess we have been critical."

"I told your father all about the tea party. And of course, we witnessed the engagement parties for ourselves. Such focus on detail."

"Fine work, Nealy."

Wow. Actual compliments from her parents. "Thanks."

"The company you work for is most fortunate to have you," her father added.

Stunned, it took a moment to answer. "I agree."

Everyone laughed, Nealy's response going a long way in relieving the tension always present when talking about her life. Her parents began to ask her about other events she'd planned. She related story after story, enjoying the positive attention for once.

"Has anyone heard from Juliet?" Anita asked once the conversation waned.

Nealy could tell from her tone she was hurt her youngest daughter hadn't called. For once, Nealy felt kind of bad for her mom. "I got a text this morning. She'll be in town next week."

"Where has she been?"

"She didn't say, Mom. And before you ask, I didn't hound her for information. She'll have plenty of time to explain when she gets home."

Anita sighed. "Fine. And your grandmother?"

"She told me not to bother her while she was on the cruise. I haven't. We'll see her Wednesday."

Anita looked around the freshly painted room. "I must say, with just a little work, Cuppa Joe is a new place. I guess I can understand why Mother held on to the business."

Wow. Her mother showing interest in Grandmother's shop *and* being nice to her. Nealy was confused and evidently it showed on her face. Lanie laughed.

"I know, right," her sister responded.

Davey glanced at his mom, then his aunt, shaking his head. "Weird."

"Women," David said under his breath.

"We can hear you," Lanie told him.

David scowled at her.

Nealy stood. "Lunch is over."

The Grainger family good-time show had officially come to an end.

As they cleaned up, Lanie pulled Nealy aside. "Okay, so I have a plan."

"For what?"

"To gain David's attention."

"Do I want to hear this?"

"Hey, you told me to try something new." Her expression grew wary. "I need to run this by someone."

Nealy was secretly glad her sister felt comfortable enough to confide in her. It meant a lot to Nealy that her approval was needed. "Shoot."

"David and I always loved to visit the old fort at Fort Desoto Park when we were in law school. We used to go there when we were studying or needed a break from the pressure of classes. We always talked about camping there, but never made the time."

"So your grand plan is to take David camping?"

"I'm hoping once we get to the park he'll remember those days when we were crazy about each other." She looked worried. "Well?"

"I was thinking more of a fancy B and B getaway, but hey, if that'll shake David out of his comfort zone, it's perfect."

Lanie hugged her. "Thanks, sis. I never would have gone out on a limb with David if you hadn't been here for me."

"I don't have to be here in Cypress Pointe to do that. I'm always available for you even if I'm in L.A."

"It's just not the same."

Nealy swallowed hard. "I'm always going to be your sister, no matter where I am."

"Well, get this L.A. fever out of your system and come home. Something tells me Juliet would appreciate it if her favorite sister lived here."

"I don't know about favorite." Nealy had been trying not to think about Juliet's prodigal return for just that reason. "She'll have you to step in."

Lanie straightened her shoulders. "I guess I will."

"So, when will you let David in on your trip?"

"After we leave here."

With lunch finished, Dane's helpers went outside to continue working. She tidied up the last of the mess when Dane joined her again.

"How much longer will your project take to finish?" she asked around the awkwardness.

"The time-consuming part is the shingles. We should get it done by tonight. The finishing will be completed this week."

"Sounds good. I have the new equipment coming tomorrow. Grandmother gets back Wednesday."

"You're still going to oversee the wedding rehearsal Thursday night, right?"

"Unless you hire a new event coordinator before then."

"Even if I do, I'd still like your help."

She thought about the hours he'd spent working here on his day off. As much as she didn't want to be near Dane, how could she decline? "I'll be there."

He still lingered, making her jumpy.

"Was there something else?"

"No. Just wondering how we would have turned out if we'd stayed married."

"It doesn't matter now. We've talked about this."

"I know, but since you've been back, I can't help but think about us."

"We wouldn't be the people we are today."

He raked his fingers through his hair, leaving tufts standing on end. Unusual for the always put-together man. Adorable, too. "I know you feel this…mutual pull of attraction. I'm trying to figure it out, but bottom line? You still intrigue me."

"I didn't ask for your attention, Dane."

"Are you denying you feel anything for me?"

No. She couldn't ignore her escalating feelings for Dane. And here she'd been so sure she would never have anything to do with the man, yet she was more attracted to him than ever.

She scrambled past him to straighten up at the counter. "What we feel doesn't matter. You have a life in Cypress Pointe, mine is in L.A. Even if you could get over your commitment problems, I don't know if I could trust you."

He shifted from one foot to the other. "The truth hurts, even if it is deserved."

"Look, I get you don't want to end up like your folks. But honestly, Dane, you're a grown man responsible for your own feelings. You aren't your father. Stop hiding behind excuses."

"Maybe my excuses came from wishing I had a do-over with you. Maybe no other woman has ever affected me like you."

"If you felt that way, Dane, you would have found me before I came back." Her insides twisted. "Distance wouldn't have mattered."

"Can you say you would have talked to me?"

"I don't know. I'll never know because it didn't happen." She shook her head. "We took separate paths. Let's leave it alone."

He moved into her space, his body warm and his intense focus on her exciting and scary at the same time. She met his gaze head-on; the longing in his eyes clear. This man would always have a piece of her heart. If they were crazy enough to consider taking a chance again, she needed to trust him first. Getting hurt again was not an option.

He reached up, thumbing off a streak of paint on her cheek. "What matters is I hurt you."

She took a step back, along with a bracing breath. "Water under the bridge, Dane. I'm glad we caught up after all these years. Seeing you again helped put the past in perspective, namely, knowing you and I will never be in a relationship."

"I need to get back to work," he said in a subdued tone.

She nodded, her throat tight, making it impossible to speak.

IN THE ALLEY behind the coffee shop, Lanie yawned as she placed a clean brush in a pail for storage.

"You look beat," David said. "Ready to head home?"

Glancing up at him, she smiled. "I am tired."

"You were up late last night. I waited for you to come to bed but fell asleep."

"I was working on a project."

"For work?"

"No. For us."

At his surprised look, Lanie laughed. "Don't be so shocked. I'm nothing if not tenacious when I get an idea."

"Should I be scared?"

"No. Excited."

His expression went from wary to interested. "This project of yours, is it—"

"I'm not saying a thing until we're alone."

Leaving him hanging, she went into Cuppa

Joe and told the family goodbye, then led him outside. "Let's go to the park."

He frowned. "I don't know. Last time we were there it didn't end well."

"Today will be different. I promise."

Containing her excitement almost did Lanie in. David took her hand, a gesture missing in their relationship of late, and she calmed down. Once at the park, they took a seat on a bench.

"You're making me nervous," he said.

Okay. Here goes. "Remember when we were in college and we would go to Fort Desoto Park to relax?"

"Sure. We'd walk the trails and get lost in nature for a few hours."

"Right." She scooted closer. "What's the one thing we always said we'd do there but never made the time?"

His brow crinkled. "Fishing?"

She chuckled. "Like you'd go fishing."

"Rent a kayak?"

"You're getting closer."

The total look of concentration on his face proved he was thinking, not trying to appease her. Finally, the lightbulb switched on and he brought his attention back to her. "Camping?"

"Bingo."

"Camping?"

"I have it all figured out—"

"I don't—"

She held up her hand. "Just hear me out."

He nodded.

"Just one weekend away. No phones, no computers, no briefs to read. We'll camp, fish, if you want, and relax. But most of all, we'll be together."

When David didn't respond right away, Lanie held her breath. What if he refused? Where would they go from here?

"You know," David said in a halting voice, "I had an idea of what our perfect life would be. Getting married, having kids, working to retirement. Exactly what we have right now."

Lanie bit her lip. David's expression was a mixture of mystery and sadness. For the first time ever, she had no idea what her husband would say. Was comfortable, dependable David happy with their life? Or wanting out because they'd grown apart?

Her heart pounded.

"Turns out I was shortsighted. These last couple months have been excruciating. Despite what you think, I noticed we weren't doing great, but didn't know what to do." He squeezed her hand. "Until my wife decided to speak up. Then I realized my vision of our future was flawed, since we're both unhappy."

Lanie blinked back the moisture welling in her eyes.

"This isn't what I signed up for."

Her heart dropped.

"Not ten-hour days and missing our son growing up. I expected camping trips and hanging out with the one person in the world who makes me happy. You."

He leaned over and brushed his lips over hers.

"I don't want to end up like Nealy and Dane, always wondering 'what if.'"

"Then let's change our future."

He kissed her again. "I want us back, but stronger than before." He grinned at her, so much like the carefree David she'd married. "So yeah, let's go away for a weekend. Just the two of us."

Lanie brushed her fingertips over David's cheeks. "True love always wins. Sometimes we just need a little help getting back there."

MONDAY FLEW BY. The new coffee brewing system arrived. Nealy and Davey spent the morning playing with the machine and figuring out all the functions. Dorinda's friend Terri arrived bright and early, pleased with the new appearance of the shop. Within an hour, she'd mastered the coffeemaker. Ed showed up as well, sporting his usual scowl.

"Place is too bright, don't you think?"

"I think it's just right."

He scowled deeper. "I still want my coffee made the old-fashioned way."

Nealy laughed and poured him a cup. "Just the way you like it," she said, handing him his usual order.

"I suppose more folks will start coming in here now. Making all kinds of noise and looking at their computers."

"I hope so, otherwise I did all this work for nothing."

Ed peered around the room. "Not my taste, but Dorinda will like it."

Hmm. A deferred compliment coming from Mr. Fussbudget. "We'll find out when she gets home Wednesday."

"Is she coming back to work right away?"

A loaded question, for sure. Since Nealy hadn't heard otherwise, she answered, "That's the plan."

Ed nodded, satisfied his world would get back to semi-normal once the owner returned.

Nealy waited on a few more customers before taking a break. She noticed Terri standing to the side of the counter, her frail hands clasped over her chest. "Give me your honest opinion," Nealy said as she stood by the older woman.

"You did a wonderful job, dear."

"But?"

Terri glanced at Nealy with a surprised expression.

"I hear a 'but' in your answer," Nealy continued.

"It's not so much a 'but' as, well…"

"Be honest."

"You've outdone yourself, putting so much time and energy getting this place spiffy and modernized. I don't want you to be disappointed."

This couldn't be good. Nealy already had an inkling of what Terri meant, but wanted to hear it from the woman. "Why would I be disappointed?"

"You know Dorinda is torn about selling. She would love to keep Cuppa Joe in the family."

"We've had a conversation or two about Grandmother putting the shop up for sale. I hope she changes her mind once she sees what we've accomplished."

Terri patted Nealy's arm. "I have no doubt your grandmother will be appreciative. I'm just not sure all this will change her decision."

In the back of her mind, she'd worried that despite everything she had done to update Cuppa Joe, her grandmother would still want to sell. Nealy knew her grandmother was being realistic. By her own admission, she couldn't run the place forever. At the same time, Nealy couldn't leave her job in L.A. Not with the possibility of Ashlee James's events coming up. With no one in the family willing to step in, what else could Grandmother do, but put the shop up for sale and enjoy retirement?

A power saw whined next door. Nealy grimaced. The sounds of construction had become a constant reminder of change. For someone who took ownership of her projects, the thought of all this work benefiting a stranger stung to her core.

"You can't be surprised," Terri said.

"No. I guess I…I'm not sure how I feel." Nealy straightened her shoulders. "If Grandmother does decide to sell, at least we turned the shop into a showplace. She'll get top dollar to enjoy her future."

Terri smiled warmly. "She will, indeed."

Shaking herself out of her maudlin thoughts, Nealy rubbed her hands together. "Enough conjecture. Back to work."

Terri patted Nealy's arm. "You never know what will happen, dear."

True, but she didn't want to accept the change so easily. Cuppa Joe had been a part of her life she didn't want to lose, but there didn't seem to be any way to keep the inevitable from happening.

After lunch, Dane's crew showed up to replace the molding around the windows.

"Oh, look, dear," Terri gushed, "The men are here to finish up the storefront."

Yes, she knew, ignoring the unwelcome twinge of disappointment when the man himself hadn't arrived. Really, she admonished, she had to get over these lingering feelings for Dane. They'd said everything worth saying yesterday. End of story.

A pang of sadness settled over her. Once she headed back to L.A., would Dane miss her? Have fond memories, thinking of her as "the one who got away"? With all the single women after him, she'd be a distant thought before too long. As it should be. It's what she wanted, right? Yet the sting in the vicinity of her heart proved otherwise. Okay, for all her mental debating, she was not over Dane, but they had too many hurdles to overcome. No promise for a future together, no matter how much she might want it.

Obviously, her emotions would be a confusing jumble right now. Being home. Spending time with her family, and enjoying it, for the first time in years. Not sure of the future of Cuppa Joe. Waiting on word about her new project back in California. Attempting to put the past where it belonged to start concentrating on her future.

The rhythmic hammering against the outside wall snagged Nealy's attention. As much as Nealy appreciated the hours the men were putting in to finish the project, she had mixed emotions about viewing the final result. Dane's vision had been so clear and right on target, she didn't want to be let down if it didn't turn out like his sketches. Either way it would be one more thing crossed off grandmother's list. One more step towards the unknown future of the shop.

Instead of going outside to see how things were progressing, she elected to stay indoors. She had enough to keep her busy with unloading deliveries and setting up other updated details around the shop. Plenty of work to take her mind off life in Cypress Pointe without her.

CHAPTER THIRTEEN

BY LATE AFTERNOON, Dane had caught up with his phone calls and poring over projections for his upcoming hotel projects. Curious about the status of Cuppa Joe's, he decided to take a break and check it out in person. He arrived ten minutes later, standing on the sidewalk, his astute gaze scanning every inch of the building exterior. Pleased with the results, he made sure to compliment the men working for him before they called it quits for the day. The last piece of the renovation, the new sign he'd ordered, would be the finishing touch on the project. Slightly nervous, he hoped Dorinda would like the changes.

Or was he trying to impress Nealy? A little of both. Nealy would be leaving soon, but he wanted her to remember how he'd taken care of her grandmother. A small gesture in the grand scheme of things, but it mattered to him.

He should head back to the hotel, but knowing Nealy was inside the shop made him walk to the front door. Things may be rocky between them, but they didn't stop him going in to see her.

For a guy who knew where his life was going, Nealy was the one part he questioned. He'd always been so sure he'd done the right thing for Nealy by having their marriage annulled. So why the questions now? Nealy accused him of not being able to commit. That wasn't the problem. He was committed to his job. His family. But lately, every decision boiled down to the one he'd made all those years ago. Maybe he'd made the wrong decision for all the right reasons. Could he just now be figuring it out?

He entered the shop. The scent of freshly brewed coffee greeted him. He gazed around the room. The Graingers had done a bang-up job painting and making the shop feel more in touch with the times. Nealy wouldn't take credit, but it was her due.

He got in line to order, noticing for the first time the new coffeemaker. Sierra manned the equipment like a pro. When it came his turn, she grinned at him. "What'll it be?"

"I take it you have more than plain coffee to offer?"

"Yep. I've just mastered lattes. Want one?"

"Sure."

He paid, and then moved to the side to wait for his order. Nealy entered from the hallway, cell phone pressed to her ear, forehead wrinkled. She passed right by, not noticing him. He hadn't intended on eavesdropping, but she stood close enough that he could hear the end of her conversation.

"Crystal, you're missing the point. I've worked with the Olsens for years."

Sierra handed him the latte.

"Yes. I'm well aware I'm not in California, but I will be back for the party. Felicia can handle things as my assistant." A pause. "No, this is not acceptable. When I get back, we're going to sit down and hash it out." Nealy turned and spotted him. Her cheeks turned pink. "Yes, Crystal, I'll be there next week."

She signed off.

"Trouble in the workplace?" he couldn't resist asking.

"More like a hassled boss trying to hand my events to a newbie." She placed the phone on the counter. "Not gonna happen."

"I've never seen this side of you. Go, tiger."

She tried to suppress a grin but failed. "I can't even escape for a couple weeks without these crazy calls from my boss. I have it all covered. The woman has never heard of the word *overkill*."

"As you've reminded me, you are good at your job."

"Crystal seems to have forgotten."

"You're hard to forget, Nealy."

Her grin froze before fading. "When I'm back next week she'll definitely know I'm there."

Sierra called Nealy over to help. "Duty calls." She made her way to the counter.

He watched her take over, admiring her sure tone while working with Sierra, her attention focused on the customers. Nealy had a way with people. Always had.

After she served the last customer in line, Dane walked to the counter. "What do you think of the storefront?"

"It was dark when I got here this morning so I didn't get a good look."

"C'mon. I want your opinion."

She hesitated, glanced at Sierra then shrugged. "Guess I can't put it off."

"Thanks for trusting me," he said drily.

Her gaze slipped away from him. "It's not your expertise I don't trust."

More like her heart. He got it.

She grabbed her phone from the counter and they went outside. She took up a position across the street, likely to get the full effect. He could have sworn he glimpsed tears in her eyes, but it could have been the sun.

"So?"

"Wow. No other shop looks like this."

"I wanted to make it different."

"You succeeded."

"So it gets the Nealy Grainger stamp of approval?"

"It does, and let me tell you, I had high expectations."

His chest grew tight. Only Nealy made him feel this good.

"I have no idea what Grandmother will think, but it's just as you explained it. If it makes her remember her trip to New England, then you hit it right on the mark."

Her cell rang again. She pressed a few buttons, closed her eyes and muttered, "Give me strength." Taking a breath, she opened her eyes and hit a button. "Crystal."

Her boss. And his employees thought he was demanding.

Once again, he couldn't miss the heated words Nealy exchanged with her employer. Apparently their cross-country communications weren't solving their issues.

"My grandmother gets home Wednesday. I'll let you know then." She finished the call and slipped the phone into her pocket.

"Another problem?"

"My boss is pushing me to come back earlier, but I want to talk to Grandmother first."

His stomach clenched. He knew she was

leaving, had known since the beginning. Still, it bothered him. "Not to put any more pressure on you, but we have the wedding rehearsal Thursday night."

"We had a deal. I'll be there, Dane."

"Look, I don't mean to push."

"I said I'd be there. At least I always keep my commitments." Guilt crossed her face. "I didn't mean about the annulment."

He held up his hand. "No need to explain."

Her features softened. "I have so much going on."

"You're stressed. I get it."

"Still."

"Nealy, don't go there."

Her face flushed and she pursed her lips together. A few awkward moments passed. As they stood there in silence, an idea niggled at him. He'd been mulling it over since the engagement parties. More so after the tea party. Going out on a limb, he said, "Got a few minutes? I've got something I'd like to run by you."

Nealy glanced at the storefront and back. "I don't think you could do anything more."

"Not about Cuppa Joe."

"Sure. I can spare a couple of minutes. I need a break anyway." She poked her head inside the shop to let Sierra know she'd be back soon.

He pushed past the kick of nerves in his

stomach. "After listening to you tangle with your boss, I can't help but think you need to lighten your stress levels."

"This is nothing. The pressure will be on once I get back to LA."

"Maybe going back to L.A. isn't the right move."

"And you would know this how? From the many events you've planned?"

"No. I do run a business and know something about workload."

She puffed out a breath. "Sorry. No need for me to be snippy. Go on."

"Ever think of opening your own business? Here? In Cypress Pointe?"

"No." She blinked. "Sounds even more stressful to me."

"Nealy, people are impressed with how you organize and run important occasions in their lives. Cypress Pointe could use a talented event planner."

She frowned. "I've never thought about doing my own thing. I like working at Milestones by Crystal."

"But you've also enjoyed being home, right?"

The quick flash of understanding in her eyes gave him the answer.

"Maybe it's time to give it some thought."

"It's kind of out of the blue, don't you think?

My mind is busy juggling the coffee shop until Grandmother gets back, with upcoming events in L.A."

"Doesn't mean you shouldn't consider the possibility."

"All my contacts are in L.A."

"So? You make new contacts here."

Her chin hitched up. "I'm due back next week."

"You don't have to do anything today. Think about it."

The door opened and Sierra stuck her head out. "Need help."

"Right." She glanced at Dane. "Um, I'll see you Thursday."

"Okay."

She went inside, leaving Dane to wonder if he'd pitched the idea of Nealy staying in town because it would benefit the population of Cypress Pointe or because he wanted her to stick around to see what happened between them.

NEALY HAD JUST approved the newly installed menu board late Wednesday morning when her grandmother bustled into the shop.

"Well, my dear, you have been busy."

Nealy whirled around. "Grandmother." With a yelp, she hurried over for a great big hug.

Dorinda took Nealy's hand and walked

around the shop, stopping to peer at the prints on the walls and the new arrangement of tables and chairs. When she made her way over to the counter displaying the brand-new equipment, she ran her fingers over the smooth metal machine. Lastly, she noticed the old Cuppa Joe sign taking up residence on the wall where pictures of Nealy once hung. She stared, blinking rapidly before turning to face the woman behind the transformation. "I don't know what to say."

"Say you like it."

"I do like it." Dorinda took a shaky breath. "When I gave you the okay to update the shop I knew I left it in good hands. I must say, you have outdone yourself."

Nealy blinked at the tears pressing against the backs of her eyes. She'd been living with butterflies in her stomach all morning, waiting for her grandmother's appearance. At her grandmother's pleased reaction, relief flooded her.

"And the outside. I barely recognized the shop."

"You can thank Dane for the change."

"Dane?"

"Long story."

"Then it's a good thing we have a new coffee

machine. Let's say you whip me up something fancy. We'll sit down and catch up."

Nealy hugged her grandmother again. "I'm so glad you like it."

Dorinda pulled back, still holding on to Nealy's arms. "How could I not?"

As her grandmother circled the shop one more time, Nealy whipped up two lattes. She handed her grandmother a cup as they sat at a corner table.

Dorinda took a careful sip. "Mmm." She took another one. "I don't know why I fought updating the shop for so long. And this coffee is delicious."

"I understand, Grandmother. It must be hard running the shop alone."

"Oh, I'm never alone. My friends always help out when I need them."

"Like Terri? She's been here every day."

Dorinda grinned. "I knew you were more than capable of handling the shop, but I wanted Terri to have something to do while all her friends were gone."

"I figured as much, but I have to say, she chipped in like she's been working here forever. I think she mastered the new machine faster than Davey and I."

"I'll have someone to show me the ropes once you leave."

Nealy felt a twinge of regret. She'd be out of Cypress Pointe soon and without much of a chance to visit with her grandmother. "Davey, too. He's so excited about the changes."

"I imagine he worked right beside you."

"Yep. Along with Lanie and David. And get this. Even Mom and Dad helped out."

Dorinda's hand flew to her chest. "Your parents pitched in?"

"They painted. Mom redid the groupings of tables and chairs. She said something about feng shui and good vibes for the customers."

"Feng shui?"

Nealy chuckled.

Tears shimmered in Dorinda's eyes again. "Oh, my."

"I know. I was shocked, as well. We all had a nice time together."

"And I missed it."

"Hey, you were enjoying yourself. Much more important."

Dorinda shrugged. "Maybe." She glanced around again. "I'm still so surprised."

"Take your time drinking it in. I know it's a lot."

"Beautiful." She met Nealy's gaze. "And the storefront. I almost went right past the place. So, how did Dane get involved?"

Nealy squirmed in her seat. Since Dane suggested she start a business in Cypress Pointe she'd thought of nothing else. Well, almost nothing else. Reliving his kiss took up a lot of her time. In just a few days she'd gone from getting over the past with Dane to, oh, no, I'm falling for him again. What should she do?

Focus, for starters.

Right.

"When I explained about the Merchants' Association hounding you, he wasn't pleased. He felt bad, and to be honest, I had no idea what to do out there, so he came up with the idea to work together."

Dorinda's eyebrows rose. "What? How?"

"Shocker, huh?" Nealy grinned. "He helped with the exterior of Cuppa Joe and, as I might have played a teensy part in Angela quitting, leaving Dane in a bind, I arranged a tea party last weekend. Once I step in and help with the wedding rehearsal on Thursday, we're even."

"You and Dane working together." Dorinda chuckled. "How did it go?"

"There were ups and downs." Nealy tightened her hand around the coffee cup. "We were able to talk about the past. Come to terms."

Dorinda sat back and regarded her granddaughter. "The bartering worked for you, Nealy. You seem more peaceful than when you first arrived."

"I am. Dane apologized. I accepted. Getting our feelings out in the open went a long way to heal my anger. It was time to let go of the past."

"Then you coming home worked out for everyone." Dorinda gazed around the shop again. "So much for your vacation."

"I didn't mind. I knew I'd be working. And I reconnected with some old friends. Even had some people ask about my services."

"People wanted you to plan events here?"

"Yes. I had to turn them down, of course, but it was nice."

Her grandmother's eyes lit up. "Have you considered staying?"

"Funny, Dane asked me the same question. After he witnessed my skills, he thinks I'd be successful."

Dorinda leaned her elbows on the table, her face filled with expectancy. "What did you tell him?"

"I have some good things going on in L.A., Grandmother. I can't think about starting my own business now."

"But you wouldn't rule it out?"

"Maybe," she hedged.

"If he suggested you stay, Dane must still have feelings for you."

"Let's not jump to conclusions. He needs to

replace his event coordinator. I'm more a means to an end."

Dorinda grinned slyly. "Sometimes life gives you a second chance."

"In our case, we closed the door on what could have been years ago. Start a new relationship now? I don't know if it would be for the best."

"There's one way to find out." Dorinda heaved a heartfelt sigh. "What I wouldn't give to have your grandfather back. You can do just about anything for the one you love."

"I don't know if love is enough in our case."

"Are you saying you love Dane?"

Nealy took her time answering. No matter how many days or how many events passed, she'd never gotten over Dane. The strong, heart-stopping love from her teens hadn't lost its luster. Yes, he made her heart race and she found herself thinking about him often. But love meant trust. She'd accepted his apology, but deep down, would she always be afraid he'd shatter her world again? "I don't think I ever stopped loving him. But we were so young. We're adults now. We have different expectations."

"Love is love, Nealy."

"You make it sound so simple."

"Sometimes we let too many things get in the

way." Her grandmother reached over to place a hand over Nealy's. "How does he make you feel?"

"Other than confused?" She laughed. "He is sorry for the whole annulment thing. As much as I can't deny I'm still attracted to him, he's made it pretty clear he doesn't want to get married again, which I can understand. I found out about his folks and how they've soured his outlook on marriage."

"A messy situation for Dane."

"Which leads us back to square one, having no idea what to do about us."

"So take some more time off. Stay in Cypress Pointe until you figure it out."

"We're going to get an answer from Ashlee James soon. If she signs on, working for her will be a sure thing, Grandmother. Waiting around to figure out things with Dane? Not so much."

"You know, Dane does have a good point about you staying here. If you started an event planning business in Cypress Pointe, we could co-own Cuppa Joe. You wouldn't have to work here, just oversee the shop. Hire employees, accountants, whomever you need. Keep it in the family."

A flicker of hope flared in her grandmother's eyes. The idea was not out of the blue, Nealy had thought of it herself this week. But give up her chance at managing a huge account? It was what she'd been sacrificing for ever since she'd opted for this career. And what about Sam? In light of her rekindled attraction to Dane, it made it impossible to stay in a relationship with Sam. She owed Sam a face-to-face when she ended things.

"Grandmother, as much as I'd love to share Cuppa Joe with you, I can't make such a huge promise. I have commitments to fulfill."

"You're still determined to head to L.A.?"

"In the back of my mind I've always thought I might return to Cypress Pointe one day." She frowned. "But now? I don't know, Grandmother. All this proximity to Dane brought back good memories and to be honest, he still makes my heart race. I could take a chance, sure, but he didn't want to be married back then. Doesn't want to be married now." She shrugged. "I can't give my heart to him again if he won't commit. Staying in L.A. is the smart thing to do. I'm sorry, Grandmother."

Dorinda sighed. "Don't be. You have your life. And I want to have some freedom to live mine before I join your grandfather." She met Nealy's gaze. "So you've made your decision, then?"

"Yes."

"Then so have I."

Nealy cocked her head, waiting to hear the words she'd been dreading since her grandmother came through the door. "I'm going to put Cuppa Joe up for sale."

DANE STRODE INTO the hospital E.R. on the tails of a phone call from Uncle Hank. His father had been rushed here, but beyond that, Hank didn't have any more information.

His uncle loitered near the door, his expression grave.

"How bad is it?"

"Your father is with the doctor now. All signs point to a heart attack."

Dane ran his palm over the back of his neck. "Is he having medical problems he didn't tell me about?"

"You know your father. Keeps things close to the vest."

Dane scanned the waiting room. "Is Mom with him?"

"I haven't seen her. From what I understand, they were together when your father started having chest pains. She called 911."

A deep ache centered in Dane's chest. The one he always got when dealing with his parents. Today, in this place, his distress magnified.

"Thanks for meeting me here, Uncle Hank."

"He's my brother. We're family."

True, but Uncle Hank had been more of a
father to Dane than his own biological one.
He'd always be thankful for his uncle's support throughout his life, but more so now in the
midst of this emergency.

A woman dressed in scrubs, a stethoscope
draped around her neck, approached them. "Are
you Mr. Peterson?"

"We both are, but this is the patient's son."
Hank nodded at Dane. "Why don't you go see
him?"

The woman smiled at Dane. "Follow me."

Heading down the corridor, Dane blocked
out the medicinal smell, a patient's groans and
the prevailing sense of foreboding.

"Here you are."

With trepidation, Dane entered the room. His
father, skin pasty and eyes closed, lay on white
sheets, covered with a white blanket. A tube
hooked him to an IV. The thought of losing his
dad, no matter the status of their relationship,
hit him full force. Dane went to his father's
bedside. "Dad," he said softly, so he wouldn't
startle him.

His father's eyes fluttered open. "Dane."

Dane pulled a rolling stool to the side of the
bed and sat down. "How are you feeling?"

"They gave me something for the pain."

"Good." Dane took a steadying breath. "What happened?"

"Your mother lit into me and we got into a fight. Started getting chest pains."

Dane controlled the fear mixed with anger. "Has this happened before?"

His father looked away. "Time or two."

Dane shook his head.

His father looked back. "Where is your mother?"

"I just got here. I don't know where she is."

"Just like Evelyn. Stir things up and leave me in the cold."

Dane didn't respond. Here his father lay in a hospital bed with an unknown prognosis, and all he could do was crab about his mother? No wonder he had chest pains.

"Love ain't worth it, son," his father grumbled. The same words Dane had heard repeated forever. "You'll end up here, just like me, heartsick and angry." He moved the pillow more comfortably behind his head. "This is all her fault. She should be here."

Did the man listen to himself? One minute he blamed his wife for making him sick, the next he wanted her with him. How screwed up was that? Look where the years of unhappiness had gotten his father. Hooked up to a beeping machine, pining over a woman who caused him misery and pain. Dane studied his father, a man who had aged before his time because of bad decisions in a dysfunctional marriage. What did it say about Dane if he ever wound up duplicating his father's actions?

"You go get her and bring her here," he demanded.

"Dad, I don't think—"

"Right now."

At his father's command, something in Dane snapped. Years of being his parents' go-between came to a head. This had to be the worst time to disagree with his father, but he'd had enough. "No."

His father eyed him. "No?"

"Look, Dad, I don't wish you any ill will, but I can't."

"You're my son. You'll do what I say."

"Yeah, I'm your son. Not a referee." The man never saw the difficult spot he always put Dane in. Or the fact that his tunnel vision about his wife had brought him to this place. "You and Mom always involve me in your problems. And I let you."

"So what, you're just gonna leave me here?" His father tried to raise himself from the bed, his face showing strain from the slight physical action. "I need you, son."

The guilt card. Effective every time.

"Dad, calm down. We'll sort all this out." Dane put a hand on the bed railing. "You're in good hands here. The staff will make sure you feel better in no time. Maybe put you on medicine to help your heart, but right now you need to rest. Talking about Mom will make you worse."

"I need her."

Bottom line. They needed each other. Dane felt tortured. All these years his parents' problems piled up and the unthinkable happened. A heart attack. This time, there was nothing he could do to make things better for his father. How could he refuse this one request when he looked so awful?

Fatigue overwhelmed him. "I'll call her. Try to convince her to come be with you."

Relieved, his father sank back into the bed. A nurse came in to take his vitals, casting Dane a questioning glance before checking her distressed patient.

"I'm going to step out for a few minutes."

"Call her," his father said, his voice weak.

Dane escaped from the room. Worry tightened like a vise around his chest. He'd call his mother as his father requested, stay until the doctor gave his diagnosis and treatment options. Once his father was on his feet, Dane would explain he was finished. No more trying to keep his parents exhausting relationship together. No more holding the family together. They had to work out the situation for themselves. If they didn't want to change, how could he make them?

He couldn't, but he could change *his* future. Nealy coming to town had made him rethink his life. Ever since the annulment, he'd run from the thought of marriage, partly because of his parents' example, but more so because he'd let Nealy down. Then, he hadn't been able to deal with his own family, let alone a new wife. What had made him think he could take care of her?

Now, all these years later, she was back in town, the beautiful, spirited woman he'd never stopped loving. What-ifs turned into possibilities. Did he have the courage to take a chance on the woman he loved? He refused to end up like his father, sick and disillusioned. No. He wanted a lifetime of happiness and love. Only Nealy would do.

He stalked into the waiting room. Uncle Hank rose from a chair. "How is he?"

"They gave him something for the pain but he looks bad. And here's the kicker. He can't stop asking about Mom. Wants me to run out and drag her over here."

Hank winced. "Let's go get a cup of coffee. Give you a few minutes to get yourself together."

They walked in silence to the hospital cafeteria. Dane took a seat while his uncle purchased two coffees. He joined Dane, pushing the steaming cup across the table.

Dane took a bracing sip. "Thanks."

"What did the doctor say?"

"He wasn't in the room. I told Dad I'd come back and we'd face this together."

They sat in silence for a few more moments. The smell of food made Dane's stomach swirl. He looked at his uncle, desperation dragging him down. "I don't want to end up like him," Dane said.

Hank blew out a troubled breath. "I get it, son."

"Do you? Do you really?"

Hank leaned forward, his face serious. "Yes. I do."

"It's like his heart is broken but he won't take the steps to heal himself." Dane rested his elbows on the table, coffee cup between his hands. "Someone has to end this cycle."

"I agree."

"I always thought that meant not marrying. All these years I'd convinced myself getting an annulment was the right thing to do for

Nealy. I'm coming to realize I might have done it for me."

"Doing the right thing is never easy, no matter the reason."

"But now I'm wondering, was it the right thing at all?" he said and glanced down at his coffee then back to his uncle. "Since Nealy has been in town, I can't stop thinking about her, about what we could have together. The spark is still there, yet we both dance around it because of my actions all those years ago." He leaned in closer. "I know I broke her heart. I understand why she's wary. But the more I've thought about it, I see the way to not end up like my parents is to marry the right woman. Go after her with everything I've got. Tell her I love her every day. I want to show my kids true love is mutual admiration, genuine affection and deep love."

"Like your Aunt Sonia and I."

"Exactly." He paused. "Sorry I never emulated your example."

"Your parents always had a strong hold on you. Set up your worldview." Hank shook his head. "You're right, though. You can't keep getting in the middle, not at the expense of your future happiness. They made their decisions. Now you make your own."

Dane couldn't break away from his uncle's gaze. "You and Aunt Sonia always showed me love at its best. Why did it take me so long to figure it out?"

"You buried the truth of your feelings to keep yourself safe."

"Once Nealy came back it all made sense. Walking away didn't solve my problems, instead it made things worse." He blew out a breath. "I want to win Nealy back. Prove to her we can make a relationship work."

"I saw this coming, you know. Dreaded it, in fact." His uncle's lips curved in a lopsided grin. "Tried everything I could to keep you away from Nealy."

Dane arched a brow. "You were pretty obvious."

"I had your best interests at heart, son."

The sentiment, as well as being called son by a man who truly loved him, touched Dane. "You've always looked out for me, Uncle Hank. I appreciate it more than you know."

Hank cleared his throat. "I've only wanted the best for you."

"Then can we agree the best is Nealy?"

"I think we can," Hank agreed. "Question is, can you convince her?"

CHAPTER FOURTEEN

THURSDAY MORNING, NEALY arrived at the coffee shop early, thinking she'd be the first family member to arrive, only to find Davey starting a pot of coffee.

"Thanks for opening the shop," she said as she stowed her purse under the counter.

He shrugged.

"Something wrong?"

"Great-Gram is going to sell the shop, isn't she?"

Okay, shaky ground here. How much did she tell him? "She has some ideas."

"She wouldn't have called a family meeting if she hadn't already made up her mind."

"I think you should hear the news from Grandmother."

"Uh-huh."

Davey stomped down the hallway and disappeared out the back door.

Nealy bit her lip. The disappointment on Davey's face mirrored her own. She'd had time to think about her grandmother's decision. She didn't want to let go, but she had no choice. She understood the older woman's need to retire. It still hurt, though.

The door opened and her grandmother came in. "You're here early, dear."

"I've gotten used to rising at the crack of dawn to make coffee." Nealy kissed her grandmother's cheek. "Are you sure you want to hold the meeting here? What about your customers?"

"They won't be surprised. And they won't be my customers for long."

"Ed's not going to like the change."

"Ed doesn't like anything."

Nealy grinned. Leave it to Grandmother to get right to the point.

They waited on customers and chatted until Nealy noticed Davey hadn't returned. "I'll be right back," she called over her shoulder.

Opening the back door, she peeked outside, her nephew nowhere in sight. She stepped into the alleyway and spied Davey sitting on a stack of crates, deep in conversation with a blonde girl. Should she interrupt? Davey glanced in her direction then spoke to the girl. She nodded and rose, walking to the back door of Rascal's Candy Shoppe located a few doors down from Cuppa Joe. Davey didn't move, so Nealy went to him.

"The meeting is about to start soon."

"I know." His glum expression turned to a pleading gaze. Nealy's heart shifted.

"You could stay," he said in a quiet tone. "You could work here. You and Dane have been hanging out. Maybe you two could get together."

And maybe pigs could fly. "I already have a job. And while Dane and I have history, I'm not sure staying in Cypress Pointe is good for either of us."

"You could quit your job. Take over Cuppa Joe. I'd help you."

She sighed. "I'm not ready to leave L.A. Besides, Grandmother is making a sound decision. Why not sell the place to someone who will love it as much as we do?"

"If we love the place so much, why won't anyone in the family take over for Great-Gram?"

Why, indeed. "It's complicated."

"No, it's simple. We keep Cuppa Joe in the family."

Nealy tentatively climbed onto the crates to take a seat beside Davey. "Cuppa Joe was Grandfather Joe's idea. His second love after Grandmother. Sometimes, even a family legacy is overlooked by the generations that follow. You and I are the only ones interested in the shop. If you were older, maybe we could arrange something businesswise, but the timing isn't right."

"You put so much work into getting the place fixed up."

"And I enjoyed every minute." A thought occurred to her. "I think the time spent with my family is what I treasured more than the outcome of this place. We'll always have good memories of Grandmother owning the shop, but more important, we made new memories when we all came together to make the shop special. Davey, we're a family, whether Grandmother keeps Cuppa Joe or not."

It took a visit back to Cypress Pointe for Nealy to understand how much she'd missed her loved ones. The years away had been busy, productive ones. She'd grown up. And now experienced a new, mature relationship with her parents. She may not live here, but she had this new phase of life with her family to look forward to.

"I guess," Davey grumbled.

Teens. Sulky and certain the world was out to get them.

Nealy slugged his shoulder. "No more grumpy face." When he didn't respond, she said, "I've noticed something about you."

He glanced at her with a wary look.

"You have a very entrepreneurial spirit. We

both have this drive in common. So here's what I think. One day you'll find some kind of business to satisfy your passion. You may not know what it is right now, but working at Cuppa Joe was the direction that you needed for your future. I predict you'll get involved in a bunch of projects before you decide what you're meant to do, but keep searching, Davey. You are going to be very successful someday."

"I do like running things."

Nealy grinned. "You are so your mother's son."

He laughed.

"But I see a lot of Grandfather Joe in you."

Davey stared at the back door of Cuppa Joe. "You think?"

"Yep."

He shifted. "Thanks."

"Okay, we've solved a few problems," Nealy declared as she carefully eased off the crates. "Let's say we go back inside."

Davey jumped off with a move only a teenage boy could accomplish.

"Show-off."

He shrugged and his face turned red. Nealy followed his gaze to see the blonde girl wave from the back door of Rascal's and disappear inside.

"Something you want to tell me?"

His face turned even more red.

"Huh. I thought you had a crush on Sierra."

"Sierra? No way. Besides, she's got a boyfriend and he's cool."

"So why were you always asking when she'd be at work?"

He hung his head. "She was giving me pointers on how to impress Madison."

Nealy glanced at the door then back at Davey. "The girl you were talking to?"

"Yeah. We go to school together. Her parents own the candy store, so she's here a lot. We started walking to school together and sometimes we meet at Cuppa Joe or her store to hang out after hours."

"Just because you have a key to the shop doesn't mean you should be in there alone after hours. I'm not sure Grandmother would approve."

"Don't make a big deal about this, okay?"

She'd give him this concession. She remembered trying to figure out her relationship with Dane when they were kids, wishing for someplace private to hang out and get to know each other better. Davey wanted the same thing.

"Well, your mother will be glad to know you're not pining over Sierra."

"And she'd think that, why?"

"I might have jumped to the wrong conclusion."

He rolled his eyes. "Thanks, Auntie."

"Don't call… Wait, I deserved that."

"Get used to the name. I plan on getting back at you for a long time."

Nealy followed Davey into the shop. At least she'd been able to get him focused on the future and not dwelling over the loss of Cuppa Joe.

When she entered the seating area, the family had commandeered two tables in the corner. A few regulars, including Ed, sat in their usual places, reading the newspaper or busy on their phones or their computers. Terri manned the counter, waiting on the steady stream of customers as if she'd been born to serve coffee.

Nealy joined the family, determined not to let them see how much her grandmother's decision bothered her.

She took a seat next to Lanie, noticing the glow on her sister's face. "I take it your suggestion went well?"

"And I have you to thank." Lanie sighed.

"Please, enough of the sappy, lovesick looks."

"Can't help it. I'm happy."

"No, really," Nealy said. "Enough."

Lanie laughed.

"Oh, and to add to your current bliss, I have

it on good authority Davey is not interested in Sierra."

Lanie smiled. "Thank goodness."

"Don't get all excited. There's another girl in the picture."

Lanie's eyes went wide.

"So have fun with that little tidbit."

"What? Who?" Lanie sputtered.

"I've said enough. I'm already on thin ice with him." Nealy leaned back in her chair and waited for the meeting to begin.

A few moments later, Dorinda began to speak. "Thank you all for coming. I don't think the reason for this meeting is much of a secret."

The group exchanged glances, but no one said a word.

"I spoke to Juliet last night. She won't be back for a few more days, but she gave me her blessing on my decision."

"She's coming home?" Anita asked in her typical bossy tone.

"Yes. And she'll explain everything when she does."

Nealy spotted the relief on her mother's face. In light of everything going on these past few weeks, her mother's actions made sense to her now. Whenever Anita was concerned about her children, she went all bossy on them. Her modus operandi for expressing concern? It sure explained Nealy's dealings with her mother over the years. Put their relationship in a new light.

"After much thought," Dorinda continued, "I've decided to sell Cuppa Joe. I have an interested party already lined up, but I need help from you, my family." She turned to her son-in-law. "Marshall, if you could take care of the legalities, I would be most grateful."

Nealy's father nodded. "I'll take care of it."

"Anita, I'd like you to help me get my house spruced up to put on the market."

Anita gasped. "Your house?"

"I've got my eye on a nice condo unit not far from the beach. I'm getting too old for yard work. I'd rather sit on a balcony and enjoy the view."

Stunned silence prevailed.

"Nealy, after the sale of the shop is completed I'll refund any additional money you shelled out for the new equipment and upgrades on the place. I'm able to ask top dollar since you all turned the shop into a showplace."

"Thanks, Grandmother."

"Any other questions?"

"Yes," Ed called from across the room. "You going to make sure this new owner still serves plain old coffee?"

The entire shop erupted in laughter. Leave it to grumpy old Ed to break the tension.

"I'll look into it," Dorinda replied. "Well, now we can move on to different topics."

The family, as well as Terri and Ed, mingled to discuss the new developments. Nealy escaped to put on a fresh pot of coffee, not eager to be part of the dialogue. She felt a hand on her shoulder and turned to face her grandmother.

"Nealy, dear, this is a good thing."

"I know. I'm just having a hard time coming to grips with the idea of someone else owning Cuppa Joe. And you moving into a condo."

"Now you know how we adults felt when you kids were making decisions. We had to stand back, watch you move forward, make mistakes, all the while knowing the choices were ultimately yours."

"It's tough watching everything change."

"These are good moves, dear. Besides, California is calling your name."

"I haven't heard from Crystal yet today, but it's still early."

"Nealy, enjoy your life and dreams. I am."

Nealy hugged her grandmother, blinking back the tears blurring her eyes. After the brief exchange, she broke free, pressing her forefingers against her eyes to stop tears from falling. "You know," she said in a husky tone, "you have no excuses to keep you from visiting me in L.A."

"Oh, don't worry, my dear. Visiting you is number one on my list."

"I'll be ready."

The conversation was cut short as customers lined up to place orders. For the last time, the family pitched in as a unit, tending to customers, filling orders and tidying the shop. A bittersweet day, indeed.

Nealy leaned against the wall, taking it all in. Her plans and hard work had paid off. The Merchants' Association representatives gushed over Cuppa Joe, claiming it to have the best storefront in town. With the new equipment installed, offering different coffee drink options, sales were up. Folks were spending more time in the shop, socializing or busy on their computers or tablets while enjoying their favorite beverages. What the family called Dorinda's living room had now become *the* hot spot in Cypress Pointe.

She'd completed her task. There was nothing left to keep her from L.A. So why wasn't she more thrilled?

THE WEDDING REHEARSAL for the Weston-Pierce wedding party awaited Nealy, who'd changed into a classic black sheath, with matching pumps and delicate pearls. Her final job here in Cypress Pointe and at the Grand Cypress Hotel, no less. Before long she'd be back in a high-profile world, thanks to Ashlee James, if she signed with Milestones by Crystal. Her boss hadn't been kidding when she said Ashlee's people would wait until the last minute to sign a contract. They had until Sunday, the day Nealy returned to L.A., to give an answer, which meant Monday would be the beginning of twelve-hour days if Ashlee came through.

While driving to the hotel, Nealy reflected on her grandmother's decision to sell Cuppa Joe. At least her parents had promised to help Grandmother with the details of the sale. Even with all the teamwork this past week, no one in the family could run the shop full-time. She couldn't cast blame on anyone. After all, she wasn't willing to give up her job any more than the others.

She also couldn't complain about her parents, who'd warmed up to her. Spoke well of her job and her successes. She never expected to hear praise from their lips. It helped temper the resignation she felt over Grandmother's decision to sell Cuppa Joe. She may not have the coffee shop to visit when she came home, but now she had her family. A satisfying trade-off.

At least Lanie and David had rebounded in their relationship. While overjoyed for them, sadness blanketed Nealy. What about her happily-ever-after? She'd always been a romantic at heart, with a bit of a realist mixed in. Once she admitted things were going nowhere with Sam, the pressure came off. The small spark she'd hoped would turn into a raging bonfire never happened. Her feelings for Sam never went beyond a modest flame. Not much to build a relationship on. Looking back, she realized Sam, or any guy she'd dated, was an excuse not to face her true feelings for Dane.

Dane had her heart. He always had. Nothing would change the truth.

On the heels of her revelation, she wondered if she should take a chance and tell Dane the truth of her feelings for him. See if they'd both changed enough to start over. It would be slow going at first, until they decided the best way to meld their lives together. The idea of being honest with him frightened her, but she'd never been one to back away from a challenge.

Arriving at the hotel several minutes before the rehearsal, she spoke to the pastor to get her mind ready for what was ahead. She'd read over the folder of notes Dane sent from his office for her to refer to in case there were any last changes. Despite everything going on in her life, plus waiting to hear about the Ashlee James project, she still couldn't keep her mind off Dane. Was she pitiful or what? She swore not to let him get to her, but it was just the opposite.

Dane would surely stop in to make sure the bride and groom were pleased with the rehearsal. The *wedding* rehearsal. The one topic between them sure to pour salt onto old wounds.

Remember, tonight is about the bride and groom, not your conflicted personal life.

"Oh, Nealy, there you are." Melissa, the bride-to-be, grabbed her as she made her way into the hotel lobby. "The last of the wedding party has arrived. Let's go outside so I can brief you on the ceremony."

Nealy followed Melissa into the beautiful, warm Florida evening. The bride's processional entailed walking from the hotel, down the white runner, to stand beside her groom in front of the pastor standing on a makeshift altar at the edge of the beach. Positioned on the altar stood a white arch, festooned with tulle and flowers. The magnolia tree filled with pink blooms added drama to the background.

A slight breeze ruffled the bride-to-be's hair. Her cheeks were rosy with excitement. As she rambled on, Nealy experienced a strange heaviness in her chest. She should have factored how dealing with a bride would make her feel.

She'd dreamed about getting married, this time in front of family and friends rather than running off to the courthouse. She envisioned standing at the altar with a man who loved her. A man who would never leave her. Who stuck with her through good times and bad, no questions asked. That man could have been Dane, had their lives turned out differently. Now she'd have to see what the future brought her.

Melissa finished her to-do list, ready to get things rolling. Nealy made it halfway up the aisle when she caught a glimpse of Dane striding toward her from the hotel. Their gazes locked. Her stomach dipped with the old familiar tingle of awareness.

The father of the groom stopped Dane. He hesitated to break the visual connection. Just before he turned away, she swore she saw anticipation in his eyes.

Before she had a chance to determine what his look meant, the bridal party gathered around her for instructions. This was like an elaborate stage play, Nealy thought, with her serving as the director, telling the participants where to stand, what to do. She pushed her personal concerns about Dane aside to let her professional persona take over.

"Ladies, inside the hotel, please." She shooed them with her hands. "Gentlemen, please stand in your appointed places." She gestured to a spot just beyond the makeshift altar. "When I give you the signal, take your places beside the groom. Then the bridesmaids will begin walking down the aisle."

Given their assignment, the groomsmen headed away. Nealy turned to the last group of important people awaiting directions. "Parents, please take your seats in the front row."

Among the chatter, they all moved forward. "No, Mr. Weston." She hurried over to take the father of the bride by the arm and turn him in the opposite direction. "You need to join your daughter indoors."

"Right." The older man adjusted his glasses. "I'm very nervous about this whole endeavor," he told Nealy in a quiet voice.

She nodded to the women mingling by the doors. "Melissa is very happy. You should be proud of her."

"I am, but I don't do very well in large crowds."

"When you walk Melissa down the aisle, keep your eyes straight ahead and you'll be fine. When you get close to the front, look for your wife and focus on her. I'm sure she'll calm you down."

That's what wives did, right?

She remembered how she always looked to Dane when they were younger, following his lead because she knew, just knew, he had her back. At least until everything between them changed.

"Thank you." He patted her hand and moved to take his place.

Mr. Weston joined his daughter. A smile blossomed on Nealy's lips. The Westons were a lovely couple and Melissa an easy bride to work with. From an event planner's point of view, anyway.

Nealy nodded to the men to take their places. Once they were situated, she made sure the bridesmaids lined up in order. Perfect. She reminded the girls to smile, urged them to have fun and cued the soundman to start the music.

As she turned to watch the girls, she bumped into Dane.

"Oof," she puffed then cleared her throat.

Dane grasped hold of Nealy's arms to keep her steady.

"Where have you been?"

"The hospital. My dad had a heart attack."

"Oh, Dane. Is he okay?"

"The doctor admitted him to run tests. I imagine he'll put Dad on some kind of medication, talk to him about lifestyle changes."

"That sounds okay," Nealy said. "How are you? Okay?"

"The ordeal kinda scared me, but I'm relieved they have him stabilized."

"Shouldn't you be at the hospital? I can handle the rehearsal if you need to go."

He met her gaze, his laser focus capturing her. "My dad will be fine. There's nowhere I'd rather be than here."

She stared at his handsome face and her heart swelled. Dressed in a dark suit with white shirt and patterned tie, he took her breath away.

"Right." She scurried out of the way, putting distance between them, hoping he hadn't seen her emotions reflected in her eyes.

The music started. Instead of the traditional wedding processional, Melissa and Ben had chosen a romantic Tim McGraw love song for her entrance. Listening to the lyrics, hot tears pricked Nealy's eyelids. The song reminded her of the night of Juliet's failed engagement party when she and Dane danced under the stars. Good grief. This wedding was making her sappy.

With a minimum of fuss, the rehearsal took little time to get through. Once Pastor James dismissed the group, everyone mingled, waiting to move on to dinner in the high-end restaurant in the hotel.

Nealy wandered off, distancing herself from the jubilant wedding party. She gazed at the beach, her mind going in so many directions that she couldn't land on one thought, until Dane joined her.

"Beautiful view," he said.

"I noticed you kept the natural feel of the area when you remodeled."

"Can't improve on something already near perfect."

She nodded, a sense of melancholy washing over her.

"So pensive tonight."

"Thinking about Juliet. How she dreamed this for her own wedding."

"Thought maybe your wistful look had to do with you wondering what our wedding ceremony would have been like, if we'd had one."

She shrugged, not willing to let him know she had indeed gone there.

"When I first bought this place, I remembered all the things we did when we worked here. Sneaking kisses during breaks, swimming in the waves when our shifts ended, sitting on the grass right here, watching the sun set." He moved closer, his arm brushing hers. "We had a good thing going until I messed it up."

"Hmm."

"What if I said I wanted to make it up to you?"

She turned her head and arched a brow at him. "A little too late, don't you think?"

"I don't think it's ever too late when it's right."

She started to ask what he meant when she spied the bride-to-be standing alone at the makeshift altar, staring at the beautiful backdrop of the sun setting in the dazzling Florida sky. Torn between having him elaborate on his meaning or helping the bride, she wavered. Technically, she was still on duty, but her heart pounded with the weight of his unspoken words until Melissa beckoned to her.

Shoot. "Hold that thought," she told Dane before going to Melissa. "Is everything okay?"

"I don't know," Melissa said. "We went back and forth about where to stand, on the ground in front of the altar or up on the platform. I agreed with the ground because I didn't have to worry about lifting my dress to climb the steps, but it doesn't feel right." Melissa stepped back. "I love the lighting right now, with the evening sun glistening over the water. What a beautiful backdrop. I want the guests to enjoy the postcard view, so I'm thinking about changing things up."

Nealy swallowed a groan. To make a change now would mean running through the rehearsal again, right when she wanted to be alone with Dane.

"If you want to make a change, we should stop the bridal party from leaving," she said.

"No," Melissa assured her. "I'm just thinking."

The young woman stepped to the right then the left as if trying to visualize the best location to stand.

"Problem?" Dane joined Nealy as she watched Melissa pace back and forth. "Looks like the bride has something on her mind."

"Where to stand."

"I thought they covered everything during rehearsal."

"You know how this goes. Last-minute tweaks."

Melissa glanced over her shoulder. "Oh, good. I need to borrow you two."

"What?" they said in unison.

The bride waved them over. "Come stand here so I can get a feel for the entire setup." She tugged at Dane's arm to move toward the altar. "Stand in for Ben." Then she pulled Nealy over. "Okay, face each other."

"Oh, I don't—"

"It'll just take a minute," she said as she spun Nealy to face Dane.

Heart thumping, Nealy met his gaze.

"This is awkward," he said.

"Tell me about it." She shrugged off the ball of nerves, willing herself not to sprint away.

A small smile tugged at his lips. "Would be

nice if I had a professional planner to navigate me through these things."

Right. She took a breath, which made matters worse. He stood too close, smelled too good and looked more handsome in the twilight than was fair.

"Beautiful. Now hold hands," Melissa instructed as she backed away from them.

"Is this necessary?" Nealy croaked.

Melissa, with her arms outstretched, called for her maid of honor to join her. "I need the full view," she explained, "to get the picture in my head."

Nealy's breath became short. She tried to control her trembling hands, but failed until Dane's steady grasp soothed her. Then, out of nowhere, the maid of honor shoved the bridal bouquet at her, forcing her to hold it instead of Dane's hand. Standing with him, where the bride and groom would exchange vows, set her off-kilter.

"You okay?"

She nodded, unsure of what to say. The bride and her maid of honor were deep in conversation.

"Look, what I wanted to tell you—" Dane started.

"I don't think now is the appropriate time."

"You don't know what I—"

"Dane…"

"I'm not going to let this go, Nealy."

She closed her eyes. Did she want him pursuing her, because his intentions were pretty obvious.

By this time, more of the bridal party had moved up to the makeshift altar to see what the bride was doing. Melissa called out, "Now, walk up onto the platform. Let's try you there."

Taking hold of her hand, Dane guided Nealy to the spot under the tulle-draped arch.

It felt right, her hand in his, giving her the illusion they were the couple getting married. Only they weren't a couple.

"Perfect," Melissa called out. "Now move closer and stare into each other's eyes."

Dane kept his gaze on Nealy, his scrutiny making her uncomfortable. She couldn't look at him for fear he'd see the hold he had on her. Nealy shifted to speak to the bride. "Melissa, maybe we—"

"Oh, don't move. Just another minute," she called. "Ben. Come here. I need your opinion."

Nealy obliged the bride and gazed into Dane's whiskey-colored eyes. He stepped closer, enveloping her in his warmth and the spicy scent of his cologne. She wanted to melt into his arms forever.

"I'm sorry," he told her.

"I know," she whispered.

"Closer," Melissa commanded.

Nealy swallowed. She could feel his breath on her cheek.

"I want to make it up to you."

She closed her eyes. "It was a long time ago."

He didn't say a word, but she felt his rapid breathing.

Lifting her lids, Nealy saw hope in his eyes.

"I didn't expect you to be so…understanding. I figured if we met up again, you'd kick me to the curb and never speak to me again."

"I needed to forgive you as much as you needed forgiveness."

"Now lean into each other like you're kissing," Melissa instructed them.

Dane's gaze lowered to her lips. Hesitated.

"It won't be all bad. You kissed me before and liked it."

He smiled. "Yeah. I liked it."

They stared at each other and Nealy felt her world shift. She loved him just as much now as she had when she was a teen. Yes, they were different now. Had taken different paths. But maybe, just maybe, they could work things out. With the couple's hushed discussion in the background, Dane moved, just a fraction closer, and their lips brushed.

The ground shook, thanks to that kiss, and it made her kiss him back with a deep longing that surprised her.

"You're trouble," Dane murmured against her lips.

"You always liked that about me."

Inches separated them. Nealy ached to feel Dane's lips pressed to hers once more. Just when she thought he'd kiss her again, Melissa clapped her hands. "Thanks so much Nealy and Dane. I've made my decision."

The loud sound brought Nealy back down to reality. She jerked away from Dane, already missing the warm connection. She shivered. The heat in his eyes still blazed.

"As much as I love the arch, I think being on the ground for the ceremony works better. We can just get pictures standing on the altar afterward. What do you think, Nealy?"

She cleared her throat, recovering from Dane's kiss. It took a second for her breathing to return to normal. "You have a good eye," she told Melissa.

"Thanks." Melissa took Ben's hand. "You guys are good sports for filling in."

She watched the couple stroll away, aware of Dane's presence as he took a spot beside her.

Now what? She'd completed her task here

at the hotel. Time to head home or extend her time with Dane?

"I'd like to show you something," he said, making the decision for her.

CHAPTER FIFTEEN

AFTER SHE COLLECTED her purse, Dane led Nealy through the hotel lobby and along the hallway to his office. Her phone rang just as they entered the room. She searched her bag for her cell. Once she had it in hand she checked the caller ID. "I have to take this. One minute."

While she stepped into the hallway to take the call, Dane pulled out the designs he'd drawn after talking to his uncle. He laid them on the desk, smoothing the paper. Uncharacteristic nerves rattled him. What would she think? Would she go along with the idea? Stay in Cypress Pointe? With him? Since talking to Uncle Hank at the hospital, he wanted to lay it all on the line, go after Nealy, more than ever. Regain what he'd let slip away all those years ago.

A few minutes later Nealy returned, a triumphant smile on her face. She thrummed with energy.

"Good news?" he asked.

She set her phone on his desk, noticing the

blueprints. "The best, but you asked me here, so you go first."

He handed her a photograph of a building.

"What is this? A new project?"

"It could be."

She glanced at him and frowned. "Come again?"

"Do you recognize the place?"

She tilted her head. Recognition followed. "The old Fowler building."

"I bought it."

"Okay." She regarded him quizzically. "And?"

"The other day I asked you about staying in Cypress Pointe. To consider starting your own business here."

"I remember."

Her lack of enthusiasm almost stopped him from carrying on, but he barreled ahead. "The more I thought about you staying, the more ideas I had. I want to turn the Fowler building into offices. Peterson Holdings could use a permanent address outside of the hotel. I want our base of operations here in Cypress Pointe."

"I don't blame you. Makes life easier." She studied the designs again. "What does this have to do with me starting a business?"

He moved to stand beside her, pointing to one of the offices in the design. "This is your office. You can set up your own event planning business right here in Cypress Pointe."

Her mouth opened but she didn't say a word.

"Plenty of people in town have expressed interest in your services. There are no event planners with your experience close by. You'd corner the market." He rushed on. "We can do this together."

By now, Nealy had closed her mouth. Her face flushed. "Together?"

"It's an awesome idea."

"No, it is not." She dropped the photo on the desk. "Doesn't this seem familiar to you?"

"Familiar?"

"You making decisions without discussing them with me first? Just like filing for an annulment and informing me after the fact. This is the same thing. You know I have a job in California yet you assume because you think this is a good business opportunity I should just drop everything and come back to Cypress Pointe."

"I'll admit, I may be getting a bit ahead of myself, but this is nothing like twelve years ago."

"From where I'm standing it's exactly the same, only this time we aren't married."

He ran a hand through his hair. "When I got the annulment, I thought I was doing the right thing for us. Now I believe moving back to Cypress Pointe is the right move for you."

"Dane, you asked me to think about it," she stated. "Me thinking and you taking it to the next level are two totally different things."

This was not going the way he'd envisioned. "Nealy, it's win-win. Your services are needed here. You could call the shots. Be your own boss. Make your own decisions about what types of clientele you want to work with. How is wanting you to be in control of your future a bad thing?"

"You're missing the point, Dane. You should have asked me. Included me in this great big plan for my life. Contrary to what you might think, I have thought about my future. Milestones by Crystal is where I want to be. Aside from the business aspect of your plan, there is no us. There hasn't been for a very long time."

"Things have changed since you've been home."

Her features softened. "Yes, they have. But, Dane, there is still no us."

"Nealy, you have to understand." He took a deep breath. Pulled his wayward thoughts together. "When I saw my dad lying in a hospital bed, the truth dawned on me. I don't want to end up like him, so unhappy with his life it made him sick. If I keep going down the same path, thinking I'll avoid heartache by never having a serious relationship with a woman, I will end up just like him. You came back to town and I realized you've always owned my heart. You are the woman I want a relationship with. I hoped the idea of helping you start your own business in Cypress Pointe would show how committed I am to us."

"Just like twelve years ago? Because that worked out so well?" She put a hand on the doorknob.

"Nealy, wait. You've got it all wrong. At the time, I honestly thought ending our marriage was the right thing to do. Now I see it as the biggest mistake I ever made."

She turned and faced him. Her expression had lost all emotion, scaring him more than any ranting and raving ever would. "Thinking you can turn my life around again, without my say-so, is the biggest mistake you ever made."

"Okay. Then tell me what you want."

"The phone call I took? It was my boss. Ashlee James came through. I'm lead planner on the project. I'm heading back to L.A. as soon as I can catch a flight."

His stomach bottomed out.

"So you see, I don't need an office here. I

never did. All I needed was for you to tell me you loved me. Three simple words."

He took a step back. "I do love you, Nealy. I always have."

"Well, I'm sorry, Dane. You should have told me how you felt before you went through all the trouble of planning my life out for me."

She was right. He had come to his epiphany too late. And then managed to screw up their new, fragile relationship. If anything proved that he'd become his father, this was it. He deserved Nealy's scorn. He'd wanted her to see his actions as a way of making up for what he'd done, not as a repeat of the past. He'd gone about this all wrong and the damage was done. "If going back to your job is what you want, is what you think is best for you, than I won't try to stop you."

"You're right. You won't stop me. This is my decision, Dane. I'm going back to the job I've worked hard to become successful at." She pointed to the drawings. "Build your offices. Rent them all out, but forget about me because I won't be here."

She walked out of the office.

Alone now, Dane stared down at the blueprints. Slowly, he rolled the plans up and slid an elastic band over the roll. He tossed the roll into a corner and stared out at the water.

He now knew exactly how Nealy felt when he'd broken her heart. She'd just returned the favor.

HER EYES BLURRY with tears, Nealy threw clothes into her suitcase in haphazard fashion. She'd already called the airline to book her flight back to L.A. At daybreak tomorrow, she'd start her day of traveling, dead set on leaving Cypress Pointe and Dane behind.

He'd done it again. Tossed her world upside down.

She sat on the edge of the bed, taking a moment to calm her nerves. The house was so quiet since her grandmother had gone to have dinner with Nealy's parents and hadn't returned yet. Nealy was glad to be alone, to gather her thoughts before her grandmother turned up and demanded to know why Nealy was leaving early.

She understood Dane had her best intentions in mind by encouraging her to start her own business. After all, she'd pondered the same idea a time or two herself since coming home. That he believed in her skills and what she could offer Cypress Pointe touched her heart. She even understood his fear of their relationship becoming like his parents' disastrous marriage. Which never would have happened. She didn't view love as a weapon, but rather a coming together to bring out the best in each other. Deep down, she believed Dane felt the same way.

But what she really wished for was Dane talking to her first, so they could figure out how best to rekindle their relationship. Yes, she'd admit she'd fallen for him all over again, but here they were, emotionally and physically, miles apart.

Rising, she tossed the last article of clothing in the case. Her cell phone rang and she glanced at the clock on the nightstand. Nine in the evening. Still early enough for Crystal to call from L.A. Nealy dropped her head. She wasn't up to it. Right now she wanted to be alone and focus on her aching heart before heading back to her job.

The ringing stopped.

Blowing out a grateful breath, she crossed the room to gather her personal belongings from the dresser top when the infernal ringing started again. Annoyed, she grabbed the offending device and pressed the talk button.

"Yes," she said curtly.

"Cuppa Joe is on fire," Lanie blurted.

For a second, Nealy froze.

"Did you hear me?"

"Yes…I'm…"

"We'll meet you there."

Once the shock wore off, Nealy ran from the house and jumped into the rental car. She made it downtown in record time. Parking a few blocks away from the cordoned-off street, she sprinted from the car. The acrid, burning scent of smoke assailed her nostrils. She ran along the sidewalk, nearly tripping in the shadows as she approached her family.

A fire truck parked at an angle on the street before the shop. Walkie-talkies squawked as firefighters and police officers scurried around the scene. Flames shot out of the store next to Cuppa Joe. The fire roared, instilled with a life of its own. Soot floated through the air. An arc of water sprayed the store in an attempt to quench the flames. Black, billowing smoke escaped Cuppa Joe, so thick she couldn't tell if the shop itself was on fire.

She shivered, rubbing her hands up and down over the fabric of her long-sleeved shirt, trying to make sense of the scene. Flashing lights from the rescue vehicles illuminated the night, making the entire scene more surreal.

Her grandmother stood behind the police line, staring at the shop, tears streaking down her cheeks. Nealy's parents flanked her. Lanie and David hovered close by. Though still in shock, Nealy slid beside her grandmother, wrapping her arms around the strong woman who now looked immensely fragile in the flickering lights.

"Grandmother, I'm so sorry."

Dorinda leaned into Nealy.

They looked on in helpless horror at the flickering glow inside the shop. Had the flames spread inside? So much for hoping the coffee shop would escape damage.

When a police officer stopped to talk to her grandmother, Nealy stepped back, bumping into a solid form. She turned and came face-to-face with Dane, his expression somber. They stared at each other for a long moment then she sank into his embrace, a move as natural as breathing. He hugged her close, stroking her back as she gave in to the free-flowing tears she'd refused to let fall. It wasn't until she heard Lanie's panicked voice that she pulled away to find out if the situation had changed. Dane kept his arm around her shoulders, nudging her closer as she took refuge in his steady strength.

Lanie, her face stricken, rushed up to Nealy. "I can't find Davey. He wasn't home when the call came in and he's not answering his cell. He should know what's going on."

With all the confusion and activity around her, Nealy felt sick. By now, she assumed, everyone in town knew about the fire. "Was he at a school function?"

Lanie shook her head. "I don't think so. He left after dinner, saying he was going out."

Dane squeezed Lanie's shoulder. "I'm sure he'll be here as soon as he hears."

Nealy nodded, but something inside niggled at her. She brushed it off. Her nerves, along with everyone else's, were on edge.

As the flames came under control and started to diminish, a police officer shined a spotlight into Cuppa Joe to assess the damage. Nealy stepped as close as she could without crossing the line to peer into the smoky interior. As the beam moved over the large room, water dripped from the ceiling, the smoky haze dispersed. She could barely make out the cash register, the coffeemakers and a familiar backpack sporting a bright orange sticker.

Her gaze glossed over the backpack then shot back to get a better look. Davey's? "Oh, no."

"What's wrong?" Dane asked.

She was almost afraid to utter her thoughts out loud. Taking Dane's hand, she pulled him from the throng. "Davey might be inside."

"Why would you think that?"

"His backpack. I saw it when the officer shined the light in the shop." She rushed toward the fire engine to find someone who would check out her concerns.

"Couldn't he have forgotten it?" Dane asked as he trailed her. "Why would he be inside?"

"I'll explain later." As she approached a man in full turnout gear, he hurried past as if he didn't see her. Frustrated, she tried again, this time flagging a police officer, but he warned her off before she had a chance to explain as a new round of shouts came from the neighboring store.

"Nobody's paying attention." She yelled for another officer, but the surrounding noise drowned her voice. After a few more minutes of yelling with no results, she turned to Dane. "Forget this."

Afraid that her suspicions might be correct, Nealy shoved through the throng of curious bystanders to run to the alleyway a few stores down the street.

"Where are you going?" Dane asked, a step behind her.

"I'm not waiting for help. If Davey is in the store, we can get in the back way."

She rounded the corner to the rear of the building. Fewer firefighters were here; those who were, were intent on their task. It seemed as though most of the damaging flames were on the front side of the building, but still, the firefighters were taking no chances.

She reached the back entrance of Cuppa Joe, but before she could grab the door handle, Dane warned her off.

"Careful. Could be hot."

He tentatively touched the metal before giving it a hard tug. "Locked."

Nealy dug into her jeans pocket, extracting her keys. She fumbled, dropped the ring, quickly retrieved it and with a shaking hand, inserted the key into the lock. With a quick turn, she pulled the door open, greeted by a wall of escaping smoke.

"Cover your nose and mouth," Dane instructed.

She brought her arm up to her face, using the sleeve of her shirt for protection. Once the majority of the smoke billowed out, she moved to rush in. Dane stopped her.

"You don't have to do this."

"Yes, I do."

"Then let me go first."

She nodded and grabbed the back of his shirt. "Go."

Together they ventured into the building, only to stop short.

She tried to see around him. "What's wrong?"

"There's something in the way."

Dane moved and Nealy saw the hall closet door stood open, boxes of cleaning supplies, along with broom, mop and other janitorial items scattered on the floor.

"Careful," Dane called over his shoulder as he stepped over the items.

Heavy smoke hung in the air. Even with her nose and mouth covered, Nealy's throat tickled. She coughed.

"Are you okay?" Dane asked.

"Yes. Keep moving."

He took her hand. "Where should we look?"

"Behind the counter."

They made their way through the shadows. As they reached the seating area, Nealy saw the gaping, charred hole in the communal wall between the coffee shop and neighboring store. She could make out silhouettes of firefighters moving around on the other side of the wall. Assessing the coffee shop, she went weak with relief to see the other three walls standing upright, covered with blackened soot and stained by water damage.

She chanced removing her shirtsleeve from her mouth as they rounded the counter. There, side by side, Davey and Madison lay slumped on the floor. Dropping Dane's hand, she crouched down beside her nephew, shaking his still form. He coughed and groaned, but his eyes remained shut.

"Let's get them out of here," Dane said. "I'll lift Davey. Think you can drag the girl?"

"I'm on it."

As they began the rescue, shouts sounded from the back door. Two firefighters ran into the shop, assessed the situation and took over. "You two, out," one commanded. The professionals lifted the teens, who were now coughing with uncontrollable spasms. The second man called the situation in and asked for EMTs.

Dane placed his hands on Nealy's shoulders and guided her to the back door. Once outside, she drank in large gulps of fresh air. The rescuers rounded the corner, skidding to a stop before the teens, who had been laid on the ground. Nealy nearly buckled at the sight of Davey and Madison sitting up, aware of their surroundings.

"Hold on there." Dane put his arms around her. She leaned into him, closing her eyes and gathering her wits about her before moving out of his embrace.

She touched his arm though, unwilling to break the connection with him. She needed the security of his strength. "Thank you."

He nodded, looking worse for wear after their impromptu rescue mission.

The fire chief approached them, a frown on his face. "You two, back to the front. We'll talk later."

Nealy opened her mouth to explain, but Dane nudged her. She noticed the caution in his look and joined him as they went back onto Main Street.

"You know, your intentions were admirable, but incredibly stupid," he told her.

"Yeah, well, I didn't see you staying away."

"And let you rescue your nephew without me? No way."

Her heart swelled with love. This was the one man who would run into unknown danger by her side, no questions asked.

They reached the sidewalk, well away from the gawking crowd. She cleared her throat, still tight from inhaling the smoke.

"You always did like being in on the action," he said.

"And you always did like taking chances."

"I'd do it again in a heartbeat." His voice choked. "I'd do anything for you."

Tears welled in her eyes. "I know."

She'd never expected him to join her, yet wasn't surprised when he followed her into the smoke-filled shop. She'd be forever grateful and, she confessed, forever in love with Dane. Facing an emergency with him by her side proved what she'd foolishly tried to walk away from. There was no other man for her. She loved Dane Peterson. Always had. Always would. Even when he made her crazy with his take-charge attitude.

He reached out, catching her chin between his fingers, cocking his head to meet her gaze. His touch made her quiver. She didn't bother hiding it. "We made a pretty good team back there," he said.

"We did. And I'm sure it'll mean we'll end up in trouble together."

"Won't be the first time."

She hoped it wouldn't be the last.

He thumbed her cheek. "Bit of ash," he explained, but his touch lingered. She moved closer, shuddering at the love shining in his eyes. He felt the same as her. So why couldn't she say the words out loud?

"We should find—"

"Nealy!"

She turned as Lanie and David joined them, their faces lined with worry. "The police chief said Davey is around back," Lanie said.

"He is," Nealy assured her. "The paramedics are checking him out."

David took Lanie's hand and they rushed to their son.

Nealy grimaced. "Once Lanie knows he's okay, she's going to lay into him big-time."

"How did you know he was in there, anyway?"

"I kinda know a secret."

One eyebrow rose.

"Davey and Madison, the daughter of the Rascal's candy store owners, like to meet in the shop after hours and talk. Davey has a key and since Grandmother closes the place in the afternoon, I guess it's their private rendezvous spot."

"Every couple needs one of those."

Just like they'd had their secret places to meet.

"So I put two and two together."

"Good thing, for Davey's sake."

"I could have been wrong, but…"

"It was a chance you were willing to take?"

She nodded.

He smiled, his handsome face shadowed by the lamplight. "That's why I love you."

He leaned in to kiss her. When his lips brushed over hers, she placed her hands on his chest, then up around his neck to bring him closer, returning his kiss, home in his arms after twelve years.

Too soon, he ended the embrace. Brushed her hair from her face.

She smiled, leaning in for another toe curler when she heard voices behind her. She reluctantly let go of Dane.

"This isn't over," he told her, winking, before her parents and grandmother reached them.

"Please tell me Davey is all right," her father said in a tortured tone.

"He'll be fine," she assured them.

Relief passed over their features.

"What was he doing inside?" Dorinda asked.

"I think he should explain," Nealy said.

"Coward," Dane teased, whispering into her ear.

"What happens now?" Nealy asked.

"The firefighters have put out the blaze," her father answered. "I informed the inspector about the ongoing construction next door. He'll be examining the building closely to determine how the fire started. They'll let us know the results and the extent of the damage after he makes that determination."

Nealy's mother circled an arm around Dorinda's shoulders. "Let's get you home, Mother. There's nothing we can do here."

"What about Davey?" she asked.

"His parents will handle him," Anita promised her.

Dorinda glanced between Nealy and Dane. "Thank you for going after him."

"It was still a dumb move," Dane said, his eyes dark and serious, "but I never seem to think straight when I'm with Nealy."

Nealy elbowed his side. "A simple 'you're welcome' would do."

He grinned.

"I should get Grandmother and me home," she said, weariness creeping over her as the excitement of the night came to an end. "And I want to get the smoke smell out of my hair and clothes."

"A shower sounds great right about now."

"Has anyone called Juliet?" Nealy asked.

"Yes," her mother replied. "I just told her the news. She sends everyone her love and is on her way home."

At the look of love on her mother's face, Nealy smiled. A lot had happened to the Grainger family in the past two weeks, but the circumstances had drawn them closer.

Dane walked with her to the car. Anita, Marshall and Dorinda followed behind. Nealy paused before opening the door.

Suddenly unsure of their next step, she said, "So, um, I'll talk to you later."

Dane opened her door, made sure she slid inside safely then leaned his forearm on top of the door as she lowered the window. "Count on it."

He leaned in and kissed her one last time, hard and fast, before straightening up to walk away.

Nealy watched him go, indecision tearing at her. Until she knew the extent of the damage and the fate of Cuppa Joe, she'd postpone her return to California. Crystal would give her an earful, but it didn't matter. Grandmother needed her. Dane told her he loved her. And while this decision to stay a little longer was an easy one, she wondered what she'd do now that her dream client required her to return to L.A. while her heart longed to stay in Cypress Pointe.

NEALY TOWELED HER HAIR dry as she walked into her grandmother's living room. Wrapped in a fluffy robe, exhaustion tugged at her. Her parents had left after fussing over her grandmother and getting assurances Nealy wouldn't leave the elderly woman's side.

"Lanie called," her grandmother informed Nealy from her perch on the couch. "They went to the hospital to have Davey checked out, Treated him for smoke inhalation, but he'll be fine."

Nealy blew out a breath as she plopped down beside her. "Thank goodness."

"He has some explaining to do," Dorinda chastised. "So do you."

"Busted." Nealy toyed with the edge of the

damp towel. "It's not like I'm keeping a big secret. I just found out about his friendship with Madison the other day. He's still trying to figure this whole relationship thing out."

Dorinda smiled. "Relationship issues never end."

"No. They don't."

"You and Dane seemed inseparable tonight."

"To hear him tell it, he tagged along with my wild idea just to protect me."

"Because he cares about you."

"Actually, he admitted he loves me."

"And you?"

"You know I never stopped."

"Did you tell him?"

"No. The man drives me crazy." She filled her grandmother in on Dane's building purchase and his plan to move her into an office so she could start her own business. "I don't want to change him, but why can't he see if we are a couple, I need to be involved in the decision making?"

Dorinda leaned over, taking Nealy's hand in hers. "Dane has always been a decision maker, at home and at work. You're smart enough to realize you can't change him, it's who he is. You two have never been together long enough to press out the kinks in a relationship. It takes time, commitment and mutual love for each other. Yes, he took the steps to get an annulment, but you took off. Would things have been resolved if you'd stayed in Cypress Pointe? We'll never know. The question now is, do you love him enough to stay? Take a chance on Dane and a business? If he loves you as much as I think he does, he'll learn to talk to you. Learn to include you in decisions. He's been making solitary decisions for a long time now, but as you two learn and grow together, he'll come to value your input. But, dear, you have to do your part, too. Running never solves anything."

Nealy swallowed around the lump in her throat. "I've spent years holding a grudge and where did it get me? In and out of relationships that never worked because no man measured up to Dane." Her smile wobbled. "But in the process I have learned to be an awesome event planner."

"I do so love your modesty."

The pressure lifted from Nealy as they both laughed.

"So what are you going to do?" her grandmother asked.

"I have two choices. Go back to L.A. and a sure thing or stay here and take a shot at a brand-new life with Dane." She blew out a breath. "You'd think this would be easy, but I guess I have my own decisions to make."

"Indeed you do."

Nealy rose from the couch, carrying her towel to the bathroom to hang it up to dry. She combed out her hair, her mind racing. She knew what she wanted, but was it the right thing?

She returned to the living room to find her grandmother still hadn't moved from her position on the couch.

"You should go to bed, Grandmother."

"I still can't get the vision of Cuppa Joe in flames out of my head." She shuddered. "Then to learn Davey was inside, it turned my blood cold."

"At least he's safe and he learned a valuable lesson." Nealy sat beside her grandmother and took her hand in hers, rubbing warmth into her grandmother's skin. "Thank heavens the entire shop wasn't destroyed. I'm sure with the insurance coverage, we can get the business back up and running."

Her grandmother regarded her with a sly look. *"We?"*

"You should reconsider selling. Seriously, after almost losing the shop, I think we should keep Cuppa Joe in the family, and you can either retire or, at least, slow down. And if we do, the rest of the family will step up and finally rethink their roles with respect to the shop. They'll want to be involved with Cuppa Joe given everything that's happened. So, Grand-mother, is your original proposal about co-owning Cuppa Joe with me still open?"

Dorinda's eyes turned bright. "You know it is."

Nealy tightened her grip on Dorinda's hand. "Then you have a partner."

"And your event planning business?"

"It'll take some doing, juggling two busi-nesses at once, but I'm up for the task. Knowing we've kept Cuppa Joe in the family is impor-tant to me. Davey will be thrilled. The idea of taking my own job experience and bringing it here to Cypress Pointe excites me."

"You won't miss the high-profile clients you've been used to working with?"

"I have to admit, I will miss working with great people and rubbing elbows with a few, but I won't miss the crazy hours and demands from Crystal. Being my own boss has a nice ring to it."

"Do you know how to start the ball rolling?"

She grinned. "No, but I happen to know just the right person to help me put a business pro-posal together."

THE NEXT MORNING, Nealy marched into Dane's office, placing a briefcase on his desk. He looked up and seemed pleasantly surprised, by the expression on his face.

"Okay, mister, we have some things to discuss."

He rose from his chair, pleasure replaced by wariness. "Do tell."

"First of all, is the office you promised me still available?"

He pushed his chair under the desk then moved to the side of the desk to lean against it. "Do you promise to use it on a daily basis?"

"I think that can be arranged." She pulled a folder from her briefcase. "Are you available to brainstorm a few different business proposals?"

"A few?"

"Yes. I'm a busy woman, have my fingers in all kinds of career opportunities. I need some expert advice. I happen to know from personal experience, not only are you a successful businessman who knows how to make a profit, but your tendency to be bossy has made you my go-to man."

"You've piqued my interest."

"As was my intention."

"I can listen. Give me a few suggestions."

Nealy grinned from ear to ear and sighed as she placed a hand over her chest. "Please repeat what you just said."

He chuckled. "I get it, Nealy. I will listen and

discuss any and all business and personal decisions with you before acting."

"Great. So we're clear?"

"We're clear. Thus far I'm zero for two in the major decision-making process. The third time around I won't strike out."

"You always said I was your good-luck charm." She dropped the folder on his desk and went into his arms. "You know it's going to take a while for us to work out our issues."

He slipped his hands around her waist. "This time we're ready."

She kissed him, pouring all her love for this man into the gesture.

Moments later he broke the kiss, his voice hopeful. "Does this need for business advice mean you've decided to stay in Cypress Pointe?"

She shrugged. "Cypress Pointe has kind of grown on me." She looked away, smoothing his shirt to ease her nervousness. "And I've discovered there's a lot to love here."

"Interesting. Anything or anyone in particular?"

She looked up to meet his gaze. "You."

"I'm sorry about—"

She placed a finger over his lips. "It's the past, Dane. I want to make a future with you."

"I do, too."

"I never stopped loving you, but a wise

woman told me I have to stop running. It was the easy way, but not the best way. Just like you have always made decisions based on doing the right thing, I reacted on pure emotion. The thing is, the emotion led me right back to you. I'm tired of running from the truth. I love you, Dane."

"I never thought I'd hear you say those words again."

"It took me time and distance, but I know what I want now."

"Even through the years we were apart, deep down, I wished for this moment." His hands held on to her waist. "We're good together, you and I."

"It's as if you're reading my mind."

His mouth covered hers tenderly and she reveled in the knowledge Dane did indeed love her. Taking this step of faith hadn't been easy, but deep inside she was prepared to fight for a love she never should have abandoned in the first place. She may not have been old enough or wise enough to work out their problems twelve years ago, but she was more than able to now.

"I'll have to go back to California, finish up some obligations and close my apartment, but I'll be back as soon as I can."

"I'm coming with you."

She froze.

"Let me rephrase. Nealy, can I please come with you?"

"That's more like it." Dane coming with her to California. Hmm, she liked the idea. "The answer is yes, as long as you promise not to be so bossy when we get there."

He kissed her forehead. "So what you're saying is, after everything we've been through, you expect me to change?"

"Um, yeah. I do."

"Trust me, I won't do anything to mess us up this time around."

The love in her heart blossomed.

She trusted him. After all the heartache, all the times she'd convinced herself the trust issue between them could never be resolved, she knew Dane's heart was honest and true.

"This is going to work, right?"

He met her gaze, staring deeply into her eyes, his usual intensity stealing her breath away. "I'd take on the world to keep you by my side."

She believed him.

* * * * *

Don't miss Tara Randel's next installment of
THE BUSINESS OF WEDDINGS
coming in December
from Harlequin Heartwarming!

LARGER-PRINT BOOKS!

GET 2 FREE
LARGER-PRINT NOVELS
PLUS 2 FREE
MYSTERY GIFTS

Love Inspired

Larger-print novels are now available...